The BOGUS Killer

NORMAN GIDDAN

CULT CLASSICS PUBLISHER   **DALLAS**

Cult Classics Publisher

ISBN-10: 978-0-9848827-5-5

Trade Paperback

© Copyright 2012 Norman Giddan
All Rights Reserved
Library of Congress #2010927993

Requests for information should be addressed to:
Cult Classics Publisher
1613A Black Duck Terrace
Carrollton, TX 75010
www.cultclassicspublisher.com

Cover Design: Nicole Tibbitt
Interior Design: Nicole Tibbitt

Printed in U.S.A.

CHAPTER ONE

Things are often exactly what they seem—horrifying or distasteful, even repugnant and disgusting. My partner and I stumbled into such. I'm a forty-year-old private investigator, an ex-cop whose wife died three years ago. My life has been a mess since then. I'm Kip Crandall and my PI partner is a wonderful lady, a Latina ex-cop, gorgeous and gay, who's thirty-three. She'd been dumped from the force due to a false allegation of sexual misconduct with a teenage prostitute.

Marty Flores usually fought like hell, but she'd taken so much crap from cops as a woman, and a brown woman at that. So much shit said inside the department that she bagged it. Lucky for me to have her as a partner.

We just met Betty Fowler's husband Chuck and her mother, Mama Waddell. Chuck's eyes lowered. His body sagged, nearly drooping on the arm of Mama's chair. Starch melted away from the crease in his fatigue pants. "I'm married to Betty. I didn't meet Mama until yesterday. Betty didn't tell either of us."

Marty said, "I can imagine. This must really be something to deal with Mrs. Waddell. You didn't know your son Butch was married, and Chuck, you didn't know Betty had Mama."

Chuck's knees wobbled. He stumbled to an ancient brown-and-yellow striped wool couch and plopped down. He said, "Neither of us knew this sex thing…" His voice trailed off in a near whisper.

I knew what he meant but I asked anyway. "What sex thing?" Even an ex-cop gets confused or angry when faced with certain realities.

Marty raised her left eyebrow, our signal for 'slow down big boy.' She deliberately veered off course for the moment. "How long have you been married, Chuck?" Out came her small notebook and gold ballpoint pen.

Chuck said, "It's been about ten years. We're both thirty-five now. We're very happy. We're adopting. We want kids. A family. There must be some mistake in all of this. Betty was arrested due to fingerprints in a routine background check. The cops got her DNA with a warrant. They say it matched some suspect twelve or thirteen years ago. Betty wouldn't hurt a fly."

Mama looked up and spoke in that too-loud voice of the elderly who are hard of hearing. "And neither would Butch. He never hurt a soul in his life."

Marty said, "A really wonderful, helpful person according to both of you." She scribbled furiously.

I said, "Are we talking about twins here? Two different people?"

"Don't get smart with me," said Mama. Her eyes narrowed, then she rubbed them with the back of her hand. "Butch loved to dress up on Halloween and Christmas. He felt good in costumes, pretending to be somebody. That must be it."

Sgt. Fowler's head was in his hands. He sobbed quietly and his voice was muffled as if he wasn't sure he wanted to say what he said. "I saw pictures Mama showed me. Betty is Mama's child. Something happened."

Marty lifted her eyebrow again, warning me.

"May I have a glass of water, please?" I said.

Chuck pulled himself up and got me a drink from the kitchen. He didn't offer anything to Marty or Mama.

I'd better go back to the beginning of the craziness. Mama Waddell, mother of the recently arrested Mrs. Betty C. Fowler, insisted on a weekend appointment. U.S. Army Staff Sgt. Chuck Fowler, Betty's husband, and Mama would provide a rough idea of what had happened and what they wanted from us. Of course, what we wanted from them was important, too.

We tooled down streets of decaying brown or red brick three-story apartment buildings in my brand new silver Corvette with one thin black racing stripe. I'd foolishly agreed to payments of $850 per month in order to feel better. That $850 would have bought me a lot of vodka or pot or Prozac. Cars don't always make you happy.

I glanced at Marty, who sported black boots, worn, frayed jeans, and a very tight black wool turtleneck. Silver jewelry flashed over her wrists and neck. She was really something.

Marty said, "Nice day for December in Ohio; just cloudy and overcast, no snow or ice yet. This thing we're getting into is a weird scene, *senor, muy loco.*"

"You're right, but maybe we don't have the story. Mrs. Waddell said it was her son, but the newspaper account said a Mrs. Fowler was the perp, maybe even a serial killer." I shifted gears needlessly and soundlessly, quite a car. My blue button-down shirt, beige corduroys, and penny loafers were all loose and baggy, since my latest diet had my six-foot frame down to 190 pounds. Diets worked for me best when I was miserably depressed and lost my appetite.

Saturday morning at 11:00 a.m. meant busy but not crowded streets. Remnants of the last storm were piled up: dirty, white, mushy snow here and there. The smooth, powerful Corvette engine guided us past the outskirts of downtown—a small jagged skyline dying to grow—near our turn-off at Central and Whitman, a solid working-class neighborhood. Streets of houses were followed by streets of apartments, and now streets of homes once again in the outlying suburbs.

Marty said, "There it is, 1202 Whitman. Looks like all the others. Put on your security system, boss, this neighborhood has changed a lot." She ran her beautifully manicured hands through long, lustrous, coal-black hair.

I parked between a yellow 1972 Olds and a battered 1969 VW bus with pop-up tent. The Corvette looked like the Taj Mahal around here. I grabbed my dented aluminum briefcase and we headed to the entryway.

The door needed paint badly, but the small hallway, although freshly painted, needed a room deodorizer. The paint must have been a fish oil-based lacquer, or else somebody had fried up a mess of battered perch. Awkward block letters read 'Mrs. Waddell' under a tarnished mail slot. I rang the bell, certain that nothing would happen. Wrong. The return buzzer was so long, so loud, that Marty jumped. We pointed down the grey dark hallway to 1B. As ex-cops, we thought that we'd seen, heard, tasted, touched, and smelled it all. Wrong again.

We padded along, confident but wary, not sure what we would

encounter. Brisk military marching would have better matched the starched, trim sergeant standing guard at parade rest, highly polished shoes spread evenly and arms flexed behind him. A grim smile crossed his face. He held out his hand finally. "I'm Sgt. Fowler. Call me Chuck." He turned his head. "They're here, Mama. I'll bring them in." His head snapped back to us. "Please follow me."

Marty pinched my left arm on the way in. She fidgeted, but her new cologne was great. I'd have to find out the name of it. I could never think of what to get her for Christmas.

Mama didn't rise from the small brown armchair covered with crocheted doilies on both arms and head-rest. She was tiny, enveloped in the chair. Her heavily wrinkled skin, ghoulishly white, contrasted with a bright red rash on her neck. Mama's black dress looked strangely like the crocheted pattern on the doilies. How much less than 100 pounds remained of Mama was anyone's guess.

She motioned us to worn, dark-green, velvet armchairs near her. Chuck stood guard at her side; parade rest, naturally.

Mama's voice struck me as surprisingly strong, given her age and apparently frail health. As she spoke, she dabbed her pale, dull eyes with a small white handkerchief and knocked off her gold-rimmed glasses. Chuck picked them up quickly. She said, "Glad you came. It's been one thing after another. I don't know if I can take it or not."

Chuck said, "Yes, you can. So can I." He was ramrod stiff at her side.

Mama's tiny white Pekingese hid behind her. She settled it in the middle of her lap. "I call him Butchie. Butch is my son. He's a good boy. He worked. He saved. Had a good job. Made good money. Paid my bills. Bought me anything I wanted. No better son in the world."

I was nervous and very curious. I checked out the pad, hiding my nerves but not my curiosity. Marty's eyes had a vacant look, but she was drinking it all in. The expensive new Danish modern furniture in the dining room, the worn and shabby armchairs, the unmarked beige wall-to-wall carpet. The odor of fried fish. Mama and Chuck. A palace of contrasts.

I felt like Joe Friday, yet resisted saying, "Just the facts, ma'am." I said, "Yes, Mrs. Waddell."

"Butchie, you lie still, now." She stroked the dog and he lay flat. "Butch was always a man. I didn't even know he was married until Chuck, his husband, told me. I guess for fun he wore girl's clothes."

"Mama, Mama," said Chuck. "It wasn't for fun. Butch didn't dress up. He's a woman through and through. I'm his husband, I mean, her husband. Butch is now Mrs. Betty Fowler."

"Whatever you say," said Mama. Unconvinced, her hot tears quickly rolled over the thin parchment of her cheeks.

Marty said, "What can we do to help? Betty's under arrest in jail and you have a good lawyer. What else do you need?" She poised her hand to transcribe the answer.

"Clear this up," said Mama. "Clear Butch's good name. He'd never harm anyone. The rest of it don't matter much. He loved to dress up."

"Yes," said Chuck. "Please help us. Mama and I are both in shock. We don't know what to think. We both love Betty, or Butch, and we'll do anything. We can sort out the rest of it when we aren't so dumbfounded by events. I want my wife back. We're going to adopt as soon as possible. Police make mistakes all the time. We'll heal and have our family together. Mama can live with us."

"What does Butch say?" I asked. I scratched my head with uncertainty as to what name to use.

"Betty told me it's all real complicated but she swore on our marriage Bible that Betty C. Fowler never hurt a living soul," said Chuck.

Marty put down her pen. She looked directly into Mama's eyes, which were slits by now because of all the puffiness. "We're pretty expensive."

I stood up. "Yes, the police wouldn't cost you anything. We each get seventy-five dollars an hour plus all expenses. We'd need a $5,000 retainer."

Chuck rose from the couch and pulled a checkbook out of his back pocket. "Who do I make the check out to?" He began to write hurriedly. "Bye-bye to my savings bonds."

"Kip Crandall Investigations is fine," I said.

Mama struggled to get out of the chair but failed. Butchie whined as he got tangled in a doily. "Please help Butch. We've got the money. Just don't tell any newspapers what you find out. Just tell us."

Marty went to Mama and held her hands. She stroked them gently. Mama's lids fluttered and her arms unfolded. "Don't you worry, Mama, we'll do our best to get to the bottom of this whole thing. We won't let any secrets out. Remember now, you've got Chuck and the two of us, so you're not alone with this thing. You're not alone. And don't talk to the police. Don't tell them anything. Do what the lawyer says."

A tiny smile crossed Mama's pursed lips. Her pale, brown eyes hid behind heavy lids. "I've got Butchie, too. He's such a comfort to me," she said. Mama clutched the tiny dog so tightly that he squealed and dropped to the carpet. "Here, Butchie, come to Mama." He jumped up to her lap and nuzzled her legs again.

We shook hands all around and left. I put the check in my wallet. It was the full $5,000. They were ready to put their money where their mouths were. Both loved Butch or Betty and would provide support and defense funds. Mama helped her loving and only son, while Chuck would go to the ends of the earth for his loving wife. After the shock and numbness ended, how would they feel?

Lost in our thoughts as we were, Marty and I slid quietly out the door to the Corvette. We sat down, simply stared at each other for a moment, then let out loud, collective "phews" and "whews" several times.

She spoke first, her beautiful dark almond-shaped eyes locked on mine. "I need an electroshock treatment. Mama's not crazy, is she? I don't think so. Did Butch cross-dress and fool both of them? She doesn't know he's a woman."

I flinched first and looked away. A cigarette would taste so good, or an ice-cold vodka. "Wouldn't Chuck have known or guessed if Butch tied off and hid his dong? Unless it was all oral and anal. And that wouldn't be too shabby for any sergeant. Not too shabby at all."

Marty said, "I don't think Butch or Betty, or whoever, is a transvestite. Even if the sergeant didn't notice her body, he would have seen some of the clothes or props and wondered what the hell was going on." She smoothed her hair and put on fresh lipstick in the Corvette mirror.

"Fooling Mama with clothes is easier than fooling Chuck," I said. "Mama can't see so well anymore. Must be in her late seventies." The engine was purring but I didn't pull away from the curb yet. "So Betty could have slipped on a pair of Chuck's slacks and a shirt when the loyal son visits Mama now and then."

Marty drummed her fingers on her notebook and twirled the gold pen. "So, boss, they're the same person but Butch became Betty. Is that it? Surgery?"

I gunned the motor; the RPMs went sky high, but so quietly we hardly noticed. "Must be. And she lied through her teeth to both of them. A son for Mama, a wife for Chuck, and never the twain shall meet. Clever. We're dealing with a very clever perp, if she's really the perp." As I slipped my car into traffic, a sense of purpose came over me. "Marty, why don't you check out our sources in the department? See what they've got—confession, newspaper accounts, and so on. I'll go talk to Betty and let her know we've been hired to help her."

Marty nodded. "Poor Chuck's pain and confusion. He might lose his wife and his chance for children and a family. You lost Wendy from cancer after a really gritty fight. My professor and I want kids, and I'm going to have them soon. Losing Betty could give Chuck an ache that never really goes away. We'll do all we can for Mrs. Waddell and Chuck. They seemed decent enough. Stop by and deposit that check, too, okay boss?"

"Yes, you bet." She observed me staring at her earrings.

"From Mexico," she said. "Professor Ruth gave them to me. Dangling strips of hammered silver with dots of amber stone and squares of enamel." She shook her head.

"They match your outfit perfectly."

"About time you noticed."

"Oh, I notice, I notice, don't worry."

Back in control, I roared past a cherry-red street version of an Alfa Romeo Spyder. The gray somber sky of morning promised to continue.

CHAPTER TWO

I dropped Marty at her car and then pointed the Corvette through the west side of Toledo, eye-balling the Gothic mimicry of the university and the nondescript 1950's modern of St. Francis de Sales High School. The Victorian buildings of the Old West End didn't need this silhouette of barren oaks and sycamores to enhance their delicate beauty, but in a strange way it did. Homes from a bygone era easily shaped into apartments or fraternity houses, while the trees hid even more memories and stories.

The light rain briefly froze to sleet and ice as I slid into downtown with its bombed-out aura, boarded-up windows of shuttered warehouses hoping for new light from the developers. Portside had failed as a commercial waterfront development, but undaunted visionaries had rehabbed several old hotels into condos that would cost millions if only they were in Manhattan or San Francisco. Past and present, hope and despair, the old and new, dark and light, short and tall—the uncertain skyline forecast the unsuccessful attempts to make this city into the best fusion of the Baltimore harbor, Las Vegas entertainment, the Red Sox ballpark, and New York steak houses.

I drove too fast, something I'd done consistently after getting rid of my 1982 Chevrolet Caprice. It was injured many times and the dented and rusted orange skin had cried out for repairs once too often. If I drove over fifty miles per hour, it had to be hooked up to an Air Force refueling tanker. So the Corvette spoiled me. It just didn't take away the pain of existence.

I pulled into the parking lot, then strolled through the handsome marble and sandstone lobby of the new police building. The guard at the desk knew me, so he hardly glanced at my PI card, just buzzed me inside. After going through a standard metal detector, I was frisked, gave up my Glock 9mm, and walked quickly into the new ten-cell holding area. This section housed citizens arrested and charged, but not yet formally arraigned or put before a grand jury. Betty Fowler was in cell number three. Snoring, but no swearing, singing, or screaming came from cells one and two as

I walked by. A police recruit of no more than twenty let me into Betty's cell. He said, "Call if you need me."

Betty perched on a built-in white metal stool, evidently writing a note. An orange jump suit didn't do much for her appearance—rough skin, small brown eyes, and crowded front teeth on the negative side, but a reasonably well-proportioned five foot seven inches or so when she finally stood up to shake my hand. She giggled. "So glad you came. Mama said Kip Crandall would be here, that help was on the way."

Something about her was different, but I couldn't put my finger on it; a touch of the mildly sexy female impersonator. All I knew was that I wanted to study her carefully without her knowing or being embarrassed by my prying eyes. I couldn't do it now. "How do you do, Betty? Nice to meet you. My partner Marty and I saw your husband and mother this morning. Nice folks. They're totally behind you. Total support."

"Yes, I'm so glad. They just met yesterday. Must be quite shocked."

I said, "Yes, you're right. Quite surprised but neither believes you're capable of murder." I pulled out a small pad and pen and my digital recorder. "Okay to record?"

Betty said, "Of course, I know I can trust you. My lawyer told me not to say anything to the police. I haven't." She sat on the stool and crossed her legs at the knees in a lady-like way. Then she picked a piece of lint from the arm of her jump suit. "I hated lying to Mama and Chuck. I was so afraid. More of what Chuck would do. I love him more than life and didn't want to lose him. I took the easy way out."

I lowered myself on to the hard mattress, covered only by a dark brown, heavy wool blanket and a pillow, gray striped. "Anyone would understand," I said.

Betty giggled and then smiled, her brown eyes widening in a plea for acceptance. "I'm a transsexual and I've killed four women. I drank their blood and ate parts of their bodies after butchering them."

"Yes, go ahead," I said. The screw-ups and losses in my personal life left me more understanding and tolerant of other people, but this story pushed me near the edge. I didn't show Betty that I felt like I'd just slurped a huge pot of coffee to wash down a bottle of ephedra pills. "Tell me more." I kept myself together.

Betty slowly criss-crossed her legs, retied a shoestring, and her pimply, doughy faced lifted to me. "Well, you know Butch did it, not Betty. I've never hurt a soul. I've been Betty for ten years, very happily married to Chuck, a good wife to him. We want kids. The adoption agency wanted a background check. I never thought that my fingerprints would do me in."

My nervous system calmed down. I told myself that I'd heard worse and seen worse as a cop. "Go ahead, Betty, you never thought what?"

"Well, I never thought I'd get caught with DNA. My lawyer says that the police had a warrant for DNA after I was arrested. There was very little evidence I'd committed a crime or knew of a crime, so no reason for DNA. Chuck and I had picked out a little girl, just three months old, to adopt. We'll be good parents. If Chuck stays with me." Tears now engulfed Betty's dark eyes. Her mascara didn't run, so maybe these were permanent lines that ophthalmologists design. "I may lose him."

"Why did Butch do these things, kill these women?" I said. "I'm sorry it's so painful for you, but Marty and I can help if we know the truth." I pictured Marty with me, eyebrow raised slightly, to tell me not to push too fast. I didn't need a confession for a DA or evidence for a grand jury, let alone a trial.

"I don't mind you asking," said Betty. "Butch always liked blood and meat. He was a cannibal. He knew he was a woman inside himself. He just waited. Once he killed the women and ate them, he'd had enough. He stopped killing when Betty, that's me, came along. Betty stopped him."

"Did Butch hate them?"

"Not really. He liked them. Liked to touch their private parts, you know." Betty's tears had dried up. Her face was composed. Eyes riveted on mine. She scribbled something on the pad of paper on the desk. "By the way, where did they find my DNA? I got rid of the first woman's body. Nothing ever turned up."

I dropped my pen. The digital recorder needed attention. I picked up the pen, then took care of the recorder. "They got a spot or two of blood from a dog, either on the leash or from the dog's collar. The dog must have nipped at the leg or hand of the person who killed Mary T. Branner. She was robbed at the ATM."

Betty's right hand flew to her mouth. "Yes, there was a dog on a leash. Maybe it did get me. There was so much going on at once. They found the dog but not the woman."

"Yes," I said. "They also found a size 10½ man's shoe print at the crime scene."

"I can tell you about the other three women, too. Butch killed them and ate them. Butch had to do it. Couldn't have stopped myself even if I had wanted to. I mean, Butch had to do it."

I needed a break. So I turned off the recorder and put it in my pocket. I patted the pocket as if the recorder was so jittery it might jump out and fly away. "I need a potty break, Betty, then we'll get some more background and some of the details. Okay?"

Betty smiled sweetly and looked down at the paper on the desk. She'd drawn a stick-figure of what looked like a pregnant woman with a huge stomach. "I need a potty-break too, so you'll have to excuse me, Mr. Crandall."

I called for the guard. I'd probably need another ninety minutes with Betty to get the additional data, which I could e-mail in my notes to Marty. I promised myself that it wouldn't be so bad; nothing could be more bizarre than a serial killer-cannibal-transsexual without insight who blames it on the guy she used to be. At least the cell was warm, clean, freshly painted, and quiet. I could take it for another ninety minutes. Betty could take it for as long as necessary. After all, she wouldn't hurt a flea. She just wanted to be a good mother and loyal wife to Chuck and a doting son to Mama.

Two hours later I lurched slowly back to the parking lot adjacent to the police headquarters annex. My head was spinning and I hadn't even turned the Corvette's key yet. I suppose Betty technically became a transsexual at the time of surgery but is transgender until that point. Was she a "transvestite" when she'd visit Mama, a transsexual female cross-dressing as a male to fool a mother into thinking that her loving son was visiting? Oh well, at least a loyal son to Mama, apart from the one big lie to her. This stuff could drive me nuts, so I wished for eight inches of that cold, white stuff to cover everything in sight, providing something tranquil to focus on and complain about. Actually, the rain had stopped, but there was still no sun or blue sky.

Marty and I work and live in Toledo. We love it. Once a sparkling industrial success, Toledo's factories continue to close, high-paying jobs disappear, people leave, and hundreds of thousands of feet of commercial space lie empty. Attempts to perk up downtown are only half successful, tax abatements and city loans to renovate housing and rehab condos backfire unexpectedly and the city loses millions. But it's a nice family town with mostly individual homes and decent schools, where you can travel anyplace in fifteen minutes and the people are very, very friendly. Who cares if the restaurants suck, the baseball and hockey teams are losers, and no one wants to come here for conventions? San Francisco, it ain't. We still love it.

The so-called Glass City, famous for its use of local natural resources to make glass products, boasts quite a history. How about the police department? In 1837, one police officer, the city marshal, was established in the original city charter. The population of the county had then reached approximately 9,000. Constables elected under state law helped, but Toledo was fifteen years old before it had a police force. That first force was all volunteer, which shows you how much value the citizens gave it. In 1866, a metropolitan police system emerged, and total cost for the first year was $13,160. The city grew, as did crime and fear. So, by 1922 the police department comprised a chief, detectives, captains, sergeants and 350 patrolmen. Oh yes, there were three matrons and three turnkeys. The first county jail, built for $4,500 in 1845 and used until 1858, sold for just $250, including building and land. Those were the days. I'd memorized the facts years ago and used them repeatedly in speeches to high school kids and community centers.

My cell phone quivered, sans pictures, messaging, or video games, and pulled me out of my history review. I pressed the magic button. There was a brief cutout. "Hello, hello," I said.

"It's me, you handsome devil. It's me, Tonto. While you had the easy job of interviewing Mrs. Fowler in a nice warm jail, I've been chasing around town. Our police snitch, Blue Throat, tells me that Betty's attorney has shut her up—just what we'd expect of the venerable Lawrence A. Goldbaum. There's no confession and no statement. Mum's the word. Betty is held on the charge of murdering one Mary T. Branner, some twelve or thirteen years ago. The woman went to an ATM and disappeared, left her small dog who wandered home. Some peculiar DNA and fingerprint evidence, also a footprint, but not much else. No eyewitness and no body. Our old buddies are working on some possible connections to other female disappearances around the same year or so."

"Good. She's keeping her mouth shut," I said.

"Right. So I went over to the newspaper archive. Ten years ago this month there's a headline on the front of the second section: 'On the Lookout for a Serial Killer.' The sheriff is standing in front of some flags. Somebody might have seen something." Marty's voice was confident and business-like; apparently, she was pleased with her progress on the case. "There were four women, including Mary T. Branner, who disappeared over a span of a year or so. Except for an arm and hand of one of them, no bodies found."

I caved into the black leather. More comfortable. The confusion of the day drained from my head and out my feet, which Chinese medicine says controls everything we think or feel or do. If I slipped off my shoes, would the process go more quickly?

Marty said, "There's more from the newspaper. At the time the police released an FBI profile of the killer. Maybe they fabricated it; but it's interesting. Killer was twenty-five to thirty, strong, ten or eleven shoe size, average socio-economic or below, job that does not involve significant relationships with the public, seems harmless, a 'nice guy,' awkward with women, risk-taker who is impulsive, doesn't handle rejection very well, and capable of unprovoked violence. You know the type, boss, so don't blame me for loving women not men. Okay?"

Who could blame her? "You did good. Very, very good. I'll e-mail you a summary of my interview. You'll go nuts. Unfortunately, the profile could be Butch. The cops probably think so." I turned the key and the powerful engine purred.

Marty said, "You're right. Blue Throat seemed strangely cocky about this one. It's Saturday night, so my professor and I are going to prowl and have fun. I'll e-mail you the rest of it."

I backed out of the parking space too fast. A police cruiser nearly clipped the Corvette's rear end. I slammed on the brakes, as did the other car, and waved to an old buddy from the force. His thumb and forefinger made a gun pointed at me as he smiled. He rolled down the window and said, "Why don't you get a real job?" Then he peeled away with his tires squealing. I could make mincemeat of any cruiser, anytime, anywhere.

I sped to the nursing home and quickly parked. Once inside, I knocked on the door of Herman and Susie Webber. No response. But I overheard them arguing.

Susie's voice was gentle but firm. "It's a nursing home, honey, accept it."

"It's not either. Don't use sugar on me. It's an assisted-living center. That's the place *before* a nursing home. A nursing home is God's waiting room. You know that much, woman," said Herman.

I knocked again. Then I walked in. Old buddies of mine, long-time, loving gladiators seated in wheelchairs facing each other.

"It is so," she said.

"Is not," he said.

"Well, well, good to see you folks, too. I came all the way out here and no one even welcomes me. Guess you'd rather fight it out. What's the victor get, anyway?" I leaned over and hugged them both. Susie kissed my cheek. It felt good. The warmth and trust of family. I'd known them since childhood. They'd known my wife Wendy and seen my struggles with booze, loss, the job—all of it. I often brought Marty.

Now in their mid-eighties, they sometimes accepted their age, sometimes didn't. Technically, their residence was the

Harborview Nursing Home, but it had been newly renovated to have the appearance of an assisted-living apartment. Small efficiency kitchen in the corner of the living area, tiny bedroom, and a bathroom with more handrails and water gadgets than I'd ever seen. It took all of their Medicare, Social Security, and both state pensions to simply pay the bill, but they didn't care. They didn't need their money for anything but their living arrangements and medicines and the doctors; they knew what their next stop was.

Herman had coached my high school basketball team and was kind enough to play me, the tenth man on the squad, occasionally— despite the fact that I couldn't dribble, couldn't pass, and couldn't shoot. He liked the fact that I was a team player and had a gritty determination to win.

Herman's thick gray mustache was the only hair on his freshly shaved black cheeks and skull. Still trim at age eighty-four, he always wore a clean, starched white shirt and a pair of baggy green slacks with a shiny seat. His soft brown eyes were clear, with no signs of the effects of the brandy that he loved. The stroke he had about two years ago really slowed him down.

"Are you exercising?" I said.

"Did you bring me a pint?" Herman said.

"Honey," said Susie, "That's answering a question with a question. And it's not even the same thing."

Susie was older than Herman, now a graceful but obese eighty-six. The chemo had taken most of her hair, so she wore a curly silver wig that gave her a more youthful appearance. Her diabetes and cancer kept her in a wheelchair or bed all of the time. Her dignified sense of humor and humanity kept her alive.

Herman's eyes twinkled, a mischievous bad little boy again. "So, did you? I put you in the games before the fourth quarter, way before you deserved it." Now he bullied me with a smile, a benign guilt trip.

I reached into the inside pocket of my blazer and out came a pint of decent French brandy. I laid the bottle in his lap.

Herman instantly slid it under the wool blanket. "Thanks, Kip. You're still a good kid. You know we love you."

Susie joined in. "And not just because you bring us stuff, either." She'd been a cafeteria worker in our school, always a smile, always upbeat. "Got anything for your old Aunt Susie?" Her dark bronze face was bloated out of its angularity but her deep-set eyes were lovingly moist, above the slight gray mustache on her upper lip.

I hugged her again and slipped a tiny box of Godiva chocolates into her robe pocket.

"Praise the Lord!" she said. "I'm so fat it don't matter. Some black baseball player said, 'If you don't mind, it don't matter' and I don't mind. By the bye, you look worried or tired or something. You don't fool me."

I relaxed on the edge of the bed. "I am puzzled. Real tough case we're working on. The person claims to have killed several women years ago and the person's mother wants us to clear the murderer's name. I don't know if we can."

Susie leaned forward in her wheelchair, and her eyes peered directly at me. Her bright red cotton robe contrasted nicely with her burnished skin, several shades lighter than Herman's. Her neck muscles were taut. "If it ain't so, it just ain't so. You can't make it true because a mother wants it, no matter how bad she wants it."

I sighed, feeling a sense of relief at my own limitations. "Thanks, Susie. I needed to hear that. When we're hired to do a job, I always give it my best. I'm getting stronger again, like I used to be."

Herman smiled, apparently putting together past and present in some way. "You always did, Kip. You weren't the tallest or the fastest, but you always gave it 110 percent."

"It's a weird case. The woman who supposedly did the crime used to be a man," I said.

"Must be some truth in it," said Herman. "Some kind of shame. Our preacher said the Lord only made men and women to love each other. Nobody'd go to that kind of trouble without a good reason." He winked at me.

"Hush, oh hush up, Herman. What do you know about police work, you old fool? Found anybody for yourself yet?" said Susie.

She got to the heart of things.

"No, Wendy's death still haunts me. I visit her grave. Think about her every day. Just keep going. Seems like I lost her yesterday, and it's been three years already." The sadness and loneliness welled up in my chest. "I should date women. I should stop drinking. I should get real tough again."

Susie said, "If I were younger, I'd make sure you had a date after church on Sunday and I'd fix your favorite fried chicken, okra, hushpuppies, and sweet potato pie."

"No greens with hocks?" I said.

She chuckled. "Mustard okay with you?"

"Mustard greens would be just fine," I said.

I loved them both. I could trust them. Herman would take a tiny nip daily and Susie would cut the candy pieces in half, one per day. They wouldn't overindulge, so I didn't need to feel too guilty over the risks of exacerbating their medical conditions with my gifts. I'd only add to their burdens by bringing them a tray of cut-up veggies with a dip. It would end up in the trash. They'd lost some interest in life, were increasingly preoccupied with their health. Who wouldn't at their stage? But I'd been with them for twenty minutes and neither had complained of pain or symptoms. They inspired me. Susie kept a box of my favorite peanut clusters under her bed, just for me.

"Listen, you two," I said. "Please don't forget those weight-lifting exercises I taught you. Sit upright in your chairs and lift those two-pound barbells like Charles Atlas did. When this case is over, I'm going to buy you your own recumbent exercise bicycle for the room."

Herman said, "Who'll put us on it?" We all laughed.

"I'll move in and take care of that. I'm getting old enough…"

We didn't say long good-byes. A quick peck on the cheek and a brief hug for each and I was out the door. "Love you both. Be back soon."

This time I sensed more of the typical hallway stench—the bleach, the disinfectant, the stale urine, blood, and vomit—which fresh paint and new wallpaper couldn't mask for very long.

I slipped on my new yellow Gucci sunglasses. To control the glare, of course, not my tears.

CHAPTER THREE

E-Mail
From: Marty
To: Kip
Subject: Mrs. F.

P.S. Blue Throat confirms what the DA's office told me. They are most likely to charge Betty with murder one on the first ATM murder. They've got more evidence on that one, matching footprint and Betty's DNA on the dog's collar–maybe more. Probably when she grabbed him and he ran away. Horrible thought to go to the electric chair based on a dead dog's evidence. Anyway, that's where they think they've got enough evidence, speculating that a partial motive may have been robbery and that it somehow escalated into murder. Still, no body, no confession, no eyewitness, and no clear motive for kidnapping or murder; unless you buy the serial-killer theory which even the police think is a big leap. Whatever blows up their skirt. I know what you're thinking; we've got to check this thing out for Mama. Well, when the shit hits the fan, we've got to find a way to tell her that Butch is now Betty and that he killed and ate four women before he got married.

So, we've got our work cut out for us (ho, ho), but I'm pretty much convinced with Betty's story. She's a fucking cannibal and I still don't have a fix on cannibals. It's a long shot but if we knew more about this cannibal thing, maybe we'd find another perp who did it. Animals do it. Some people do it. There are reasons—get smart, get strong, you know the old, Broadway show tune, "You Gotta Have Heart!" Stay close to your friends, but closer to your enemies. Eat them; you can't get any closer than that, can you, boss? If this weren't so serious, it would be a riot. How the hell do we get into these things? How the hell did Mama and Chuck get the bread to pay our enormous fees? I guess Chuck's savings and Mama's retirement are gone with the wind.

We've got people to interview in a block on the north side of town, where the victim originally lived with her husband, Willie Branner, a truck driver turned insurance salesman. Blue Throat says the police carefully interviewed all of these neighbors and family years ago, but couldn't come up with anything on any of them except there were all kinds of motives to kidnap or even kill Mary. We'll move fast because we probably won't come up with anything new here. I'll give you a brief summary from the files I saw.

Her daughter, Shari Lynn, worked in a slaughterhouse and meat-locker company, too. At the time of the murder, she was twenty-seven and married, but had a daughter of twelve named Tami. Shari Lynn had been a wild kid who wasn't playing with a full deck and she'd been very sick and crazed when Tami was born out of wedlock. Psychiatrists gave her meds and a judge declared her unable to care for the child. So, loving mother Mary swooped in and took Tami with the help of the biological father, Damone Jackson, Jr., who evidently didn't give a shit and got bought off— paid for his rights and no child support. Mary lied to the state and county to pay for Tami's upkeep. Basically, Tami was a cash cow for more than a decade for Willie and Mary. Well, that would give Shari Lynn plenty of reason to hate Mary—to seek vengeance and to try any means to get her daughter back.

The apple doesn't fall to far from the tree. Mary evidently was a victim of mental illness, given to extremes. Sloppy as hell, wouldn't cook, big gambling debts, drove Willie crazy with all of her shenanigans. Didn't make her a very good mother for Tami, but the courts let it stand all of those years. Willie was Mr. Mom, in addition to vain efforts to earn enough money to support Mary's habits and excesses and all of her doctor and hospital bills, to boot.

Then there's this guy Damone Jackson, Jr. He was thirty-five when Mary was killed. His thing was young girls. He knocked up Shari Lynn, then took no responsibility for anything. After Tami's birth he told a few lies and pretended to want what was the best for Tami. Shari Lynn was left to brood about her lost daughter all of those years while Willie raised her after Mary died. Damone was a small-time numbers runner at the auto plant nearby, then was sent to jail briefly for receiving stolen property. He recently got a SBA minority loan to help his struggling landscape company survive and works nights as a bartender.

The other neighbors should be considered, too. The brothers, Boomer and Bubba Kwiatowski, shared a house next to Willie's. They are factory workers who inherited the house but have made it into a pig-sty. Bubba served time, about six years. Boomer got drunk and shot his .22 pistol at a neighbor, then was arrested by the SWAT team after nearly being killed by them. Bubba had him arrested for selling coke at the factory, but the charges were dismissed when he ratted out his supervisor, his main supplier in the scheme. These two guys, B & B as they are known, were always into it with Willie and Mary, arguing over a fence's location, who should rake the leaves from whose trees, or whether a dog of one should shit on the lawn of the other.

Neatness counts is the motto of Robert Archer who lives on the other side of the original Branner location. As messy as Mary was, Robert was the picture of cleanliness and organization. He scraped, painted, nailed, washed, cleaned, shaved, swept, dusted, and so on all day long. After washing and polishing cars, painting gutters, hanging new screens, and putting in a new stove, he still found many tasks. He did not work outside the home, but his wife and five kids did. He couldn't stand Mary. She was everything he feared and hated—sloppy, messy, disorganized, and impulsive. There were rumors that Robert's parents had mysteriously disappeared while on a trip hunting elk in the west.

Poor Mary T. Branner. Everybody in the world hated this bitch's ass.

E-Mail
From: Kip Crandall
To: Marty Flores
Subject: Interviews with Mrs. Betty Fowler

Hey, Marty. I tracked her down in the county lock-up. Once she knew Mama had sent me, she was extremely cooperative and very talkative. I interviewed her twice. We can see her together next time. No, you see her alone.

She's had a lot of friends try to visit and they've delivered more cakes and pies for her than I've seen at most funerals. Guards and cops eat well. Here goes. You'd better sit down. Betty doesn't spare the details.

Butch loved red meat. He'd grown more flexible in adulthood, also ate pork, but preferred aged beef over veal, lamb, or goat. Aged red meat was tops, eaten raw, broiled or roasted. He didn't care if it was charbroiled or chopped up with oil and garlic, organic or not, tender or tough.

Butch hated vegetables. He especially hated green vegetables. Lettuce filled space and wasted time, and spinach, kale, and greens were a nightmare. However, corn, okra, tomatoes, and potatoes were okay a few times each year—but only if served with some kind of a red meat sandwich or stew.

He often bragged about his skills with a knife. While he was in high school, he worked part-time at the dry-dock marina area, carving replacement parts for the handmade oak, cherry, and walnut interiors of the rich people's yachts—railings, moulding, built-in shelving, and so on. He even worked in stone but he didn't like it so much because of the heavy chisels and hammers; he missed his knives.

Butch loved to fool people. He was medium height and thin, with stringy, oily, dark hair that had no body or luster to it. His hair stuck to his skull as if glued down. He wore cheap clothes, the colors clashed and the fabrics were wrong for the season—wool in summer and flimsy cotton in winter. People usually ignored him or shunned him, or occasionally were openly hostile.

He thought he would become one of the most feared and hated criminals in the world, a dreaded and horribly successful serial killer, one who loved the blood, ate the meat, carved the human rump roasts to perfection, and then hid what was left of the bodies in his frozen meat locker. He felt he should be referred to as 'The Butcher.'

Mama hooked up with Ralph Waddell. He promised her that he would pay most of the bills. He promised Butch that he'd read books to him. Mama and Ralph got married downtown by a judge. It didn't take Mama long to realize that Ralph was as poor as she was. He bought a fifth of Jim Beam twice a week, but not much else. He didn't even know how to read and never went to church. No pew would hold his 350 pounds of blubber.

After a year or so, Uncle Ralph left Mama. He stuffed himself into his old Chevy, back seat loaded with all of his earthly possessions, and drove away in the dust. Butch followed him to a run-down boardinghouse on the edge of town. Butch snuck into the house, found Uncle Ralph's room, and knocked softly. The door opened slowly, revealing Waddell in his brown, smelly underwear. Butch stabbed Ralph directly in the heart and made an L-shaped deep cut. He wiped the Bowie knife on Ralph's shorts, licked off the remains, and walked to his bicycle for the long ride back to Mama. He hadn't waited to see Ralph slide to the floor dead. He swore to himself that he'd get rid of the name Waddell some day, even though Mama had insisted he take it whether it was legal or not.

When he was seventeen, the vocational-education department sent Butch a letter. It began, "Dear Mr. Waddell," and asked him if he wanted to get real-life experience on a work internship and be paid for it. Twice as much money as his bowling alley job. He replied yes. He picked an internship in a wholesale slaughterhouse, learning the trade of butcher.

Mama smiled when he told her, then she cried with happiness. The money helped, but she told him that this opportunity could really lead to something. He could be somebody; a butcher was always needed and usually respected.

The first afternoon at Churchill's meat-packing plant, Butch knew he'd found a home—he whispered the word 'heaven' to himself. The smell excited him despite the cold. Red-faced butchers cut, sliced, chopped, sawed, sewed, hung, gutted, and packaged all kinds of weird-looking carcasses and chunks of meat. A huge poster displayed all the different sections and organs of a steer. He had a lot to learn. Blood was everywhere; bright red on aprons, dark on the floor where spots had dried and couldn't be swept up or cleaned away completely. Nothing was wasted.

Everything was so beautiful, so orderly, so wonderful. Someday he'd try to discern the ingredients in the odor he loved, pungent, sweet, overwhelming. Was it the blood? Whatever, it was heaven on earth. Butch knew this was the beginning for him.

The placards on the wall made him smile: "We don't grow it, we just mow it," "You stab it, we slab it" and "Doctors bury their mistakes, we grind ours".

His chosen profession helped hide a secret part of Butch. Covered in a bloody white jacket, apron and a tight hat, face pimpled and scarred inside a plastic shield, others saw little of him except his chipped gray teeth and wispy mustache. He'd pluck it on Sundays rather than shave, but it grew back to torment him. Butch fought hard to hide an inner truth from himself for most of his first seventeen years; potentially it could blot out every other sensation or emotion that welled up. He fought it hard. He walked fast. He cut quickly. The meat axes and saws moved like glistening white lightning in his hands. The boss said he was the best intern he'd ever seen. Butch had a great future ahead.

Then those three words would blast through his brain, fire through it, bounce around. If he could have brain surgery, they could be removed. The tumor could be excised. He'd have surgery later, when he had the money. Then he'd have, what did the school counselor say…then he'd have self-esteem. "I'm a girl." He pounded his head against the cold steel door of the meat freezer. "I'm a girl."

He'd really known this truth since he was seven or eight years old. His hips weren't broad or rounded, he didn't get a period, rarely imagined himself as a mother, but he instinctively realized that he was misplaced, really a girl in a boy's body. He wanted to change himself some day, the real thing. Then he would be a girl, later a woman, and dress and act and be treated like what he really was. He'd change his name, but he would be true to the genuine Butch. He didn't even know that the name Butch had other connotations.

In the meantime, he would hide himself, tell no one his secret, force it out of his consciousness as much as he could, never mention it to Mama, act like a boy, and tell himself that he would be whatever he had to be later. He was alone with it. It was a horrifying, empty loneliness, but he chose it over the risks of exposure, the wrath of the world, and Mama's eternal disappointment with him, her "brave little boy," her "son who helped out like a real man would," her "Who needs a husband when I've got my little Butch?"

That's Betty-Butch's story so far. Stay tuned. I need to re-charge my batteries, as they say.

CHAPTER FOUR

I realized my old buddy Vince Johnson needed a haircut. He also needed to perform about one hundred crunches daily for a month or so. His belly hung over the tight elastic waistband of his extra-long blue running shorts. Tall and slim by nature, he was unhappy with his new-found belly, a product of too much beer and pasta. Cops always celebrated with beer, shots, pizza and pool. They had a lot to celebrate lately at my old precinct—two successful murder convictions, with Vince the lead detective in both of them.

When he called me, literally begging to come to Wildwood Club with me to workout, who could refuse? I knew that secretly he just wanted to see me, see how I was doing, share a laugh or two, and that he was sure if he offered golf, pool, beer, movie, bowling or whatever, I'd find some lame excuse. That had been my social MO since I lost Wendy. I'd find a way, nice or not, to say thanks but no thanks. I knew it was a mistake.

I threw on my black tank top and a pair of yellow knee-length nylon shorts, a Los Angeles Lakers wannabe. My own little gut still needed work, but it was so much more comfortable to observe and evaluate Vince's problems.

We were about to depart the locker room. Vince said, "I may as well get it over with."

"Go ahead," I said.

"We want you alone, or you and Marty, or you and someone, to come over for dinner, or go out to catch a movie."

"What else?" I said.

"We've got a neighbor, cute as hell and a widow with two young kids, just for a drink or a coffee date. She's only thirty."

"Yeah?" I said.

"The Captain and the gang at the job want you to come to the Thursday all-night poker party. Just once. Like old times."

"You know I appreciate it. Not quite ready. Soon, maybe. You'll be the first," I said. I had to admit it felt good to get the offers. One of these days I'd be back.

"Use it or lose it," Vince said.

"I lost it a few years ago."

We both laughed, tied the laces on our cross-trainers and bounced out of the locker room to the work-out area, complete with running track and basketball court on the second floor, weights and body machines crowded into the lower level. TVs and hip-hop sounded everywhere, night and day. Almost as cold as a surgery center, mysteriously the place did not smell like a gym or locker room. Probably some cancer-causing chemicals surreptitiously added to the heating and air system eliminated odors. All these sprays sugarcoat the world just before they kill us.

We hopped on adjoining treadmills, elevated them slightly for a twenty-minute run to start the evening off. Not bad shape for a couple of guys about forty, but none of the heads on top of gorgeous young female bodies in tight black spandex exercise suits turned our way—yet.

"Cap says he'll retire soon. Got nearly twenty-five in and he's still alive. I've got a shot at it, or at least watch commander," said Vince.

"That's great, Vince. You're one of the best. You never took anything and you never ratted out anybody who did."

"It's a fine line. At times I felt holier than thou, but managed to get re-assigned. Told myself I wasn't Internal Affairs so it wasn't up to me."

We were both sweating now. Our speed was at about a seven-minute pace with a medium elevation. I felt good, not in a zone, but distracted from the usual worries, and the obsessions about the past seemed remote for the moment. I peered at Vince and he had a contented look, though he was breathing harder now to match his reddening skin. He was funny, with a sense of humor that came out when he drank or relaxed.

"Oh, I almost forgot. When you come over next time, you can have my wife," he said.

"Bullshit. I want your sister."

"She's in a nursing home. She'll be able to walk again soon," Vince said.

"No wonder people hate cop jokes. We are raunchy. Comes with the territory, I guess."

A brawny, tanned body-builder type strolled up to Vince's treadmill and pulled the plug. It lurched to a sudden stop and Vince nearly fell over. "Okay, asshole. You arrested my brother Tony Sanchez. He didn't do nothing to nobody."

The guy grabbed the treadmill side rail and shook it furiously. I put a chokehold on him from the rear, while Vince smashed him twice in the gut. The guy fell to his knees in pain.

He said, "Don't look over your shoulder. I'll be there. Sooner or later, I'll get you. You're a lying bastard cop."

I leaned over quickly and gave Mr. World an elbow in the mouth. Blood spurted out. It was a quasi-disguised blow in the best tradition of an NBA center or power forward—just turning in the pivot.

I picked up a towel and pressed it to his mouth and nose.
"I've got some cuffs in my locker. Be right back," said Vince. He ran off.

A small traffic jam developed near the treadmills. People were scared and curious. Most had missed the action because it was so fast. We each grabbed an arm and walked Mr. World to the lobby, called a cruiser, and had him escorted downtown.

The manager quickly told anyone who asked about the event that there had been a misunderstanding, everyone was safe and no one was hurt, that it was all over. The rhythm of the mass workouts resumed quickly, the narcissism of lean hard bodies outweighing any fear or danger related to Mr. World's antics.

We stretched out on thick padded mats. Vince said, "Nice work, partner. I thought the guy was going to spread-eagle me into the goddamn machine. Thanks. His brother's a fucking psycho, beat up his wife and his kid last week. He's a body-builder, too, owns a tanning parlor."

More stretching. First, full body, then legs, next pushups, finally crunches and more crunches lying on our sides. Humped over like a cat, head pressed up like a lion. Then squats. The only easy part was the finish. It had to be over at some point. Guys with stiff joints hate to stretch. Vince and me. At the end we lay exhausted, breathing very hard.

"No pain, no gain," he said. The standard line of gym rats.

"Speak little, do much," I said. Worn out, this saying fit me better at the moment.

Cold water at the fountain was irresistible. We gulped like we'd been marooned on the Sahara for days. Then we sat at a table full of newspapers and magazines, artfully managing the chairs for maximum viewing of the female species at work on their bodies.

Vince said, "I finally killed a perp. He wrestled my gun away. I got it back and it went off. One shot. Bam. Right in the chest." He wiped away beads of sweat from his brow and upper lip. His small gray eyes narrowed with the painful memory. He shook his head several times and perspiration flew from his buzz cut.

"Yeah, I read about it. Sorry. Must have been awful for you."

"Young kid of seventeen. Robbed a liquor store. His family was heartbroken," Vince said. "With all the really bad guys I've arrested over the years it had to be this one. A goddamn kid. I was on administrative leave for a few weeks." Vince moved his chair back and abruptly headed for the showers.

"Not your fault, old buddy," I said. "I know you. You never took—no money, no drugs, no sex. Good cop. Good guy. Hell, I even considered making you my partner someday." I sat pondering the crosses we all have to bear in our lifetime.

"Come back to the job, asshole." Sweat dropped from Vince's body and pooled around his feet.

I brushed my fingers over the four-inch scar running from my left ear down to my chin, thick and hot now. Exercise, stress, booze—they all got it going and sometimes at the most embarrassing times. It turned red and sore-looking, too. Marty told me. Mr. World's antic took me back to my last fight. A wino with a cheap jug wine in a brown paper sack, living near the high level bridge, had asked for help. We were putting him into the patrol car to take him to the mission. He suddenly cracked the bottle on the car door handle, the broken glass sliced through the paper, and he swung. An inch or so one way or the other and I wouldn't have made it. The plastic surgeon said that he could make it look better, but I'd left it alone, with the stitches done by the emergency department resident. That was several years ago. He was an up-and-coming surgeon now. The ER doctor, that is. The drunk is dead. That was my last assault while a cop.

After the steam room and a hot shower, I felt much better. My scar calmed down. Abandoned, unused muscles relaxed to the point of tolerable pain. The shower and shampoo were always good. I considered an aspirin but said no to that specific artificial crutch. However, giving up so much bodily fluid to the steam and exercise, the thought of a beer crossed my mind.

"Are you thinking what I'm thinking? It's only 8:30 p.m.," Vince said.

"Man, we are definitely on the same wave length. Arnie's for a quick beer. Maybe two."

"Race you. Loser buys," said Vince.

I drove the Corvette as slowly as those horses would allow without simply falling down. It was good to see Vince, and I wanted to show my appreciation. I missed him, missed working with guys like him. Good times with beautiful, sexy Marty; she was a damn fine cop and investigator. It was different with the guys—tough, strong, no bull-shit.

Arnie's was closed, renovation or something like that. I couldn't read the sign clearly in the dark. Vince arrived first, slumped behind the wheel of his '89 Nova sedan, smirking at me. He lowered his window with the hand crank, while my power system took care of the driver's side opening.

He said, "You must have known. I win nothing so far. Loser pays. You lost."

"Double or nothing," I said. "Whoever buys a six-pack first at the closest carry-out wins. Okay?"

"You're on. Slowpoke. See you there." He peeled out of the empty parking lot, wheels smoking. I turned off my engine and counted to one hundred backwards, then I tooled out into the traffic.

Vince strutted out of the store proudly holding up a six-pack. "You owe me twelve bucks and change, wise-guy. Double or nothing, right?" He knew I'd dogged it, but he played along.

We sat in the luxurious leather listening to a CD with Sinatra, Ella, and Sarah favorites. Vince popped open a beer for each of us. He'd added some pretzels, "on me" was his description. So here we were, like it was high school. Drinking cold beer, sitting in a car in the parking lot of a carry-out, hoping the police don't chase us out, nibbling on a pretzel now and then. I handed cash to Vince. "Keep the change. That'll cover the pretzels, too. I lost."

"Nice car. The PI business must be good. My old Nova is ready to explode any day now." He admired my car's interior, eyes darting to all the gauges under the dashboard.

"Not bad," I said. "Marty and I do a lot of stuff for attorneys, especially Goldbaum. Always try to get back on track but haven't done it yet. My sponsor dumped me. All kinds of people have plenty of advice." I felt relaxed for the moment. I trusted Vince. The tension and stress drifted upward from toes and legs to shoulders and neck. It went out of me somewhere in my brain.

Vince chugged his beer and opened us each a second can. He handed me a pretzel.

"Thanks, mother. Tastes good even in the winter, doesn't it? See, this sadness takes over. Wendy and I did everything together. I had the job and my partner. But everything else was with her. At first I didn't care if I lived or not. I blamed myself. Better care, better doctors, better hospital, better husband—something could have saved her." I tilted the can and half of the beer slid down my throat.

"Wish we had some schnapps, a couple of shots would go down with the brewskies," said Vince. "Or a plate of tortellini."

"Then I got over the guilt. I just plain missed her, and I was so fucking scared. I drank at six in the morning. First white wine, then I settled into a fifth of Jim Beam every day, usually by late afternoon. Some days I ate, some days I didn't. Never answered the phone or the doorbell. Resigned from the force, lived on savings and Wendy's life insurance. She'd always handled the money. I'd splurge and order a double-pepperoni pizza. I'd give the kid a ten dollar tip; I didn't give a rat's ass about anything. Then I got pissed, really pissed. I'd break stuff, bought a punching bag."

Vince said, "Pissed off at the whole goddamned world."

"There were times when I had no desire to go on. No purpose. Nothing meant anything to me. Not even drinking a six-pack and watching an NFL game. So why should I take up space on this earth?

Vince said, "Sounds like the bottom of the barrel."

I shifted positions so that my legs weren't so bunched up, twisting my torso for relief. Recalling the loneliness and grief of Wendy's loss, I could sense the melancholy stiffen my joints quickly. "Almost. One day I drank a quart of vodka by noon. I decided to put one bullet in the Glock, no semi-automatic shit, just one bullet and see what happened. I put the Glock on top of the TV stand and waited for something. It's weird but I surfed to a Benny Hinn revival show in Berlin of all places. You know, the dark-skinned evangelist in those Nehru-type white suits. Probably a giant con with all of those miracles. I watched it through my personal haze, psychological cataracts that made every thought so blurry I couldn't turn one into action. Something snapped in me, and my brain registered a tiny bit of hope. I thought to myself, if he can fake a cure for cancer or stroke, why can't I fake a little bit of something for myself? So, I loaded the gun with a clip, put it back in the holster, shaved, showered and went out to eat a plate of eggs, bacon and grits."

Vince said, "Hinn would take credit, I guess."

"He may deserve it," I said.

"Finally, Marty got me back to AA. I got a new sponsor and stopped most, not all, of the booze. That's been over two years we've worked together. We've had some very bizarre cases and we do drink together now and then, but mostly we're recovering and trying to live one day, shit, one hour, sometimes one moment at a time."

Vince opened each of us a third beer. We both chugged it down.

"That's it, old buddy. Got to go. Cap said you were one of the best. Took charge. You'll get through it." He'd had enough. The car door opened and he was gone.

CHAPTER FIVE

E-Mail
From: Kip
To: Marty
Subject: Continuation of Mrs. Betty Fowler

At eighteen, the foreman offered Butch a job as an apprentice butcher. He hurried to work at 5:45 a.m. every day, ahead of the others. For the next ten hours each day he was in a kind of trance, what some would call a zone. It was a mixture of contentment, achievement and effort—and the thrill and simple enjoyment of blood and guts; the taste, smell, texture, color—well, really the *feel* of butchering. Butch was quite successful at his job, and by the time he was twenty, he was a full-fledged butcher.

At twenty-one, Butch got restless in his job about the same time that the boss offered him the chance of a lifetime. Would he consider being a driver, as well as a butcher, and a bit of a salesman to boot? Would he! He jumped at the chance to be on the move and active, get out of the slaughterhouse and the butchering room, see the world, meet people briefly, and still be around his beloved meat all day long. Butch toasted himself when he was alone one night with a thimble full of beef blood. It whet his appetite for more, but he left work quickly because he was still so fearful of being caught.

Life was perfect. He loaded the cold truck around 5:00 a.m. with his orders for the day. Sometimes he had to do some butchering himself. Usually the orders were prepared and packaged for him. If a restaurant or store changed the order, he could "cut and paste" as he put it, while the truck was parked. His route took him to small mom-and-pop stores, huge supermarkets, an Italian sausage factory, catering businesses, and a small Amish slaughterhouse that couldn't get sufficient supply from its own farmers. The customers liked him. He had the respect of the other butchers because he was actually one of them. Butch always had a smile, a superficial, "How you doing?" or "What can I get you?" No one knew that he was a girl inside his body, and that as a teenager, he had already killed one man. They all liked Butch, the young guy who took good care of his customers.

Butch developed the most successful and lucrative route for the company. He got several salary raises over the next eighteen months. Several momentous events occurred at nearly the same time. At twenty-two, Butch had the idea of creating a secret compartment for his truck. The boss asked him if he'd drive further on his route, even stay overnight in other cities occasionally if the return drive was too long. He agreed immediately.

Butch then asked for three or four days off so he could build the false wall and door that he'd create in the rear of his white panel truck. The space would be about 4 feet x 8 feet x 8 feet, the size of a narrow closet. He attached hooks to the ceiling identical to those in the truck that held whole sides of beef, lamb, or goat. The hinge for the doors to the secret compartment was hidden by hooks on which he placed his dirty white jackets, aprons, or hats. The compartment was perfectly camouflaged; it simply appeared to be the back wall of the truck's interior meat locker.

He now hauled only the finest aged, dark-marbled New York strip steaks and choice tender racks of lamb. When the fire and police departments needed hundreds of pounds of the best baby-back ribs for their annual barbecues, Butch delivered post-haste. Small, ethnic butcher shops and traditional Jewish delis counted on Butch for goat, brisket, and veal shanks. He was pleasant, efficient, and helpful and delivered only the best.

Around the same time, Mama ordered him a $500 set of knives from a TV ad. He was so grateful that he hugged her too hard, scattering small black and blue marks on her baggy arms. She told him it was nothing and would heal. He argued forcefully that he should take her to a doctor but she refused with equal strength. The last thing in life that he wanted was to hurt Mama in any way.

Butch was now ready to start his sideline. The secret compartment was built, he had plentiful implements, the butcher's tools of the trade, and he traveled the state. It all coalesced without much additional thought or strategy, the opportunity, the implements, the concealment, and the motive. Butch didn't like to think about the motive. Why did he want to kill people? He'd killed Uncle Ralph and never given it a second thought, because Waddell deserved it for the way he'd treated Mama. That was fair play.

The kind of killing he thought of now was different, and he really couldn't understand his reasons. He was successful in his job, saved money from his good salary, enjoyed lots of freedom and, most important, Mama was immensely proud of him. She said that the good Lord had smiled on her the day Butch was born, that his birth made all of her suffering worth it. But Butch knew in his heart that he wanted to murder people, actual strangers, and then eat some of their bodies, drink their blood, and freeze the remainder to keep in the rear compartment of his truck. He named it Butch's Fast Freezer in his mind because he was a speedy butcher and because meat and bones would freeze quickly in a small space kept at temperatures below freezing.

The first murder actually took place at a bank ATM on a late fall evening. Heavy clouds and a chill wind rolled over a parking lot where the money machine was placed at the poorly lit end near the street. He thought he'd kill a man first, but here was a sloppily dressed middle-aged woman who had walked up to the machine holding a miniature brown dog. She put the dog at her feet, held tightly to the leash, and withdrew some cash with her card. Butch drove his truck to within ten feet of the kiosk, shifted into park, kept the motor running, and opened the rear doors. He walked up to the woman, said, "Good evening," slit her throat with his Bowie knife, and dragged her into the rear secret compartment. He hung her bleeding body on a hook and drove off, humming a half-forgotten childhood melody to himself.

It had gone so smoothly that he surprised himself. No witnesses. And he had an extra $200 in cash that she'd withdrawn simply sitting in the tray for him. Someone would assume robbery. He had the money, her bank cards, and purse, but as he grabbed the sweet little dog by the collar it had scampered away. A dog could never identify Butch, especially a tiny thing with only a name tag on it. Perhaps someone knew she was walking to the

ATM to get cash, perhaps not.

Butch drove slowly and cautiously for a distance of fifty miles. He pulled into a highway rest stop and slept for a few hours until dawn. Then he stopped for coffee at a truck stop.

Butch proceeded to a campsite near a lake where he sometimes parked the truck. He would rest, maybe sit in the sun for a bit or go for a brief swim. The unmarked white panel truck was one of many, so police would have difficulty identifying it, even if a witness had observed it.

It was nearly 10:00 a.m. when he finally stopped in his usual site near the lake. Butch slipped the "Do Not Disturb" sign on the rear latch and climbed into the truck and shut the door. The motor was running and the refrigeration was too cold since he'd made all of his deliveries. He was trembling.

There was no overhead light. He had to use a large camping lantern in addition to a smaller flashlight that he carried in the glove box. The flickering yellowish light provided a weird back drop for the limp body hanging in his inner sanctum. She was dead, her face contorted in fear. The towel around her neck had soaked up blood, but plenty of it covered her jeans and blouse, and some was beginning to congeal on the floor in an incredibly neat circular pool. Her legs were dimpled, very swollen and purplish. Butch couldn't wait to look at her breasts and vagina. Before anything else, prior to dismembering her and eating and drinking, he wanted to see and feel and examine her sex.

Butch undressed her slowly and carefully. Her vaginal area was mysterious and rewarding. Butch touched and poked and smelled and stared for at least thirty minutes even before he'd completely removed her panties and slacks. He'd have one like this someday, the beautiful folds of skin, the rose-like appearance, soft, moist quality, even with so much blood drained away. He knew more than ever that he wanted what Mary T. Branner probably took for granted.

Butch followed his instincts now, as well as his training and experience. He gutted Mary, butchered her body, keeping the inner glands and organs separate. Then he cut up the legs and arms and torso with a twelve-inch steak knife called a "ghetto special," and packaged them in freezer paper. He planned to burn her clothing later. Next, he took part of the heart and liver, cut them up, soaked them in red wine, then started a beautiful wood fire in the pit outside and fried them in butter, onions, and more wine. After lunch, he sipped a little of the fresh blood and napped. When he awakened at dusk, he had the crazy thought that maybe he really was a vampire, since they slept during the day and came out in the darkness. So, he climbed outside, into the last remnants of daylight. He was no vampire.

The next day TV news had the story of her disappearance. The woman had lived near the bank and, as she often did, walked to the ATM to get cash. She did not return; however her dog wandered home. Police didn't know if foul play was involved, but no trace of her surfaced after leaving her home. No one had seen her or her dog. Her computerized account showed $200 withdrawn that evening, so police speculated that robbery may be involved. What a laugh, Butch said, that someone could be killed for $200. Murder was much more important to him than a mere $200, but he was glad to have the cash for Mama.

And that brings us to the present, in which Betty's mother, lovingly known to all as "Mama," has sought our help to clear her only child's good name. A mistake? False confession to me? Serial killer? Coincidence? Have fun with the next interview. How do we get into all this crazy shit? I got into police work to make a difference, make society a better place.

CHAPTER SIX

Marty scheduled her interview with Betty for Tuesday. We were up in the air over all the Betty stuff. Her story was bizarre but believable, weird by anyone's standards, yet with a certain consistency to it. She didn't strike us as a woman who would brag about her past or show off for the world. Unless there was a very deep cave of guilt and shame, why would anyone confess to murders of women with cannibalism thrown in at no extra charge? Why would she falsely confess? If she were telling the truth, why did she cannibalize? Why not just kill the women, maybe molest them while alive, or dead, and be done with it? Why not cut them up and dispose of the bodies? Few ate their victims. We wanted to get ahead of the police on the cannibalism in case they added it to her charges. More information might even help clear Betty.

I hoped Professor Ernesto Agatucci could answer the riddle. He was a professor and director of an institute at the university and known as something of a bon vivant around town since his wife of fifty years died last year.

Marty set up an appointment for us with the professor late on a Monday afternoon, the usual "Thank God It's Monday" time. I parked the Corvette in a small reserved lot next to a one hundred-year-old Victorian beauty near the campus. The woodwork was exquisitely trimmed in baby blue and sunflower yellow while the countless layers of wooden siding reflected a bright white enamel. Extensive restoration had paid off. This was a gem. A shiny bronze plaque near the door read "Institute of Anthropophagy."

"What the hell is that?" I said.

Marty said, "It means studying cannibals. You know Hannibal the Cannibal. Well, this is Professor Aggie, the cannibal expert. That's what they call him." She straightened my blue-and-gold rep tie, worn to impress others. "Stay strong, boss."

Marty was ready for action and dressed to kill. Her legs were covered in knee-high black suede boots under a simple black A-line skirt topped with a white cashmere turtleneck. Gold glistened from her wrists and ears.

"I don't get it. You can touch my clothes, straighten my tie without permission, but I can't ogle you." She knew I wasn't really annoyed. I loved the by-play.

"That's it," she said. "You've got it and remember, you're the boss. Sexual harassment is very real." She blew me a kiss.

I pressed the buzzer. Then again. At long last a very old, hunch-backed woman wearing a heavy black wool shawl opened the door. The cold air blew her thin gray-blue locks into bangs. "Come in. Hurry. It's cold." She held the door open barely enough for us to pass by into the broad expanse of hallway and entrance area. Dark oak floor panels shone with wax and at first glance, it appeared that the entire first floor had wood-paneled walls with a different wood in each room. The effect was mysterious and other-worldly. Plasterboard walls in the suburbs could never compete with this.

"I'll turn on some lights. I'm Gina. I've worked for Professor Aggie for forty-nine years. Please sit." She led us to crimson-red velvet chairs, something you'd see in a huge tent in the Sahara. Would Vincent Price appear soon? The floors were covered by magnificent Middle-Eastern rugs that would be wall hangings in most places.

Before we could get our bearings, out popped Professor Aggie from an inner office. I should have guessed. Was it Edward G. Robinson with a mass of curly gray hair and neatly trimmed, nearly white beard, or was it Richard Attenborough, the scientist from *Jurassic Park*? He was perpetual motion as he shook hands and pulled us into his private office. "So glad you're here. So very glad," he said.

Gina called, "Can I leave, Professor? I've done the typing."

"No, you can't," he said. "It's not 6:00 p.m. yet. We need sherry in here. You're not going out for drinks with your boyfriend, are you?"

Moments later, a loud cough preceded Gina's entrance laden with a tray of sherry, paper-thin slices of fat Italian salami, several kinds of green olives, thin Tuscan wheat crackers, and brie cheese.

"Looks wonderful, Gina. Thanks so much. I thought brie was

a French cheese, not Italian," said Marty. She quickly reached for the food and drink.

"It is," she said. "And the sherry is Spanish." She walked out slowly, turned her head slightly over her right shoulder. "He's a man of the world."

Professor Aggie tucked his multi-colored ascot back into the white spread-collar shirt, whose top buttons were deliberately left open. Gray sharkskin slacks were a perfect fit to his short, slender frame. A baggy hand-knitted black sweater with suede elbow patches was no surprise, but white running shoes were. Yes, quite the man of the world—Madrid, Venice, Paris, New York.

The office walls were hidden by books, magazines, and newspapers on shelves that soared from floor to ceiling. I had expected a collection of skulls or, at least, bones of ancient animals or humans who'd been eaten by each other. A striking, blackened, iron pot about two feet in diameter had been made into a stunning desk lamp and next to it was placed a stand-up sign that originally read 'You Are What You Eat.' The 'what' had been crossed out and replaced with 'who'.

We sat while he hopped around like a bird in a cage. "So glad you're here. Eat. Drink. Enjoy. Americans don't take time to enjoy good food, wine, olives—the blessings of the gods."

We did as we were told. Who could deny anything to this delightful man so obviously caught up in the lust and passion of human existence? His face, wrinkled by a sardonic smile and long creases from electric blue eyes to his ears, was a moving target. Eye contact was nearly non-existent. He sipped his wine, nibbled on a cracker, and spit an olive pit into his hand before he wrapped it in a napkin; made it into a ball, shot it into a waste-basket and said, "Two."

"Professor," I said.

"You don't need to explain, young man. People only come to see me for one reason. I know why you're here."

I glanced at Marty. She raised the eyebrow. "Of course," I said. "You're the expert."

"I've made a short list of recent books for you. In fact, I'll loan you my copies. Here's Goldman with his categories and criteria of cannibalism." He ran to the wall that held the door. "The Aztec gods ate human hearts and drank blood. Here's Sartore's text and this is the book by Tannahill, which is good on blood covenants with the living, the dead, and the gods." He handed the three books to Marty with a deep bow from the waist. The ascot loosened and his cheeks reddened considerably.

"Thank you so much, Professor. We'll study them," said Marty.

"Ah, yes," said Agatucci. "This book by Hanson makes it clear that you can't legally kill someone even if you're starving. Usually, the sailors would cast lots to see who was eaten. That was different." He dropped the Hanson book in my lap. "And here's Askenasy's book with a map of where cannibalism took place in both prehistoric and recorded time. Very interesting." He turned to the map and appeared to be studying it. "Is that enough for your story?"

"Thank you so much for the books and the ideas. We want to know about cannibalism because we've got a client who's confessed, in confidence, to being a murderer and a cannibal. Some killers eat victims, have sex with them, keep their bones, and that stuff. We're private investigators. I'm Kip, in charge of the case, and this is my associate, Marty."

Professor Aggie sat down in the straight-backed, hand-carved wooden chair piled high with cushions behind his desk. He stared ahead. "You should have told me. I thought you were newspaper reporters. You looked like newspaper reporters. Small writing pads. Good listeners and all that."

Marty said, "We should have been more specific with Gina when we made the appointment. Sorry." She was so good at allowing people to save face. Her eyes warmly invited the professor to continue as she sat motionless with her hands covering the tomes in her lap.

"We've been eating each other for a very long time. Sometimes for food, sometimes it's the enemy killed in battle, or we feed the gods or it's been magic or witchcraft, or even vampires. We've eaten our own family, tribal or village peers, in order to gain strength, courage, and intelligence."

"So many reasons," I said. Beads of perspiration formed on my upper lip. I poured a second glass of sherry for myself and slowly chewed slices of salami.

"Yes, indeed, cannibalism is an ancient behavior performed for varied reasons at different times with activities and purposes that played central roles in many cultures despite the taboos of today." Professor Aggie jumped to his feet again and strutted around the small room with his hands locked behind him.

I said, "Is it one of the deepest and most profound impulses in mankind?"

He stopped dead in his tracks. "It is to me, of course. Forgive me, but it can reduce a human being to excrement or it can be a spiritual experience of the highest order. An old teacher of mine used to say we're all at risk of 'flesh to shit' and 'dust to dust,' really 'flesh to dust' if you allow enough time to go by and that's what anthropophagy is all about—enough time to go by." The twinkle in his eye was replaced by a bloodshot dullness thanks to several nips of the excellent sherry.

Marty said, "Excuse me, Professor.   May I use the restroom?"

"Of course, it's on the right-hand side down the hall." He needlessly pointed to the right as Marty rose and walked out of the door. His gaze followed her. Under his breath he said, "Beautiful creature, very beautiful."

"Yes, Marty's beautiful and a consummate professional. Very good at what she does."

Professor Aggie actually looked directly into my eyes as he stood just a few feet away from my chair. "You know, early on there was the idea that human flesh led women to conceive. The dead person's life was absorbed into a woman and then born again, so to speak."

Purely my idea, but maybe Butch ate women to become a woman and mother. It's not my job, but Goldbaum could use an insanity defense if we can't locate another suspect.

He went on, "Of course, today we do other things to take body parts and bodily fluids from one human and put them into another—transplanted organs, blood and plasma infusions, even surrogate motherhood with the husband's sperm or a donor. We harvest organs from the dead, even the living."

Where was Marty? My scar felt hot. I kept trying to ignore it. This talk of death and surrogate parenting seemed relevant to my own life, but I couldn't quite put my finger on it. Perspiring, I could feel my heart race. The sherry didn't quite do it, I wanted vodka.

Marty strolled in leisurely, revealing perfect white teeth in a wide smile. "That's quite a collection of skulls in that curio cabinet in the bathroom. I guess it's just the top half of a skull."

Professor Aggie returned the smile. "Yes, the soul was in the head for some societies but primitives also used the skull as a cup to drink from."

Marty said, "Gulp." We all laughed. "Did anyone lie or distort being cannibalistic?" she said.

"Oh, yes, still a big controversy in anthropology today. Since many reports are anecdotal, people aren't sure what's valid. Some societies claim more cannibalism than really existed, a way to shock and instill fear in enemies or exert control over their own people."

"Any contemporary individuals or criminals confess to cannibalism when it's not true?" I asked.

"Crazies might belong to demonic cults or use bones and group witchcraft. They could suffer from shame or guilt, or self-aggrandizement, or secretly hope to be killed. I'm not an expert at the individual psychological level." The good professor frowned, next chug-a-lugged a brimming glass of wine, noisily chewed a handful of crackers, crossed himself twice, blinked his eyes, then managed to find his chair and plop down awkwardly. "Of course, confession is good for the soul. Then there's the sacrament with the body and blood of Christ."

Professor Aggie nodded off instantly, so we tiptoed out. Marty said, "I'll call him tomorrow and thank him for his help. I'll thank Gina, too."

CHAPTER SEVEN

E-Mail
From: Marty Flores
To: Kip Crandall
Subject: Confidential Interview of Betty Fowler

Read your memo to me with great interest. What a son-of-a-bitch Butch was, or is. Did I miss something or did the asshole show any contrition or remorse, or feel any guilt or shame, or need for punishment or hope for redemption? He's just a goddamn cannibal, a primitive who doesn't belong in a civilized world but will probably get away with it. I thank my lucky stars that we don't have to judge him or convict him. I'm just going to keep my butt up in the air over the idea that the more we can find out, the closer to the truth we come, the more we can help out poor old Mama. This He-She stuff is awkward, so Betty will be "She" later in the memo. Okay, boss?

Betty's arrest only took place because of the fingerprint match. She and her husband, Sgt. Chuck Fowler, were in the midst of an adoption process when the routine testing turned up the thirteen-year-old crimes. Blue Throat gave me further rumors on some other disappearances, not yet confirmed. There was skin and hair under the fingernails of the hand on the severed arm and two types of blood on the torn piece of a firefighter uniform—possible murders that were miles and months apart.

Caught a glimpse of Sgt. Fowler today in the lobby of the jail and we chatted briefly; trim, athletic, brass all shined, polished shoes, and pressed pants. He's a sergeant with the three stripes on top and one underneath. Is that staff sergeant? He still loves her to death and doesn't believe the charges. He can't imagine himself, a real macho stud, marrying another guy. If she wanted to, Betty could prove it easily with medical, surgical, and dental records, or else the sergeant could search for scar tissue! Originally, Betty gave Chuck some cock'n'bull story about having had an abortion as a teenager that was botched so badly that she is sterile.

Sgt. Fowler totally supports his wife's innocence. He's not only hired a very expensive criminal defense attorney, but a publicist, if needed, to shape public opinion in Betty's favor. Killers, especially cannibal types, aren't very popular with the media. Mama's exhausted most of her savings.

Betty is sort of thin. She wore prison orange slacks and an overshirt like nurses wear. Her hands were soft and delicate, well-cared for. There's a kind of giggle she does, or maybe it's a choking kind of laughter just before she talks. Like, you ask her something, and she giggles while she's thinking of what so say, then stops and says it. It has a rehearsed quality to it.

Here goes some details, mostly from Betty but fleshed out with information from Blue Throat. Betty said that she wonders if Butch's need for a woman was to strengthen his own femininity, to take on the style and grace of a woman's body.

When Butch saw Kerry Sanders at the Jericho Deli he observed her small, well-shaped breasts and her narrow hips at the top of long shapely legs. That's what he liked and, of course, would want for himself some day. Kerry was friendly and outgoing, a high school junior of seventeen, last year's captain of the cheerleaders, and a peer counselor in math for freshmen. She was planning on attending the local community college after graduation. Must have been real cute.

Butch delivered pastrami and corned beef to the deli. Kerry now worked from 3:00 p.m. to 6:00 p.m. each day. She left work by the rear door, yelling, "See you guys later."

Butch knew her routine. One day, he waited. He pretended to write bills and notes on his ledger pad, and when Kerry flew out of the store, Butch asked her if she'd ever seen the inside of a frozen-food locker truck. She said no and that was it. She climbed in, Butch closed the door, hacked her aorta, hung her to bleed, and drove off. No witnesses. No Kerry. No suspicion of Butch. Police had tire prints of all of the cars and trucks in the rear and front parking lots, and that's all of the crime scene evidence they could find. That wasn't very useful because Kerry walked to her boyfriend's house every day after work and no one knew where her abduction took place, if indeed, it had.

Months went by before Butch killed again. He was saving money for his surgery, getting the strength and courage he'd need to make the physical and psychological transition ahead. How would he tell Mama? Could he? What would she think of Butch as a woman? As he drove the highway late one evening after an arduous round trip, he almost ran over what looked like a young man hitchhiking, dressed in jeans and a sweat shirt, with spiked white hair and huge gold hoop earrings. Butch stopped for him. He hopped into the truck's passenger seat. To Butch's surprise, his rider was a thirty-one-year-old, light-skinned Latino who said her name was Es Martinez. She was a known prostitute who hung out at truck stops. She offered to do things to Butch. He responded by stabbing her in the heart three times at the next truck stop and freezing her remains immediately. He later ate some of her stomach and thighs for sexual strength, well really for sexiness, but would not drink her blood because he feared disease. Police found a severed arm and hand along that highway a few days later and linked the prints to her.

Less than a year after he had first killed at the ATM, he made a special run to the Firefighter's Annual Picnic to deliver extra pork ribs for the barbecue. A firefighter lingered in the truck and seemed interested in the life of a butcher and freezer truck driver. Sheila McMartin was twenty-seven and was destined, she felt, to some day be a battalion commander. Sheila told Butch he was cute and that she liked the coolness of the truck. She suddenly kissed him; Butch was frightened, nearly repulsed, but he covered it up.

They made plans to see each other when she got off work around midnight the next day. Butch picked her up as she parked her old Honda in front of the apartment building where she lived alone. He drove to a remote area near the big county dam site. Sheila fought hard. Butch put the Bowie through her right eye and cut her throat. He put his lips to her aorta, then drank the spurting hot red blood to his fill. He had cut his hand during the fight, so he fixed the wound and drove off. The bagpipes eventually played for Sheila, but her body was never discovered by the police.

Butch was more lucky than smart. He was never questioned

by the police and never became a suspect in any of the four murders. Without going into more gory details, he butchered and ate parts of all four women, disposed of the rest of the flesh at the slaughterhouse dump, sold the bones in a bag to the perfume factory as was common at his company, burned the clothes, and then abruptly he decided to stop killing. He simply said that he felt whatever he was doing was finished, that, in some sense, he'd completed his mission. He felt that what he did was necessary, a cover-up—that he had to do it, and for whatever the motive it was a series of murders that protected Butch. From what?

At the time Butch stopped killing, the police had very little crime-scene evidence. There was a shoe print and fingerprints and blood on the dog from Mary, several questionable molds of tire tracks from Kerry, prints on a severed arm and hand from Es as well as material under her fingernails, and a piece of torn uniform from Sheila. Butch's prints were present on the dog's collar and were probably the partial prints on Es's hand. Otherwise, the police had no suspect, no confession, no bodies, no eyewitness, and they had no connection between these four missing women for many years.

Butch told his boss that he had been robbed and his truck stolen. The boss filed a police report and collected the insurance. In fact, Butch sold the refrigeration equipment to a second-hand dealer, then sold the truck to a shady operator who shipped it to Argentina. Both thugs are long dead and their activities taken over by others. Butch actually got a bonus and commendation from his boss for his courage during the robbery.

Mama wants the truth, she says, but I don't see how a seventy-seven-year-old woman could handle all of this garbage about her loving, only son. It could all be bogus, but that's our job to check it out. We're way ahead of the police investigation.

Betty was tearful off and on during the entire three hours with me. "I'm so sorry." "I feel so ashamed." "Guilty as hell." "I thought it was all behind me." "I'll never live it down." "Mama and Chuck will hate me." That's what I got. Butch apparently had no remorse. Betty was all shame, guilt, fears, and tears—maybe crocodile. She might even be a suicide risk. She wants to make amends, if she can, to the victims' families, to Chuck, to Mama. But, and here's the hooker, she didn't do it; Butch did it. You know, the butler did it. Butch is a different person, a prior identity. Now she's Betty and has been married for ten years. And the babe truly and sincerely means it. Betty is innocent of any charge of murder. She could get herself a pussy, a bunch of silicone in her chest, but she couldn't change her fingerprints or the DNA. Woulda, coulda, shoulda.

Let me pick up the story where I left off with the Butch piece, and I'll stop wandering all over the place. Butch saved up a bunch of money for the surgery. He told Mama he was going on a long vacation and bought post-cards from exotic locations to send to Mama. Actually, he got a job at Wal-Mart as a checker, took hormones, and for a period of a year and a half or so, he entered counseling required by the surgeon.

Betty had to be sure of her decision, since the physical changes were only part of the process. She had to be comfortable and sure of herself as a woman, prepared for what she wanted—marriage, children, and a white picket fence. Betty was cocksure of herself, knew for fifteen years that she was a woman.

The counselor helped Betty get a better job at the Army base commissary. Betty told the counselor everything except about the serial murders, the earlier killing of Uncle Ralph, and the cannibal shit. People don't tell their therapist everything, but the counselor must have been a dumb shit not to have sensed that something wasn't right. Betty expressed feelings and emotions that had been pent up for years, and at times she said that she wasn't sure if she made up the feelings or if they were really there. The loneliness, the angst, the frustration, the anger, the sexual inhibition, the desperate desire for friends and to help Mama, the absence of genuine social skills; basically, what I get is the flat, unexpressive, superficially friendly person she'd been. She either learned to be a sensitive, caring, supportive woman, or else she faked it or both.

The counselor taught her social skills where she learned to identify emotions and respond appropriately. She didn't need the usual voice training; her inflection and throatiness were perfect. Another step along the way consisted of Betty attending a three-day Transgender Conference in New Orleans. The counselor said that she wouldn't feel so alone with her life and her plans, that it would help her to be with other adults who also had unusual life paths. Betty had a ball. At the conference, Betty attended seminars and discussions that were very relevant to her life. She felt accepted and one of the gang, so to speak. It was a new and treasured feeling. The seminar on marriage and family life meant the most to her.

Then she met Chuck at the Army base store. She was in the middle of the transition, already dressing as a woman, hormone therapy eliminating hair on her face and body, when she met Chuck. She abruptly left him and her job for a month, ostensibly because of a family medical problem that was urgent. Really, she had the surgery, and then two weeks in the hospital to recover, and one week to get a new apartment, to see Mama, and to buy herself a new wardrobe.

The surgeries were a huge success according to Betty, as well as the doctors. The breast implants were completed in one morning in the plastic surgeon's outpatient office; pointy with big reddish-brown nipples that looked good to Betty even before they fully healed. She could hardly keep her hands off them, so the nurse bundled her up with plentiful white gauze bandages. One month later her new, beautiful vagina was constructed during a hospital stay. She was excited beyond belief, never frightened or nervous during any stage of the surgeries. The doctor's role was simply to reveal to Betty her true nature, what God had intended her to be. I was afraid she'd ask me if I wanted to see some of the surgical results. She didn't, thank goodness, but she did comment in an off-hand way that Chuck liked the results.

About six months after the surgery, Chuck proposed. They were married by the Protestant chaplain at the base, with Chuck's buddy and his wife attending them. Chuck found a convenient two-bedroom apartment in the enlisted men's married housing complex. Friends gave them furniture and they bought some new things, more towels and kitchen utensils and, voila! They were in business as happy homemakers.

Betty threw herself into married life. She shopped. She

cooked. Sex was fantastic. She loved Chuck completely. His orgasms satisfied her as well. She worked full-time in the base store and was employee of the month several times. She was offered managerial positions gradually. She was involved, maybe over-involved, with clubs and organizations. She would babysit a friend's kids at the drop of a hat. Betty organized parties, dances, blood drives, and tours. The other wives saw Betty as a role model and went to her apartment for gossip and cooking lessons.

Betty came close to telling Chuck her true identity but never did. She wanted to, but feared that he'd find her repugnant and leave her, probably divorce her. She reasoned to herself that it wasn't that important, or even that relevant. The past was past; Butch was not Betty. She was now herself. In Betty's mind, Butch was dead and buried. Chuck believed that she had no living family. It was just easier that way, and solved two problems—neither Chuck nor Mama knew the true identity of Betty, and she had no need to introduce Chuck to Mama, since Mama didn't exist. Betty is no fool.

Betty is not a multiple personality. She truly believes that Butch Waddell was not, and is not, Betty Fowler and that she did not change identities to elude the police. She simply became herself. I suppose she'd say, if pressed, that what Butch did was connected to his inherently becoming a woman, that it was necessary in some convoluted way to Betty's emergence; almost a matter of self-preservation that Butch was a serial killer. But can she walk away from killing five people by simply saying Butch did it? She's insane, *muy loco*, I think. Yet, maybe a psychiatrist could have a hard time proving she's psychotic or killed in self-defense to promote self-preservation. Butch killed to protect the life of Betty. How's that?

I need three huge strawberry margaritas. Then I'll hit my head on the wall, pull out my hair, and fall asleep for days. This whole thing is just too bizarre for words. Boss, I'm so glad you're in charge of this case. Take care and see you soon.

On a particularly lonely Thursday night in December, reading Marty's report didn't help my mood. I drifted over to the West Side station house about 10:00 p.m. First time in months I'd done it. Occupying the first floor of an old elementary school, it was full of gray metal desks, phones, computers, fax machines, file cabinets, and cigar smoke but no holding pen. That was downtown. Needing to see old pals and drink some coffee or have a beer, I'd showered and shaved, put on fresh clothes, brushed my teeth—like a first date in school with a new girl. My armpits were clammy as I contemplated questions such as 'How would they feel about me?' and 'How would I feel about them?'

I ran down memory lane. Chasing crooks in back alleys with Vince, a scam we cracked with long nights studying computer print-outs, talking down a jumper from one of the bridges, the surprise party our wives threw when we both got promoted, Wendy and Vince's wife Sandy planning a cruise we never took, the day I left the force, the unwavering support of Cap even when he disagreed so vehemently with me.

I got lucky. Captain Miles and Vince were there getting ready for a shift change, so the bowling league was next. Cap was head of the detective bureau, a burly, strong Irish guy with curly gray hair who shopped at the Big and Tall Shop and would give you the over-sized shirt off of his back. And good old Vince, my people. Why did I avoid them like the plague? Hell, they probably knew me better than I knew myself. Of course, that just might be the reason.

"Have I died and gone to heaven?" said Vince. We shook hands. Then he hugged me, the grip of a python, and handed me over to Cap. Arm around my shoulders, he simply squeezed so hard I choked. Nobody answered the phone.

Relief ran through me. I was home. "It's me who died. You guys sure are a sight for sore eyes," I said.

"We've got an extra, its bowling night," said Cap. He threw me a canary yellow extra-large T-shirt with one word in large black letters on the back—COPS. "They're beautiful, aren't they?"

I slipped mine over my white turtleneck sweater. "You guys remember, don't you? I'm a shitty bowler."

"Who could forget?" said Vince. "The only thing you're worse at is keeping score." We all laughed.

Even in my, "Give the tough case to Kip, he's like a dog with a bone" heyday, I wasn't a regular on the team. I'd made a terrible mistake on the scoring one time, counting strikes as spares, or some kind of freaking mathematical misfortune.

We'd walked to the bowling alley before I realized it. Lost in thought, I'd just luxuriated in strolling between Vince and Cap. "Keep him in the middle. He can't escape and we won't need the cuffs," said Cap.

The Bowl More Alley, nearly a historic landmark, begged for a facelift. An exterior stucco front on the one-story flat-roofed structure sported a second coat of primer. That had been applied two or three years ago. Somehow the finish coat had been forgotten. The cracks in the stucco returned, and the primer coat failed to control a heady mixture of mildew, rust streaks and water stains. The inside was equally shabby, with worn orange-flecked linoleum and threadbare brown carpeting in the bar area. Now a family fun center, one corner of the entryway featured video games, and a small area behind the shoe rentals had a sign "Child Care" on the door. Who would bring a kid of two or three out at midnight while mom and dad drank beer and bowled?

As we claimed a table, I remembered why I had never liked bowling. Loud talk, crude shirts, frustrating curve balls, impossible scoring, blue smoke and stale beer, stinking insoles of rented shoes, thudding balls pounding wood floors, popping clack of ball on pins, screams of well-wishers and glad-handers, high fives, "buy you a round," strikes and spares, then do it all over again like washing dishes or mowing grass.

Two other guys, both rookies I barely knew, joined us at our table. "Good shirts, Cap, they'll know who the hell we are, anyway. Nice to meet you, Kip," said the short, dark-haired patrolman. Both newcomers shook my hand. They all put on their bowling shoes while I held my nose and rented a pair.

Thank God the place was so loud. There couldn't be much counseling from my friends; do this, do that, time heals, get out more, become a regular on the team, and so on. We'd barely be able to hear anything given the din here, so I felt a certain kind of safety. I wouldn't have to apologize or explain or complain, just drink beer, laugh, swear, and lie a little bit.

The rookie bought the first round of beer. "This is horse-piss, kid, you'll never ever make corporal," said Vince. He knocked his can over on the tray. No bubbles. The kid jumped up and brought back a pitcher.

"Now we're cooking," said Cap. He retied his laces. "I remember when you fell on your ass, Kip." His large-featured, pock-marked face softened with warm reminiscences.

I sipped on the beer. "How could I forget? Must be seven or eight years ago. One of my first times here. The ball was too heavy. I lost my grip and slipped on the goddamn oily wood halfway down into the gutter."

Vince laughed. "I'll never forget it. You were flat out. And your bowling never did improve much. You're one of the shittiest bowlers on the job, past, present, or future."

"Thanks. That makes me feel good. You won't expect much." I petted one of the old black balls that I used. The others had their own personal balls, initialed and kept with their bowling shoes in small lockers here at the alley. My hand never fit the public balls very well, but that's no excuse.

"Go ahead, Kip, roll one," said Cap. He chugged his second beer, unfazed by the cheap brew. "The other team isn't here yet. Those firemen must be working overtime."

"Just so those fuckers don't show up dripping water all over us, or full of smoke," said Vince.

"Maybe full of shit, just no smoke." Cap laughed, so did the two rookies. "We should make them promise to shower before they bowl."

I stepped up. Held my feet together, ball in two hands chest high, poised for my first roll in years. I paused for effect. Put the ball down in the rack, wiped my hands carefully on the towel, chalked my hands lightly, then toweled off a second time. Then I quickly took the position and rolled a beauty. Straight down the lane after an extremely hard landing. All the pins flew.

"You goddamn sonofabitch. Jesus Christ. Where'd you learn that shit? Perfect strike," said Vince. His green eyes were bright with pride.

I felt like a million. "Weren't nothing, Marshal," I said. The others applauded me, loudly because they were working on their third round.

I sat down promptly and drained my glass. "Next one's on me." So I went to the bar and returned with five cans and a huge bag of barbecue chips.

"Business must be good, Kip. Thanks for the brewski," said Cap.

"We've got some very weird shit. Very weird. One of those murder cases for Goldbaum. Our perp is a girl who used to be a boy. Please don't tell anyone. Confidentiality," I said.

Vince roared. He choked on some chips, then coughed. He was our own Blue Throat but he didn't know that I knew. He gave us a helping hand, access to records and photos, and here I was bragging about confidentiality with a client.

The others threw practice balls. Vince's form was impeccable, a red-headed guy rolling a marbled red ball, feet bedecked in red-striped bowling shoes. Strike.

Cap lumbered up to the line, a tiny bit wobbly, even with the arch supports in his well-worn shoes. The back of his shirt blared COPS at us as he gently lowered his ball and it hit its customary curve. Ten pin up. Spare.

Mind clogged with memories, ears plugged with the alley's constant cacophony of sounds, aromas mostly an insult, I felt immunized to the world's sensations. Vince leaned over as we sat next to each other on the bench. He said, "Sandy is sick but we're not sure how bad it is. We'll know soon."

"Jesus Christ. Hope it's better than Wendy." I put my arm around his shoulder. Tried to keep the gaping hole in my psyche from festering and opening up. My eyes teared up from the smoke.

Cap interrupted. "Where are the chicken-shit firemen? They're always late when you need then. After we have six beers each, they forfeit the match. That's the rules." Everyone nodded, knowing he'd just made up the rules.

"No women on the team," I said. "You've got a couple of women sergeants now." Had to keep my feelings in check, so out came a diversionary topic.

"They came once. Two guys got in a fight over one of them, the one with the wooden leg. So we only use them as subs. Like we used to use you, you SOB," said Cap. He rubbed his hands together, then moved his fingers quickly, as if to fight off some discomfort. "The holes in my ball have shrunk, goddamn it."

Laughter and round number five arrived. One more beer and the firemen were fucked. They'd never hear the end of it.

Cap pulled out his cell phone. He listened. "Oh, shit, okay." He sat down suddenly and slipped off his shoes, grabbed his ball and stuffed it into his bag. "There's a huge warehouse fire downtown. They aren't bowling tonight. Anyone who can stand or drive is needed."

Out we went. Hell, we didn't get to discuss sex, SWAT teams, politicians, political protests and murder, street crime, how it felt to be overworked, underpaid, and "nobody gives a shit about you until they need you." We walked out singing some old Irish ditty about firemen and their massive problem with erectile dysfunction. I kept my new shirt. I loved it.

But I had changed. The attitudes toward female cops turned me off, and the idea of half-drunk cops going to an emergency situation seemed deranged. The real change was inside me—the feeling for other people, not just an investigator's suspicion of a perp's motives but a deeper appreciation of human feelings and needs. Most important for me was the increased acceptance of my own angst, which showed through attempts to conceal it with a cop's hard-boiled veneer of objectivity. Cops had guns, clubs and gas, but they could be scared shitless, like the rest of us.

CHAPTER EIGHT

Were it decent weather in spring or summer, we might visit the engaging Toledo Zoo or one of the city's many attractive metro parks to relax. Marty and I faced a dilemma in winter. Should we go to the Wildwood Club now, work out, build muscle, drain away our sins in a sauna and steam bath? Or should we head quickly to Arnie's to eat, drink booze, and absorb everybody else's cigarette smoke, even if we ourselves abstained? Arnie's had pool tables and more huge TV screens to show sport events than existed in an entire electronics warehouse. Pool tables clinched the vote, two-to-zip, for Arnie's.

We tooled along in the Corvette into the west side after I filled its tank at the cheapest service station near downtown. No pings in the engine yet, so the gas must be good enough. My thoughts were troubled at the station because a large collection of homeless folks and bag ladies hung out near there, actually a half block from the county drug-and-alcohol treatment center and a food-distribution warehouse. There but for the grace of God go I. My own recovery needed vigilance. Too many visits to Arnie's cost me my most recent sponsor. He told me to stay away.

The weather was fickle; some light rain followed by freezing rain succeeded by a light, wet snow that stopped quickly. Dusk came early on mid-December days so the automatic headlights shone already, though it was only a few minutes before 5:00 p.m. Potholes meant nothing to my huge, soft-riding tires, though winter was creating plenty of spring work for the street maintenance and repair department.

A burst water main on Central created a diversion blocked off with crime-scene tape, and two cops in orange vests directed traffic. Fire engines sped by us, screaming and blinking their way to a house fire where one prayed the hydrant worked.

Perversely, the second floor of a building had pots of red geraniums on a ledge outside the window, maybe just for a quick watering before coming back into the safety and warmth of an office or apartment. The day gave us a grim gray sky, with the dark, rolling white-black clouds that were so ugly this time of year. Evening promised a starless sky with slim possibility of even a glimpse of a patchy moon. Hell, we'd make our own fun. We always did.

The wetness slithered off our jackets but the moisture and chill clung to our bones. We shook our parkas furiously as we entered Arnie's, fighting off the instant onslaught of cracking pool balls, thick, ubiquitous, smoke, and screaming hordes cheering on some unknown college team playing football in a heavy downpour at an obscure Southern bowl venue.

Marty looked fantastic in the haze of our booth. Low-rise jeans highlighted the diamond stud in her navel, abs flat and beginning to ripple. A tight white mohair top clashed beautifully with her bronze skin and jet black hair worn in a chignon today. I made a renewed pledge to improve my appearance, work on the stomach and hips, do my free weights on a more regular and disciplined basis. If I didn't, people would stare at us and muse that I must be so rich or powerful that a gorgeous babe like Marty would go for me.

The waitress stood above us. I said, "The usual?" Marty nodded and smiled. "Let's see now. Some cheese poppers and hot wings. Two vodkas and olives with anchovies inside them."

"Be right back," said the waitress.

Marty glanced at me, trying for that comfortable, nonchalant blank face to hide her usual discomfort at the thought that everyone, male or female, in the place stared at her. She said, "Maybe I shouldn't wear this sweater. Too bright."

"Not for me. I love it. Bigger and brighter, the better. You know what I mean." I blew her a kiss.

"Boss, you sound horny and you look beat up," said Marty. "Wendy's been gone three years. She'd like to see you get laid and have some fun."

"That's what Herman and Susie said, too. But in a much nicer way—was I dating anyone, you know?" My eyes itched so much that I coughed. Should have worn a mask in here.

Marty reached up to help the waitress with the drinks and the chow. Arnie's always had big, cold drinks and hot, tasty hors

d'oeuvres. It was unspoken that we were going off the wagon.
We knew enough 12-step philosophy not to blame it on Betty and
Mama and Chuck—but if pressed, we would have. A cue ball
flew off of the closest table and rolled to us, so I picked it up and
threw it soft and underhand to a guy who thanked me with a twirl
of his cue-stick.

Marty cupped her glass in both hands and sipped. "My wife
and I are thinking about selling the duplex and buying something
in the country. You know, with some land for horses and a small
pond. Get away from it all kind of thing."

She trusted me but still referred to Professor Ruth Gillespie of
the university's English Department as her wife, rarely mentioned
her name. They'd been together for five years but lived in a duplex
to cover the relationship.

Neither felt completely secure being gay. Ruth lived with so
many rumors around the university about her sexuality that she
felt that her professional life and job were better protected with
the duplex, each with her own apartment. Marty had been dumped
from the force due to a false allegation of sexual assault and rape
when she'd really had a consensual quickie with a former female
prisoner. Poor judgment, but the greedy lawyer who got $25,000
from the city police force for the case didn't deserve it. Marty, one
of the most promising of the new breed of police officers, didn't
fight very hard, so she lost her job after several administrative
hearings. She was fed up with all the bullshit female cops got. In
the back of my mind I always suspected that Marty and Ruth were
not completely committed to each other—the duplex spelled some
degree of distance and ambivalence.

"Sounds great. You'll be together. You both love nature
and horseback riding. A Thoreau thing." I gulped my drink and
grabbed a popper. The explosion of cheese, pepper, anchovies,
and vodka on my palate was miraculous.

"Maybe kids, too," said Marty. She swirled the olive round
and round. Her eyes softened into deep, dark pools. "Maybe
kids."

"Uncle Kip will visit and help spoil them. I promise." Familiar
urges welled up somewhere in me; jealousy and hurt tinged with

resentment. I rubbed my eyes again, so much blue haze and the reminder of Wendy's death and my own loss of a family. She'd been thirty-three and married to me for seven years, ready for kids and then the cancer, the big C, came along. An unusual leukemia, with chemo and radiation producing exhaustion, lying on a couch vomiting for six months and later, no more Wendy, no more hope of kids, no more family. "This smoke is horrible." I used the napkin to catch the tears. "Uncle Kip will be there."

Marty didn't need to do therapy today. She said, "Speaking of family, what about Mama and Chuck? Are we taking money under false pretenses? Betty has confessed to us that she murdered five people, four women and one man, and ate parts of each of the women. You tell me, boss, how in the hell do we clear her name for Mamacita?"

I gulped the last few drops and looked for the waitress. As I caught her eye, I held up two fingers. She nodded.

I said, "Now, now, right to the point. That's why you're such a damn good partner. No lost motion." My gaze traveled to her diamond stud. "Hell, they'd have a lot to deal with if it were just the Butch-to-Betty thing and meeting each other for the first time."

Marty poked a popper open, then put it down. She drained her glass. "Has she taken a lie detector test yet?"

"No, not yet. She refused. If she failed it, that would help us. She won't do it. Her lawyer explained he'd arrange it, not the police. She just giggled."

Marty handed the waitress our two empty glasses, which were replaced with two new drinks. They looked even bigger and colder than their predecessors.

"Two cheeseburgers with everything and fries, please," I said.

Marty nodded and smiled. She held up her drink in a mock toast. "To the best boss a girl ever had."

I gulped mine. "If she eventually gets charged with all five murders, I'm thinking that a jury would look at Betty and think she's absolutely crazy, so perverse she should be locked up in a looney bin, maybe too nuts to even stand trial."

"Maybe she could be defended as a dual-identity person, Jekyll and Hyde type, and that the bad guy was gone and replaced by a good woman. But the cannibal shit, nobody will walk away from that. No juror in the world."

"You're right," I said. "If she's lying for some reason, how in the hell will we know? No lie detector. We can't read her mind."

"No one can. There's not much evidence the police have to compare with Betty's story. Why would she confess to us? This is no typical serial killer. Is she so guilt-ridden? Doesn't seem to be. Seeking publicity? No. Hurt Mama and Chuck? Seems to love them both." I raised my hand to hold up two fingers.

Marty pulled it down as the waitress appeared. "Let's eat the burgers first. Okay? There's only one way out of this thing for us and for her. One way to clear her name for Mama. Somebody else did it. She's not the one. Forget what she told us, or most of it. It's manure, so let's look for the pony." This time the waitress slid the burgers in front of us without Marty's assistance.

"Two more, please," I said.

Marty nodded without a smile this time.

The waitress said, "Burgers or vodka?" She laughed and hurried away.

Marty was logical and focused. She meticulously repositioned the lettuce, tomato, pickle, and onion inside the bun, which already absorbed the blend of mayo, mustard, and catsup. She took a swipe at it, teeth bared. "Mary T. Branner is the department's number-one case. Most evidence there. They'll charge Betty with murder one and then search for any kind of a pattern in several disappearances of women. No other bodies yet. If we could find another perp, or raise some doubt about Mary T. Branner, that could do it. It wouldn't be satisfying, but that could do it."

Some red juice, catsup mixed with medium-rare burger, dripped slowly down Marty's chin. I dabbed at it with my damp napkin. "You're a bit of a cannibal yourself. I like your idea."

Marty stuffed her mouth with fries, really getting into the food. "This Hell Street where Mary lived was something. The people I found out about are all still alive and there. Our own Blue

Throat let me read most of the interviews. That's how I got the picture. So many with motives and opportunity. Mary was very unpopular, sounds bipolar to me, and a bitch to live with."

"Good, good. I like it." I pushed the half-full glass aside. Back to work. "So, we've got the husband, the daughter, the granddaughter, two brothers on side of the Branner house, and another weird guy living on the other side. Plus, the biological father of Mary's granddaughter. Mary's two other kids were so young at the time we can rule them out. Poor old Mary."

"We'll just do our thing," Marty said. "Begin at the beginning. Re-interview everyone. See if we can get a different take on it. Cops never solved it. It's been an open disappearance or homicide for ten years. If we get Betty off on this one, then Mama and Chuck can spend the next few years getting to know each other and Betty can patiently fill them in on her life." She leaned over the table, stretched to the max, and kissed me on the forehead. "I'm drunk, boss. Let's go." Marty's flushed cheeks and milky eyes appeared to speak of a need to get home quickly, into the waiting arms of her lover and soul mate.

Me, I'd had my perfunctory peck. The nascent sexual response that traveled somewhere between my brain and my groin abated rapidly. I knew where I stood with Marty. So I paid the bill and left our waitress a twenty percent tip. Maybe she could have fun with her boyfriend tonight.

We arrived at the car with my thoughts suffused with plans to buy tires, the best and biggest street tires available. Then I could go fast, smooth, long, and hard. The Corvette, that is.

Marty said, "I'm disappointed. Usually we play nine-ball and winner pays the bill. Usually, we laugh more than tonight. Usually, you make a play for me. And usually, I tell you 'no, but I still love you.' Are you losing it?"

"Yes," I said. "I've lost it. This case has me very uneasy, not just perplexed or confused. There's something about it. I know I should take charge of the investigation but I'm really not sure. Not sure at all."

Marty frowned but her eyes twinkled mischievously. She said, "I know what you mean. It's probably why we drank so much vodka tonight instead of beer and lime."

"I was hoping you'd tell me more about what you and the professor do under the covers. None of my business, but hope springs eternal."

Marty answered with action. She slipped her digital recorder from her purse. "This is more your speed—Butch and Betty." She turned up the sound.

Marty: "Betty, do you have any more ideas why Butch did these things?"

Betty: "Not really, I'm not much of a thinker. Never was. When we studied a story in English class in school, I couldn't understand the characters very well."

Marty: "Well, I don't want to make you uncomfortable, but do you think he wanted to feel powerful and be able to intimidate other people? That's why some tribes or societies do it in faraway places."

Betty: "No, that doesn't seem right to me."

Marty: "What does seem right?"

Betty: "Well, Butch liked hot things hot and cold things cold. He liked to drink warm blood. He always cooked a thigh or piece of heart and reheated it if it got cold."

Marty: "So he enjoyed the drinking and the eating?"

Betty: "Oh my, yes. Butch thought there was nothing so sweet and tender as a broiled piece of thigh or butt. And the blood was so warm and thick. It felt good going down."

Marty: "Go on."

Betty: "He knew they wouldn't mind a bit. They were already dead. He knew it was all so good for him."

Marty: "Uh, how was it good for him?"

Betty: "He screwed them, pardon the expression."

Marty: "So, it was rape and then murder and then a feast."

Betty: "It was different. He cared about them. They were nice. They were pretty. They taught him. He knew he was a woman, so he thought to himself, how do women have sex with women? He bought a real nice black leather strap-on dildo."

Marty: "He pretended he was a woman. He didn't use his own, umm, penis."

Betty: "Butch never used his own. He wouldn't do that. He knew some day he'd be a happily married woman."

I pushed the 'pause' button. If I'd had a cigarette handy, I'd have lit it. "There's more, isn't there?" I said. Marty nodded, so I turned the recorder on again.

Marty: "Butch knew he'd be Betty, somehow, someday—a woman."

Betty: "So, he'd strap the dildo on to them and try to you know—have sex. It was hard to do. Chuck does it great now, by the way."

Marty: "Anything else?"

Betty: "Well, he'd come, you know what I mean, have an orgasm, and mix it with blood and meat—kind of a stew…"

Marty: "Uh, huh."

Betty: "Butch practiced oral stuff on the dildo but it tasted bad. Chuck tastes so nice and hot." Laughter and giggles. "Hot things hot."

Marty: "Quite busy wasn't Butch before he got rid of what was left of the bodies?"

Betty: "Yes, he was. He got an idea from a Chinese health store that they ground up certain animal tusks or bones and ate them. He sold most of the bones, but he cleaned and soaked and dried a few of them from each woman. Then he ground them and put the powder into blood. He could keep going for hours like this."

Marty: "Did he save any bones? Some people who do what you say Butch did, save things—for good luck or to feel they still have a part of the person with them. Did he?"

Betty: "I'll never tell." Giggling. "That's for me to know and you to find out." Giggling.

Marty: "Sorry, I didn't mean to pry."

Betty: "It's okay. Butch ate part of Mary's heart and he loved Sheila's blood. He nibbled a tiny piece of Es's, but got scared because she was a whore. She probably had diseases he could catch."

I turned the recorder off. My stomach churned and gurgled. The vodka and burger and fries were suffering an identity crisis. I didn't know whether to laugh or cry, because it all had the ring of truth.

Marty said, "Take me home, boss. It's late. She's such a nice lady, with her kidnapping, cannibalism, and plain old-fashioned murder."

We fell silent as I drove. We needed to cool off in mind and body. I turned the heater down and cracked my side window. "Should I open the moon roof?"

"Yes, that would be nice," said Marty. "We need to lighten up." The night chill swirled around us, a partial antidote to dear old Betty.

I thought that the stuff in the e-mails was raw, but this recorded garbage was really sicko. Sex and cannibalism bound up together, a bizarre pattern of behavior. We sure wouldn't want this in the hands of the prosecutors or, especially, the family. The language alone would shatter the ladylike, loving-wife image Betty created for Chuck.

Yes, there was crime scene evidence but nothing conclusive or foolproof to link Betty to murder. That is, except Betty's statements about Butch's killing spree, a confession the police would never obtain. I was sure that there would be alternative explanations for the paucity of circumstantial evidence that the police had. But Betty should be behind some kind of bars somewhere—a prison or a psychiatric hospital or a gulag in Siberia. She was so damn convincing. How the hell could we clear her? The other guy did it. That was Betty's story. Butch did it. Maybe someone else killed Mary T. Branner, despite Betty's prints and DNA on the dog's collar.

Once in my apartment I made a mental note to call Goldbaum. Asleep suddenly, I awoke at 3:00 a.m., head throbbing, T-shirt dripping with sweat, startled by the fragment of a dream. I was a farmer, wearing a white baseball hat, brown denim coveralls, and heavy black high-top shoes. Perched high up in the driver's seat of a huge yellow harvester, I smoked a cigarette, trolling through the fields at a snail's pace. The truly frightening part was the crop itself. I was harvesting body parts, human body—hearts, livers, lungs, eyes, hands, arms, legs, feet. The organs and extremities were attached to corn stalks, collected by the harvester machine, then bundled and dropped in neat piles scattered around the field.

All this cannibal shit was evidently getting to my subconscious. That thought gave me strange comfort as I decided we were all cannibals in some way or other. Gas, clothes, houses, food, the environment–our eat-more, drink-more, get-more culture with its pressure on successfully consuming nature and each other was a kind of cannibalism.

I pulled off the T-shirt, dried my body, and fell back to sleep, smugly aware that I had a brain. I wasn't some dim-wit, corrupt, drunken ex-cop turned PI—I also promised God that I'd start going to AA again, real soon.

Four hours later I felt better. I'd shaved and showered, brewed a big pot of heavy dark roast coffee and read the paper. I did a half-hour on the treadmill and promised myself that I'd go to Wildwood three times a week to work out. How in the hell could I reconcile introducing weightlifting to Herman and Susie in their eighties and then not follow through myself? Very easily. I was as full of contradictions as the next guy.

A horn beeped twice, then a long burp. Marty was there in her huge red Suburban. I chug-a-lugged the rest of my waker-upper mix, two raw eggs, bran, honey, strawberries, half a banana, and vanilla soy milk. Sometimes I wouldn't eat until dinner. I toyed with the idea of a tiny, colorful tissue umbrella to put in the side of my drink.

No time to make the bed, gather my clothes, do the dishes, vacuum the floor, or take out the garbage. I galloped down the stairs and out to the Suburban. As I slid into my seat, Marty was ready with a high-five for one hand and a steaming cup of coffee for the other.

I slapped her hand twice, sipped the coffee and put the cup in the holder. "Thanks," I said.

"No problem, boss. You're the one. Spot-on, as they say."

The coffee and the kind words made me suddenly aware of how lonely I really was. Living by myself in a one-bedroom bachelor pad was not my fantasy of where I'd be in life at my age. I leaned back into the heavy leather seats and let the roaring, throaty

Suburban engine do its thing. The 350 horsepower reminded me of a shuttle take-off.

Blood-shot eyes and a slight case of the shakes didn't deter me from noticing how beautiful Marty was today. She must be celebrating something or someone, dressed in an all-white pants suit with delicate white suede boots. Wow! The high cheekbones and stunning gold on her ears set off the bronze skin and ruby-red lips. Between my waker-upper drink and Marty's appearance, the day was beginning to make some sense.

"We're going to see Willie, in case you forgot," she said.

"I'd go anywhere with you. New things on your ears?"

"Things, you say. These are serpents who eat snakes, so watch out, boss. Just twists of gold. Wish it were a Latino legend, but it's Scottish."

I said, "I could make a very off-color remark, but I won't. Just out of respect."

"That's a novel approach for you."

The sun stared at us as we headed due east out of town. Most of the snow had melted into greasy, black pools of water, and the roads were clear except for zillions of salt pellets. New subdivisions, several on lakes or quarries, flew by with no real promise of ever growing sidewalks or trees. People probably stayed inside to use their personal gyms or family media rooms anyway. Of course, they might have to take the garbage to the street. Quickly, the rural scene prevailed. Houses were acres apart and varied from manufactured homes with decks to ancient farmhouses with ramshackle barns nearby.

I said, "We're going to old county road 29, then a left and two miles, and on the right is Willie's place."

"You're so damn efficient." Her head turned slowly and she let me see the whites of her eyes, the way movie directors do it with starlets or Antonio Banderas. "I got lucky, boss. I got lucky."

Patches of elm and sycamore trees appeared. Some were planted to provide shade for a barn or home. Others were grouped to line a field or demarcate one section or owner from another.

"What do those bare trees remind you of?" I asked.

"Well, now that you mention it, my Mexican grandfather had

long, hard black hairs growing out of his nose and ears. No, I take it back. They're like the stiff hair on the top of a rhino's head, or what I bet Hitler's thin little mustache felt like to Eva Braun."

"Speaking of Hitler," I said, "I had a bad dream that I was a cannibal of sorts. But I feel better. Did you notice that Betty superficially mentioned the victims' families? We've talked to her for several hours, and we've got tons of background stuff and intimate admissions, but nothing in detail about how the mothers and fathers and sibs and friends of the victims felt or suffered or anything. Once they were dead, Butch could do anything he wanted. She's not only not playing with a full deck, she's playing some very bizarre game."

"I didn't really notice that," Marty said. "It's like it was just Butch and the victim, and it stopped right there. Maybe it's all bullshit."

The Suburban lurched to a stop in a gravel driveway that circled the front of a nondescript, one-story red-brick ranch house. The gutters and shutters had flaked off most of the white trim paint, and the winter-brown lawn showed mounds of dirt or sand scattered erratically, suggesting gardening tasks started but not completed. Dull evergreen shrubs called out for a good trimming. A shiny coach light was attached to the left side of the door, but its counterpart was hanging by a thread on the right side.

Wasn't upkeep what rural folks did during the winter months? Things they couldn't do while planting and harvesting in the other seasons? Of course, this wasn't a true farm, more like a ranch house on several acres in a semi-rural area—inside plumbing and all the amenities. The beat-up '69 Ford station wagon in the driveway didn't do much to counter my initial impression as we parked behind it. Marty gunned the Suburban's huge power plant and, for just a moment, I feared she would simply push the Ford out of the way. People who drive Suburban's often have the mentality either of a tank commander in the Sahara during World War II or a star in an action movie.

Marty turned the key. "We're here, Willie, ready or not."

I said, "He sounded surprised when I called. Told me he'd been interviewed so many times that he didn't mind one more.

That he only told the truth."

Marty unlatched her seat belt and opened her door. "Just once, I wish somebody would say they lied. Just one goddamn time."

We hit the ground about the same time, Marty light on her feet, me with sharp pain in both knees. The Suburban rode high and mighty, but it was a long drop for a middle-aged guy with bum basketball knees.

I pushed a rusty doorbell several times. It didn't ring, yet there Willie stood at the open door in a dirty, white sleeveless undershirt set off by well-oiled black suspenders, a huge beer gut, and more thick black hair covering his chest and arms than I'd seen in quite awhile. Not much on top though, as he took off his filthy baseball cap to welcome us in a toreador bow. "Glad to see you. Which one is Kip? Could go either way," he said. His belly jiggled with laughter and so did the cold beer he held tightly in his other hand. "Come on in."

Marty and I entered. I closed the door behind us because Willie's hands were still full of beer and the baseball cap.

The house was a shambles. The inside made the outside look good. It appeared as if the cops had tossed it many years ago searching for evidence and Willie said to himself, "The hell with it. Why clean it up? They'll be back." Beer cans were everywhere, pizza boxes in varying stages of decomposition, stacks of dirty laundry, and several shirts that had been ironed to the point of burn marks. A child's rocking horse was overturned, and the far wall was dominated by holes where someone had completely missed the dartboard. An oversized TV—apparently new, as the screen was clean and unmarked—covered half of one wall, blaring a game show. Willie quickly pushed the mute button.

The aroma was a near-combustible combination of stale beer, overcooked boiled potatoes, cigar smoke, and a room spray, likely Spring Morning. "The little ones are at school. Lisa Marie is fourteen and Bryan is sixteen. They don't know nothing," said Willie. He plopped down on the floor and sat between us, cross-legged, gulping beer, then crushing the can with his hands.

Marty and I dropped on some ancient leatherette footstools opposite each other. "I'm Kip," I said. "Kip Crandall and this is Marty Flores. We're private investigators, as I said over the phone, looking into the case of Betty Fowler. She's suspected of having something to do with your wife Mary."

Willie looked up with bleary, tired eyes. "It's okay. You can say my 'wife's disappearance.' She's been gone or dead or whatever for thirteen years. You can talk straight and not give me the sugar-coated bullshit."

Marty didn't raise her eyebrow, so I could go straight at it, not deflect or divert or talk in euphemisms to protect Willie's tender feelings.

"Thanks for seeing us," said Marty. She drummed her nails on the note pad, ready to get under way.

Willie said, "I'm no host but there's plenty of cold ones in the fridge."

I said, "Thanks, Willie, but we're working. Tell us about Mary." My nostrils were talking to me, my nose and septum, too, up to the swollen pockets under my eyes. I sneezed. "The country air, I guess."

"Mary was a slob. A goddamn slob. She didn't cook. She wouldn't clean a bit. She hated to change the baby's diapers and they had real bad rashes."

"Must have been rough on you," said Marty. She slowly brushed her hair back from her ears. Then she carefully wiped some dust or cat hair from her white pants legs. It didn't work. Must be something else that soiled this beautiful white suit that didn't simply brush off easily. She held on to the pen throughout the attempt to groom herself, using the side of her hand for the cleaning. Now she gripped the pen tightly again.

Willie said, "It sure was."

The beer looked good. I was afraid if I had one I might puke all over this place. What a pigsty, but Willie didn't appear to mind or feel any embarrassment over his home. In fact, he seemed proud of his crudeness and slovenliness. Next time I give a lead at AA I could recount this scene, but then, I didn't know if Willie had bottomed out yet.

"Willie, I know you've been over it may times. But if you don't mind, tell us what happened," I said.

"Sure thing, Kipper, glad to." He belched loudly. "We lived in the city. In the top floor of an old house. Real nice. Three bedrooms. Me and Mary, the little ones, and our granddaughter Tami, who was about twelve then. She had her own room, real nice one, too. We also had use of the attic above our apartment."

"Nice place, huh?" I said. I looked over at Marty, who wrote furiously on her pad.

"The place was nice. Mary ruined it. She could ruin anyplace. She was a fucking nut case. Messy. Sloppy. Dirty. Wouldn't keep house or cook. Ate fast-food at least twice a day. Gained fifty pounds in one year. Wouldn't take her medicine. Sometimes I'd crush them pills and fool her and put it in her rum. She loved rum with lemon or lime squeezed in it. Said it reminded her of the South Seas—shit, she'd never been further west than Wichita." Willie struggled to uncross his legs and stand. He was having difficulty.

I slipped into the kitchen, grabbed a beer and tossed the can to him. He chugged about half of it. The he laughed, a blood-curdling howl. "What are you going to do, Kipper, old buddy, when I have to take a piss?"

The time I saw Marty's eyebrow go up several times in emergency mode. I didn't say or do what I felt; clock the guy, or pull out my weapon and point it at his head. Maybe fire it, too.

"Don't be an asshole," I said. "Go on, Willie, tell us more. What happened that night?"

Willie hiccupped several times, then belched again. I'd swear he was trying to sense our reactions to him; if only I could read minds. I couldn't, so we simply waited him out. If he'd asked, I'd have told him we were, indeed, grossed out by him and the house.

"Well, she was something, my Mary was," said Willie. "As usual she was flat broke, credit cards up to the hilt, borrowing on one to pay a new one. I gave her a five dollar bill each day. She had to pay for food, buy the kids stuff, and feed her own face at a fast-food joint with the five spot."

"Must have been hard on you to have to watch her so carefully," said Marty. The empathy went right by Willie. He gulped down the rest of the beer and twirled the can on the floor. When it stopped, it pointed at him.

"Then she got some goddamn new card. She went to a machine and took out money. I'd just learned about it. That's where she went that night. Our apartment was two blocks from the bank machine. She went out in the dark to get money," he said. Willie made a half-hearted attempt to rise Indian style but didn't make it. What would he do when he had to pee?

Sour gastric juices formed in my gut and began their ascent. This toxic garbage made me want to vomit right there in the living room without saying 'sorry' or cleaning it up. Willie would understand. "Go ahead, Willie, what then?"

"She didn't come home. I fed the little ones and told Tami to watch them. I searched for her for awhile. Called the cops sometime the next morning. Called hospitals. I thought she ran away. Still not sure. She'd left before."

Marty perked up. She stood, arched her back and stretched her arms behind her, gaze riveted on Willie, as if trying to penetrate into his brain to get a fix on the guy. Was he truthful? Could we trust him? Was he really a Mr. Mom as he suggested? "So, you're not entirely sure she was kidnapped or murdered?" said Marty.

"You got it," said Willie. "They found her goddamn little bitty dog the next day outside the house, but the tiny spots of blood don't prove nothing. Not a dang thing. She could have faked it. She just needed Lithium, cheeseburgers, and a rich guy to say yes to her constant buying. And a guy who could be a household maid or else buy one for her." Complete surprise to us, Willie bent his head forward and his body shook with sobs. No tears, just gut-wrenching sobs and a kind of wild animal howl. "But I loved her. I've never stopped that. I'd kill the guy that got her."

I went to the fridge to get Willie another cold one. After I handed it to him, he held the can to his forehead and cheeks. "Anything else we should know?" I said.

"Well, people didn't like her. We'd adopted Tami cause Shari Lynn was screwed up. Some of the neighbors picked a bone with her. But nobody would hurt her. She was a mess, in and out of hospitals, crazy as hell, a lousy mother but she was mine. I quit driving trucks to take care of everything here. Sold insurance since then. Not very good at it either. Church helps us out. Government, too. We get by."

Marty was on her feet first, her face a perfect blank. It was probably going round and round in her brain but she revealed nothing to me or Willie. The only thing I detected was that she appeared to be more pale than usual. "I don't feel so hot, guys. I'm going outside." She ran to the door. I heard her retch several times near the old Ford.

Willie rose. He had to piss. Fortunately, the alcohol must have lubricated his joints. He stumbled; nearly fell as he lurched awkwardly into the bathroom. The plumbing squealed, at least a hopeful sign that it was being used. I was more than ready to follow Marty outside.

Willie stood tall in the bathroom doorway, his posture improved but still the morose, hairy drunk, the wannabe WWF wrestler—fingering a black switchblade knife. He opened and closed it several times, the dull click announcing each change. "You bug me, Kipper. I just decided I don't want to do no more talking today."

"Put down the knife, Willie. You're an asshole. Are you going to hurt me?" I stood and shuffled backward a few steps. The guy was probably good with a knife. I had my Glock but I didn't want a confrontation with any angry drunk.

"I just might do that. Sick of going over all this shit. Like I'm a suspect or something." His knees wobbled again and his words were slurred. The flash of power and strength was just that, I hoped—only momentary. "I loved her. I'd slice up anybody who laid a finger on her."

Her voice low and cold, Marty said, "Put it down, Willie. We're not the enemy." She stood immobile just inside the front door, her gun pointed directly at Willie's head. "Please put down your knife. You've had a little too much beer. I apologize if Kip said something wrong to you."

He snapped the knife shut and threw it over his shoulder into the bathroom. It bounced around, attacking a few tiles until it settled quietly in some of the sludge. "I'm sorry. I got kind of screwed up. All the memories."

Marty lowered her gun. I took my hand away from my holster. I nodded at Marty. She turned on her heel and walked out.

"Thanks, Willie, we'll be in touch," I said. My neck throbbed and my Al Capone slice was hot and sweaty, probably quite red. I touched it, magically hoping it had healed and disappeared. It had been fight not flight. We were just PIs doing our job.

"Always got a cold one for friends like you Kipper, old buddy. I doubt if that woman they've arrested did it. People might hate Mary but no one would kill her. She was too pitiful." Willie stood there. Nothing else from him now but the huge blast of a beer-head's fart.

Once outside I picked up my cell phone and dialed Sgt. Fowler at his apartment at the base. He deserved an update while our meeting with Willie Branner was still fresh. Well, the "fresh" part was a play on words.

"Sgt. Fowler here."

"Hey, Chuck, it's Kip Crandall. Marty and I just paid a visit to Mary's husband Willie. We've decided to re-interview the people originally part of the investigation. We wanted you and Mama to know our plan. We hope to find out what really happened to Mary Branner."

"Yes," said Chuck. "Sounds good to me. Don't worry about the money. Do whatever is required by your battle plan. Don't spare resources." Chuck's voice was strong and resolute, the perfect employer. The cell phone cut out.

Marty gave me the keys. The Suburban was surprisingly quiet at high speeds. I drove much too fast on this county road but couldn't put enough distance between us and Willie. Quite a guy with quite a story. Marty slept instantly, loud snores occasionally punctuating her slow breathing. She'd finally relaxed after the revulsion of the interview.

I redialed. "How you doing, Chuck? How's Mama feeling?"

"Mama still has strong doubts. She doesn't believe what happened to Butch. I don't mean the murders. I mean the Betty thing. Thinks she's just in a costume, or at a party."

"And you?" I said.

"Kip, the shock is beginning to wear off. I'm frightened, sometimes I feel repulsed. Why in the hell couldn't Betty have trusted me? Why didn't she feel my love would be strong enough? Why didn't she feel I could take the truth? Now, it's all worse because she lied." Sadness and confusion weakened Chuck's voice, blurred his painfully honest words.

"I think I understand. It's a lot to deal with. At least, the truth is there now between you and Betty. It's there to deal with. We'll find out the truth about the Branner case and maybe others. There's some reason for hope, but I admit that Betty's explanations are quite believable. She's apparently very honest and above-board in describing what occurred so many years ago."

"Do you think someone else did it?" His voice was pleading.

My hand tensed on the steering wheel. I paused, jaw tightening. What to say? "That's our theory. To find the perpetrator. That's the best way to clear Betty's name. We'll focus on the Branner case."

"I need help. I need counseling. I'm going to get it privately. I don't want all this stuff in my service records. Don't know who I can trust."

"That's a good idea," I said. "There's a lot to sort out. I know you mainly want to show support for Betty now. Jail is no fun for her, while the cops decide what to officially charge her with and what to eventually reveal at a hearing. The community will want blood. They hate cannibals."

The loving husband spoke now. "Betty didn't do it. I'll swear to that, put my life and honor as a soldier on it. She didn't. It's some kind of horrible nightmare."

"We'll stay in touch, Chuck, I promise."

Marty stirred, yawned and coughed. "Who was that on the phone?"

"Chuck. Dawning on him he married a guy who may be a murderer."

"Oh." Back to sleep.

CHAPTER NINE

We found Tami at her job in a north side grocery store a week before Christmas. Now twenty-five, she stocked the shelves in the canned-goods department, having graduated from an apprenticeship as a bagger. She agreed to see us after work, if "you take me out for pizza. I just love it."

We did. Several hours later Marty, Tami, and I squeezed ourselves uncomfortably into a small booth in a long black-and-white painted dining room in Gino's pizza shop, famous for its layers of swirling, hot multi-colored cheeses. Tami consumed half of a medium and two sodas before saying much. Marty drank black coffee while I ordered an Italian sub, cut in half. Marty's appetite would surely return soon.

In the vernacular, Tami defined the concept of a piece of work; almond-shaped hazel eyes, thick curly hair, tipped both green and red, several tattoos, and a sexy Caribbean look. Slightly buck teeth prevented her heart-shaped face from being truly compelling. Her clothes, jewelry, and manners were cheap.

"Mary was a bitch, if you must know," she said. She spoke in bursts between bites. "Treated me like shit. Wouldn't let me see Shari Lynn, my real mom. Christ, I hated her guts."

Marty said, "Please talk more slowly, Tami. I'm a little bit hard of hearing." The tin ceiling tiles painted with three generations of white enamel bounced the magnified sound all over us.

"Sorry. Mary and Willie raised me up after Shari Lynn couldn't. My real dad, Damone, didn't do much but give me a little color. They say I'm real pretty." She swallowed the rest of the soda, put in a straw, and sucked loudly.

"Another one?" I said.

"Yessiree. Nice and cold. Could I have another small double cheese, too? The more pizza I eat, the hungrier I am." Her hip huggers, bare flat stomach, and see-through gauzy pink blouse belied Tami's love of pizza.

"What about Willie?" Marty said. "He was your grandfather, but he and Mary adopted you."

Tami blushed a reddish-cocoa color. The red blotches started in her neck and spread quickly. "Did he tell you what they did?" She tried to wipe away the redness.

"Please tell us," I said. I fingered the sandwich. Marty grabbed half of it and took a huge bite, as I'd expected.

"They put me in the attic. We had the top floor of this old house. Willie did stuff. Mary didn't stop him. He's a worthless piece of shit. My boyfriend didn't even make me do that. Willie didn't ever take a bath when he got home after driving trucks for two or three days." She downed half of the third soda, which the waitress had quietly delivered. The second pizza came next. Her hands went to it instantly. Both hands displayed rings on all five fingers, the type that used to arrive free as cereal-box prizes.

Marty said, "Do I understand you to be saying that Willie abused you? What an asshole." She took another huge bite.

"You got it, lady. He messed with me when I was eight years old and kept it up until I moved out with my boyfriend. Sometimes it was okay. In the attic." The straw in the soda reached bottom again.

"Another soda?" I said.

"Yessiree, that'd be good. I love pizza with soda," said Tami. "I tried to tell people. No one believed me. They said I was a tramp and a ho and a liar. I did do certain things at any early age, but I didn't lie about Willie. Mary knew it was the Lord's truth. She just cared more about Willie." Tami slid out of the booth on her way to the women's room. Those were twelve-ounce plastic cups of soda with ice she'd poured down.

Marty reached for the other half of the sub. I instinctively grabbed her hand. "I'm starved now, boss." I smiled and let go. She swiftly bit off a large mouthful of the sub, chewing and swallowing salami, mozzarella, bologna, and ham before Tami returned.

Tami said, "That was good. I needed to get rid of those sodas. Whew, it builds up. Where were we before we were so rudely interrupted?" At least she didn't belch like Willie, though there were other clear parallels in their behavior.

"Your birth mother? Did she believe you?" Marty said.

"Yeah, she did, but it didn't help none. Nobody believed Shari Lynn. They all thought she was crazy and a bad mother. But I love her just as much as I hated my grandmother. Shari Lynn always sent me nice gifts at Christmas and never forgot my birthdays. I wanted to live with her but that bitch Mary stopped it. Willie liked his deal, too, if you take my meaning." One of Tami's long, fake, pink fluorescent fingernails stuck in the crust. The cuticle was bitten to the quick and had scabs where it bled. She put the finger in her mouth repeatedly, nibbling around the edge. "Mary made money on me. She lied to the welfare. Shari Lynn explained it real clear. So, they got money and sex and pretended to love their granddaughter."

Marty said, "Must have been awful." She finished off the few bites of submarine.

"You bet, got out as soon as I could to live with my boyfriend and work at a grocery store. Quit school, too. I don't need no education to get a good job like I got. I'm lucky Willie didn't knock me up along the way."

Marty had not raised an eyebrow so I decided to go for it. "Tami, you seem like a nice young lady. You didn't do anything to hurt Mary did you? Did you want her dead?"

Tami's high pitched, fast-talking style suddenly slowed down behind the narrowed, suspicious hazel eyes. "Look, mister, I said I hated that bitch. I never did anything to her. I was a kid then. Should have. Shit, she probably ran away with some guy with money. Want me to show you?"

"Show us what?" I said.

"Where it happened. The money machine and where we used to live. Have you seen it yet?"

"That'd be just great, Tami. Thanks. I didn't mean to imply you'd done anything."

"Let's go then," she said. "I can't spend all night with you. My boyfriend is insanely jealous. He wants his Tami next to him when he drinks his six-pack and watches TV." She brushed crumbs from her lap as she stood up. I hadn't noticed the three small gold bands in her navel until now. Yessiree, she'd say, there's three of them.

Once outside Tami suggested that we walk, since the bank ATM and their original home were only a few blocks away. This Toledo neighborhood had suffered in the past decade, garbage and litter here and there, a few street lights shot out, and several boarded-up small businesses with "For Lease" signs. Small cottages and homes on either the river or the lakefront peeked out at us, the working and middle-class answer to Palm Beach or LaJolla. One-story bungalows on the water with creaky wooden docks hid the hopes that no significant pollution had drifted in from Detroit or Cleveland. Most people ate fish caught here at most twice a month, though never if you were pregnant or had a compromised immune system. Lake Erie was a work in progress.

An old gas station transformed into a brightly lit, all-night carry-out beckoned. A methadone clinic sat dark next door. Tami's trendy slip-ons with two-inch heels forced her to walk in a loping slide. She bent down occasionally to force shoe and foot together, nearly an occasion for the jeans to split open, but it didn't happen. "We turn at the corner. We lived down there. The bank is nearby, too."

Cars, trucks, and old dented campers crowded both sides of the street along the curb. Driveways occasionally held a small boat on a carrier or a rusty car up on blocks. These small dark lawns would never recover by spring. The upkeep of these residential properties had suffered along with erratic fortunes of local businesses. "That's it," she said. "That big old white house. The owners lived downstairs and we lived upstairs. Me and Willie and Mary and the two babies. The attic was above our place."

The house needed paint badly; chipped and peeling white paint had been layered over some dark color years ago. In the dim light from street lamps, the cracked sidewalks and irregular landscaping played shadow games. Here a bush, there a tree. A light fog gave the house a slightly ethereal look. I stumbled over an old basketball and kicked it into the yard.

"Yessiree, we were there a few years. I'd like to forget them years. Mary never bought me nice clothes or nothing. Shari Lynn says she lied and stole money from Uncle Sam. She never cooked nothing good, either."

Marty apparently was absorbing the ambience of a

neighborhood still full of cops and firemen and their families, not yet the crack houses and burned-out frames suggesting arson. She said, "Those two are certainly different. One is so neat and carefully maintained, and the other one, well it's a real mess." We were looking at the bungalows on either said of the Branner place.

Tami explained. "Boomer and Bubba were nothing but trouble, especially after their folks died. Never did anything. Never went to church. Smoked dope all day. Mr. Robert Archer and his family live in the other one. All he does every day is take care of the house. They say he killed his folks. I don't know. Mary was into it with all of them. Maybe they smoked her. Our place was 2702 Hill, but I called it 2702 Hell."

Tami led us down the block and turned the next corner. We passed Gino's on the way to a small, old, ornate branch bank and at the end of the parking lot stood a brightly lit ATM. We eyeballed the machine, while a police cruiser turned and circled nearby. "This is where Mary came. She had a card. Willie hid it from her, but she'd always find it. They say her little terrier, Sweet Pea, was with her. They found Sweet Pea outside our house."

Marty appeared bored with Tami, no emotion in her question when she asked, "What do you think happened to Mary?"

Tami stopped and gazed at the heavens. She said very slowly, and clearly, with more sincerity than anything she'd told us, "Probably ran off with a guy who owned a McDonald's. She loved cheeseburgers."

Marty said, "The police think someone kidnapped her here in the parking lot, then killed her. Her body was never found, you know."

Tami laughed. "Mary had blown up to over 200 pounds. She was a mess. Maybe she's in some hospital. Willie had her in and out of hospitals."

"You don't care much, do you?' I said. I walked around the ATM. It would have been an easy abduction. The lighting was very new.

"Not really," said Tami. "Is there anything else? My boyfriend needs me."

"Yes," said Marty. "After Mary was gone, what about you and Willie?" Marty had only appeared to be drifting away.

Tami's eyes breathed fire. She frowned, skin wrinkling at the sides of her mouth. Then her cheeks puffed and she blew out the air. "It's none of your goddamn business, lady. Well, you'll find out anyway. I sort of took Mary's place. Willie was nicer to me then. I slept in his bed for a few years."

Marty was relentless. "Did he miss her?"

"Not so's you'd notice. He did everything around the house anyway. I took care of the babies. He said I was better than Mary ever was in bed. He stopped driving truck and sold something or other." Tami ran her hand over the ATM machine. "I'd sure like to learn how to use one of these. I could borrow my boyfriend's card."

I said, "I guess that's about it. I hope you've told us the truth. The pizza in prison sucks. We may see you again."

Tami said, "They've got a thing at Gino's. If you buy two pizzas for ten dollars, you get a third one free." Her eyes pleaded as she reached out her hands, cupped together.

I reached for my wallet and slipped her two fives.

"One night when he was real drunk Willie told me that his dad was part Mexican, that his real name was Miguel Gomez and that he'd changed it. Said he'd been in jail as a kid for some kind of assault. Willie might have been bullshitting me."

The cruiser whirled around the lot again. A spotlight shone at our feet. "Everything okay over there?" the cop asked.

"Yes, officer, we're just out for a walk. We're leaving," said Marty.

"Thanks for the pizza," said Tami. "And the sodas." She was off in her inimitable slippery glide. The cop's searchlight followed her for a moment. "I don't live far from here."

Marty and I stood in the space near the floodlight above the ATM. Time stood still. We didn't need to speak. What a family— Mary, Willie, and now Tami. In some ways they were a natural counterpart to Mama, Butch, and Chuck. These people were not really so unusual with the abuse, alcohol, violence, lies and fractured relationships. Kids suffered most and no one seemed to care.

Marty finally spoke. "Now, I'm really hungry. I want a pizza."

"Me, too."

We picked up speed in order to get back to Gino's before it closed. We ordered, we devoured, and we left. I ordered a medium extra-cheese with sausage and pepperoni to go. "Guess what," I said.

"You mean, guess where or guess for whom, don't you," said Marty. "I know what you're doing."

I drove straight to the nursing home. It was after 9:00 p.m. but the night clerk let us in, bribed by a steaming hot slice of Gino's best.

Herman and Susie usually read or watch TV until 10:00 p.m. Many other residents went to bed two hours earlier, so they were night owls, relatively speaking. We tiptoed down the hall feeling very conspiratorial, breaking the rules, mostly not wanting to wake anyone else.

After a light knock on the door, we walked into the room. "Pizza man is here," I said.

Susie looked up first, placing her embroidery work on a nearby table. "Smells good. Who could this be?" she said.

Marty threw her arms around Susie, then embraced Herman. She'd been here many times with me and loved them, too.

Herman was watching basketball on a small, hand-held color TV I'd given him last Christmas. "You two shouldn't have, but how did you know we had a lousy cream of chicken on toast for dinner? Smells good, Kip. Love ya, Marty."

"We were in the neighborhood and thought we'd stop by. We've got just a few minutes. The night nurse wasn't very happy to see us," I said.

Susie said, "She's new. She'll learn. It's people that keep us alive. Not all this medicine." She'd already taken two bites of a large wedge.

I pulled a sliding table across Herman's lap and set a huge piece of pizza on a napkin in front of him. "Looks too good to eat. My favorite sausage. Hope there's no anchovy. Hate it."

A tap came on the door. Night nurse, stern-faced, held one finger to her lips, took her hand away, smiled, and closed the door again.

Marty perched on an old hassock. I sat on the edge of the bed and said, "Been interviewing the husband and some young girl in that case I told you about. We're trying to find who killed the woman in question thirteen years ago. The people involved are not—well, they've got big-time problems."

"Watch out for that husband," said Herman. "It's the people you love who do it. And don't forget that he-she person. Sinful to mess with God's work."

Susie said, "Marty, can you get this guy to go out on a date? Kip'll be a lonely old man in a nursing home and no family, no wife. Old is bad enough."

Marty went along. "You're so right. He won't listen to anyone. He believes in the idea that 'life goes on' but he doesn't live like it. Give him some wisdom, Susie. He won't follow my suggestions." Marty excused herself to use the restroom.

Susie said, "She's awful pretty, Kip. Isn't she sweet on you?"

I said, "She's involved with someone else."

Herman had quickly munched his piece and only left an edge of crust. Unceremoniously, he'd fallen asleep in his chair, chin lowered to his chest. Snoring already.

Susie said, "I married a younger man. No manners. Take a piece of candy, under the bed."

I took one and handed the box to Marty, who had returned. She said, "I love chocolate turtles."

"I sure do love those earrings, honey. They're real pretty. They jiggle, too," said Susie.

"Thanks. Solid fourteen-carat gold hoops. Handmade. From the art fair. If I lose one, it's supposed to be good luck."

The nurse rapped on the door. "Time's up." We kissed Susie good-bye and handed the pizza box to the nurse as we left. She'd remember us next time. Two pieces remained.

CHAPTER TEN

"She was fifteen when I was born. Then I was fifteen when out popped Tami. At least Tami hasn't done it." Shari Lynn quickly packaged meats in a plastic wrap, covered them in a heavy white paper, and dumped them into a refrigerated box. Employed by a specialty butcher shop, J & J's Meats, and now forty, she'd worked at this job for more than fifteen years.

Shari Lynn, short and fat, wore no make-up. Her hair was reddish-brown and apparently had been colored, permed, and set recently into a tight group of curls and ringlets. She leaned over to pick up a rib roast from the floor but every curl stayed put. She'd invited us to "drop by my office anytime," laughing loudly at the self-deprecating humor.

We stood on either side of Shari Lynn, winter parkas zipped up to the neck to fight off the chill of this meat-packaging room. I kept my gloves on, too, but Marty's were off so that she could take notes.

Shari Lynn shoved white gauze hats at us. We slipped them on in the fashion of French berets. Nausea was immediate, an onslaught that hit nose, eyes and stomach, in that order. The odor was difficult to identify, more of a moist, slightly misty, all-encompassing something or other. Marty eyed me and stuck her finger in her mouth. If we didn't cut this short, we'd both flip our cookies here.

Shari Lynn was the perfect hostess. She said, "We keep it lower than fifty-five degrees from that big cold air vent. It don't smell so good. That bone-barrel is full of cut-up meat and bones, and some of them are spoiled. Some people say it's like what a dentist smells and others say it's like a garbage dump."

Two cute signs above the bone-barrel read, "If it's green, it's mean," and "Black is beautiful, but not on meat." My eyes watered and I felt that I literally had a bone in my throat. A tall-boy dominated one corner of the room, approximately six feet high; it was a rolling rack to hold large trays of packaged meats. Stacks of boxes carelessly littered the space, and huge white enamel doors leading to the "cooler" were chipped and rusty on the edges. Someone had spray painted "Pile it high, watch it fly," on one of the doors.

"I love Tami to death. Never missed a birthday," said Shari Lynn. "But the way Mary treated me, I hated her with a passion. She took my baby away from me. She and that asshole Damone. He knocked me up," said Shari Lynn. Her hands were busy, her face impassive.

I said, "You hated Mary but loved Tami. Mary and Damone took Tami away."

"Bingo." Shari Lynn loved to gamble.

Marty wrote furiously. Her hands trembled from the cold air. I was annoyed more by the odors, which I still couldn't quite place, but blood and sinew and bone were the basic ingredients— old, new, hot and cold. Shari Lynn and Marty now appeared oblivious to this concatenation of aromas, so maybe it was just a man thing.

"I never speak ill of the dead, but you asked," said Shari Lynn. "She's dead these many years. My common-law husband died two years ago. I seldom see Damone."

"What about Willie?" I said.

"I hate that motherfucker, too. Do you know what he did to Tami? He made her his wife. You know what I mean. That bastard." The anger didn't show itself anyplace except in Shari Lynn's words. She kept packaging, folding, tearing, and taping with great efficiency. Her face above the wool scarf at her throat was flat and changeless, gray eyes dull and lifeless. But the words were enough to understand Shari Lynn. When she said she hated somebody, she meant it. And she had her own good reasons.

Marty shoved the pen and pad into her purse and slipped on some colorful native Alaskan knitted mittens. "Shari Lynn, wasn't Willie really Tami's grandfather, who became sort of her 'father' when he and Mary adopted her?"

"Bingo. Then he put her in his bed and in charge of the two little ones. He'd drive truck for a couple of days. Then he changed jobs."

Marty and I silently exchanged places. We were cold and

simply moved around for the warmth. Shari Lynn just kept working, like an auto mechanic or a good barber or hairdresser who knows the job so well that he can engage in a conversation without losing a work beat. I reminded myself we were looking for a murderer, someone with motive, opportunity, and means. Hatred and revenge were here, but so many people thought ill of Mary T. Branner, including her kin.

I said, "Let's start at the beginning. How did Mary and Willie come to adopt Tami?" Long pause, no response. "Why did Tami get raised by Mary?" I grimaced in frustration; I suspected Shari Lynn wasn't totally up front.

"I heard you the first time, mister, I'm not deaf. It's not a nice story. I was real sick after Tami was born. My seizures acted up in the hospital. They said I was psychotic. Took strong medicine. I don't remember too much, but I kept thinking that somebody wanted to steal my baby girl. I just didn't know who."

"You were sick in the hospital after Tami's birth and Mary got her legally?" We needed the facts.

"Bingo," said Shari Lynn.

"Couldn't a lawyer have helped you?" Marty began. Her sad eyes looked furtively at me.

"Bingo. Tried it. Got nowhere. They had a judge rule that I was an unfit mother and a danger to the infant. So they took her and the welfare money, too. They got away with lying on all of the paperwork."

Marty stood ever closer to her in a show of concern and empathy mixed with confusion. "Visitation was possible wasn't it?"

"Bingo. Mary just decided one day I could only see Tami on her birthday and at Christmas. I did some stuff," said Shari Lynn. "I'd been young and foolish." Her dove-gray eyes begged for acceptance.

"Go ahead," I said. Shivering, I slapped both arms hard against my body several times.

"Well, I had a thing for guys with light-brown skin. Damone was a Caribbean type. One time I was hospitalized after a breakdown and the nurse found me giving a blow job to two male psychiatric attendants at the same time in the men's john."

"Do you really mean at the same time?" said Marty. She slumped in a huge shrug of dismay.

"Bingo. At the same time, in this here same mouth." She pointed to her thin, chapped lips with the first finger of both hands. "I was kind of a hell raiser."

The Branner family was remarkable. As wacky as Mary and Willie had evidently been, the court had deemed them more responsible as parents than Shari Lynn and let them adopt Tami and take full custody. It all began to make some sense.

Shari Lynn said, "And I married one of them, sort of common law. But he died two years ago. I always kidded him that if he and his buddy ever made me do them both again, I'd bite it off. He never did." Shari Lynn did have a sense of the absurd, but was it her absurdity or ours?

I said, "So, now you live alone and you get together with Tami whenever you want to. Is that correct?" I said. I was working on the theory that all's well that ends well, and that Shari Lynn and Tami could still enjoy each other and discover some of the mother-child bond impossible at an earlier point.

"She stayed with Willie and then she moved in with the boyfriend when he knocked her up. She lost the baby. She was around fourteen. She loves me but has no time for me," said Shari Lynn. She ripped off her rubber gloves and her face finally revealed a touch of animation—gray eyes brightened and widened, while her nostrils flared in recognition of what she'd said. "I'm so hurt, so lonely, she's all I got in the world."

"You've had a tough time of it," said Marty. "Real tough."

The dam burst. Shari Lynn grabbed a handful of thick red steaks and threw them on the floor, directly into the sawdust. A half-wrapped rib roast hit the wall after she swiped it with a side arm. Then she picked up a meat cleaver and chopped down hard on the steel door to the freezer. She ran to the wooden chopping block and beat on it repeatedly with a mallet, next slicing the edge with a small bone saw. "I hate everyone!" she screamed. "I hate every fucking person in the world!"

We backed away from her.

"Did you kill Mary?" I said. A protective instinct energized me in case she turned on us with a weapon. I patted my back where the Glock was holstered. My scar heated up in warning. Fight or flight.

"You fucker," she said. "I wish to Christ I had. She deserved it." Shari Lynn collapsed on the floor, sobbing hysterically. I expected other employees to barge in but the noise from the refrigerators and fans was so loud it must have muffled Shari Lynn's outburst. "All I ever wanted was to be a mother. Tami was it. My little girl. I was a real woman. Then they took her from me. My own mother and father stole her. Why wouldn't I kill Mary? I should have killed them both. Those assholes." Her body shook, breathing was labored and rapid, and she lay prostrate sobbing and humming to herself. "Mary had a little lamb, little lamb…"

I was afraid she might have had a seizure. We helped her stand and then seated her again on a stool. She dried her eyes, and the hiccups passed quickly.

Marty filled a glass with water from a sink in the corner. She said, "It's okay, Shari Lynn. Everything is okay. We know you didn't kill Mary. You hated her but you needed her. She wasn't a good mother to you and she wouldn't let you be a good mother to Tami. Everyone understands."

Full of admiration for Marty, I thought to myself what a wonderful mother she'd make someday if she and the professor could get it on. Shari Lynn dried her eyes again with her apron and put her gloves back on. She recovered as fast as she'd fallen apart. "No more psychotic stuff for me. I take my meds, never going back to that hospital."

I said, "You look great, Shari Lynn. Thanks for sharing so much. I've got one more nasty question."

"Bingo."

"Is there any chance Willie did something to Mary? How was he after she disappeared? How did he act?" I stopped short now that Marty's eyebrow rose to a warning level.

Shari Lynn stopped working. I couldn't decide if the look on her face was thoughtful or just vacant. She gazed at each of us, eyes searching for something. Could be hiding something. Maybe we appeared to know the truth. "I never thought of it. None of us missed her much. Willie had Tami and he did all the crap around the house anyway. He never got down—you know, real sad. Still went fishing and hunting whenever he got the chance. Helped the police. They always figured a stranger got her, or else she just ran away somewhere."

"The police are looking at every angle, even the unlikely possibility of a serial killer," said Marty. "Someone who kills many people." She moved away from Shari Lynn as she spoke, preparing to leave. I felt the same way.

"Beats me," said Shari Lynn. "Going to see Damone? He's a part-time bartender at the Oasis. Still gorgeous. Still do it with him when I get real, real horny. Tell him to call me."

Obviously, Shari Lynn didn't forgive easily, so her need for Damone must have overcome the several strong reasons to avoid him—he sold her out as Tami's mother and then abandoned Tami completely.

As we trundled out, I fought off the impulse to grab Shari Lynn and dump her in the frozen meat locker. She'd gotten a raw deal in life, but she had to take some measure of responsibility, for God's sake. Her medical condition when Tami was born might have been temporary, yet her wild behaviors could easily turn off a judge trying to find a solid, stable home for an infant. She had quite a temper, too. How would she have reacted to a toddler messing up her diaper, or an infant girl dripping her cereal onto the high chair, then the floor? Quite a temper!

Maybe, just maybe, her boss and the other employees knew her well enough to let her work alone in a cold room with four icy walls and very loud mechanical equipment. She could chill out, hurt no one, and work efficiently.

The walls were slick and mottled white, spotted here and there in red, with several gashes near the door where, I suspected, Shari Lynn had thrown a tool or else smashed the wall herself with a solid right uppercut. Fourteen-year-old boys who couldn't concentrate in school or who were on their way to a stealing, drinking, and fighting career often had walls in their bedroom that resembled

Shari Lynn's workspace.

"I guess we've got to see him," said Marty. She'd picked up Shari Lynn's habit of using pronouns without any clear reference. "By the way, did you notice the cigarette paper and tobacco pouch? That woman rolls her own."

We trotted to the Corvette, anxious to put this experience behind us. I stopped at a nearby service station to wash up, an effort to get the grease and grime of all that meat from my hands and face. The soap and towels didn't remove the peculiar odor that lingered.

Marty huddled near the heat vents, warm as toast when I returned. The heaters worked in a matter of seconds. She said, "I know where the Oasis is. Let's see him. He's Mr. Damone Jackson, Jr., small-time hustler, part-time bartender, and father of Tami and Lord knows who else. He's originally Jamaican, still wears dreadlocks, and has the body of an eighteen-year-old Adonis."

"Sounds like you've got the hots for him."

"Very funny," she said. "Eat your heart out, big boy." Marty twirled the green cabochon ring worn on the middle finger of her left hand, a recent gift from her loving professor.

I tooled down Bancroft Street to Upton and turned right to a small neighborhood bar in an area favored by those from the Bahamas, Jamaica, and Aruba, as well as recent immigrants from Central America. The reggae beat spoke to us as we parked. I snapped my fingers to the beat but wondered how it was to live with this loud music blaring in the area every night. We had recovered our body warmth by the time the door to the bar opened wide for us. The security guard stamped our hands but did not ask for an ID. To his credit, he didn't ask for a senior-saver card either.

We kept our parkas on, partly so that Marty wouldn't be eyeballed by everyone in the place. The music came from a jukebox and the place was smoky and nearly empty. Our man leaned on the counter behind the bar, mid-forties, cocoa-shade with full black beard and chiseled features topping off an expensive-looking black silk shirt and creased white linen slacks.

We sat down at the bar. "Hey, Damone. Long time no see," said Marty. "How about two beers and one for yourself?"

"Well, well, Marty. How you doing? I still make good rum drinks from the islands. Want one?" said Damone. He moved to us and threw Marty a hot, seductive smile.

"Another time. Can we talk? This is my boss, Kip Crandall."

"Sure," said Damone. He put two beers in front of us and a plate of mixed nuts. "How you doing, Kip? What's up?"

Marty said, "Just some questions about Mary T. Branner's disappearance. We've got a private client." She took a sip and nibbled on the nuts.

Damone's wide charming smile faded. Jaw clenched, he stroked his short, neatly-trimmed beard slowly several times. "That was a long time ago." He walked to the end of the bar, slid some clean glasses on to a plastic tray, the wiped the bar several times until it was dry and shiny again.

"The story we got is that you're Tami's biological father and that you helped Mary and Willie adopt her."

"Hey, wait a minute," Damone said. "The judge did it. Shari Lynn was sick. She couldn't raise a kid. I couldn't."

Both Marty and I raised our voices, making sure that the few patrons heard this embarrassing interchange.

"I've got nothing to hide," said Damone. Two thick gold chains around his neck clinked together when he bent at the waist to pick up ice or a glass. "I don't owe money. They paid me. Tami's okay."

I said, "We're here about Mary, only to see what happened to Mary." I raised an eyebrow to Marty.

In a matter-of-fact tone, without shame, Damone said, "Shari Lynn and I were a hot item. Then came Tami. We were kids. Mary and Willie adopted her when Shari Lynn was so crazy. I wouldn't have been a very good father. They gave me money to give up all my rights. I didn't owe nothing to nobody. It was done real legal and all that." His eyes were undressing Marty. She must have observed it, too.

"Do you have any idea what happened to Mary?" I asked. "Would Willie or Tami or Shari Lynn have hurt her or done anything?"

"They all had their reasons. Shari Lynn always blamed Mary. The only thing I know is that Willie controlled Tami at that point. She was his, well, you know—his alibi. And she'd have died for him." Damone served another customer, then came back to us. "Another beer?" he said.

"No, thanks," I said. "By the way, Shari Lynn said to say hello."

"Yes, I've got to call her. It's kind of a mutual service club," he said. He paused to see if we knew what he meant.

A large party of Caribbean people arrived in a cloud of marijuana smoke. Damone opened long-necked beer bottles quickly and threw together a big pitcher of rum punch. He turned up the volume of the reggae music. We eased out of the place.

CHAPTER ELEVEN

The loud, deep horn from the Suburban startled me as I finished shaving the next morning. Marty was early. I'd defer my decision about growing a beard or a mustache to a later time. Marty knocked, so I quickly threw on a thick wool turtleneck and chinos and opened the door. "Hey, you're here. Good. Have coffee," I said.

She plopped herself down in my old, rust-colored velvet arm-chair, the one comfortable spot in the apartment. I poured her a cup of freshly brewed Colombian roast, heavy and dark for any eye-opener. "These people we've been seeing, boss, they trouble me. Bunch of jerks but I don't know if they're kidnappers or murderers. They've all got alibis for the night Mary disappeared, according to police reports," she said.

"Jerks is a nice way to put it," I said. "Assholes might be better. Or, pitiful assholes, but I'm no social worker."

Marty blew on the coffee. "Hot," she said. "The neighbors are left. They weren't exactly suspects, but the cops were interested in them. Maybe they saw something or remember something now. Maybe they didn't hate Mary as much as her family did."

A half-hour later, Marty pulled the Suburban to a stop in front of the original Branner home. We'd called Bubba and Boomer Kwiatowski earlier and they grudgingly agreed to talk to us. "We might be more talkative if you bring a case of beer with you," one of them said. No 'please' or 'thank you'.

"How about meth?" I said.

"Yes, if you've got it. Sure you're private, not cops? Not setting us up, are you, shithead?" said one of them.

We had no illusions about this pair of losers. They lived in what had once been their family's attractive bungalow, probably built before World War II. Now, it was a mess, front porch full of dented, rusted appliances, broken bicycles, boxes of old newspapers and magazines soaked by winter snow and a kennel with two black, hungry-looking Rottweiler's barking and snarling. A mason-contractor and a painter, armed with about $25,000, could have brought the outside of the house up to snuff or at least to look as attractive as the Robert Archer home on the other side of the Branner place.

The weather was a fooler, up into the mid-sixties suddenly, just three days before Christmas. Marty and I left our parkas in the car; she was warm enough in a long cashmere cardigan and thick black corduroy slacks. My turtleneck was fine. Surprisingly, one of the brothers opened the door dressed in jockey shorts and high, dirty white socks—a sybaritic version of Tom Cruise dancing. "Hi, I'm Bubba." He held out his left hand with the letters B-U-B-B-A tattooed on the knuckles.

We walked in and then another hand reached out. "Hi, I'm Boomer." The right hand with B-O-O-M-E tattooed on the knuckles. He laughed crazily. "I can't spell for shit. Flunked third grade twice. Forgot no room for the 'R'."

I didn't try to shake hands. I grasped the case of beer tightly. One of them grabbed it, the other tried to wrestle it away. Then it was down on the floor and two cans were flipped open and drained. After belches, Bubba spoke. "Let's talk quick. I've got to shower. Got a date."

Marty said, "Should we stand or sit?"

Boomer said, "Suit yourself, little lady. Bedroom is in the back, if you need it." They both chortled.

Marty said, "Do you have a robe or a pair of jeans, Bubba?"

Obediently, he grabbed a pair of denim shorts on the floor and pulled them over the underwear. He turned his back to us, shirtless with a huge tattoo of a purple Harley ridden by an elderly gray-haired woman and a young boy. "That's my Madonna and child."

"In case you didn't get my drift, lady, I'd like to get in your pants. That's what the bedroom's for." They guffawed. We didn't.

"In case you don't get her drift, Boomer, go fuck yourself," I said. "Or, better yet, go fuck Bubba."

Marty didn't really need my help. She knew just what level of discourse—the proper tone and appropriate language—was required by most situations. Seldom scared or genuinely insulted by idiots or jerks, she gave as well as she got. I couldn't recall the details exactly but she seldom drew her gun, and hadn't shot anyone, even at anyone, for years. Her words usually did it. She might mean, 'don't talk to me that way' or 'I wouldn't touch you with a ten-foot pole' or 'you're the ugliest, crudest dude I've seen,' while her simple "fuck you" usually did the job. She'd even surprised men with the "C" word, seldom a female expletive. Marty took no shit.

I played it straight. "We're here to look into the disappearance of Mary Branner. We're private, not heat. It's confidential."

The brothers were identical twins, horrible as that seemed to us. Maybe six and a half feet and 280 pounds each, with big beer guts, plenty of acne, long brown hair in ponytails, and the most unkempt, ugly walrus mustaches God ever created. For starters, the house should be condemned.

"So, what do you need to know, Miss Pretty Eyes?" said Bubba. He chugged another beer. "Have a brewski."

"Don't be crude, asshole. What was your relationship with Mary?" I asked. I sat down on a card table chair that creaked with pain and age. Marty stood.

Bubba eyed us both through slits, carefully trained, according to his rap sheet, by six years in prison to appear friendly but trust no one. "She was bad. Tried to get us to mow her grass or clear her sidewalks in the winter. Why couldn't old Willie have done it?"

"Couldn't stand her?" I said. The chair wobbled. I was prepared to jump if necessary.

Boomer swung leisurely in an old webbed hammock. "We didn't hurt her none. I'd had a run-in with a kid in her house. I got drunk and thought he was going to hurt me, so I shot my pistol at him. SWAT team put me in a mental hospital for a week or so."

Bubba agreed. "We never hurt nobody." His arms were full of smaller, imperfect, thin tattoos, homemade in prison with pens, ink and pocket knives—crosses, swastikas and phrases such as 'Jesus Saves' and 'God Loves Us.'

"That little dog of hers was a pain in the ass. Got our pit bulls all upset," said Boomer. "She called the cops on us a couple of times. We had pit bulls way back then. They were real bad."

Finally, my chair gave in to gravity and I slid off and stood. I'd stand for the remainder of the visit. "Did either of you have anything to do with Mary's disappearance, or do you know who did?" I said. Marty's eyebrows went up pronto and I touched my backside to reassure myself that my weapon was there. My scar did not react to the twins, but it's not a perfect judge of imminent peril.

The hammock stopped swinging. "Get out," said Boomer. "We tried to be nice! Nobody could stand her. The cops told us we had a perfect alibi—each other. Get out now."

Naturally, we followed their suggestion in an orderly way. No show of fear or panic in the face of these two bruisers. That would only incite them, or their dogs, or both. Nobody paid us enough to get into it with this foursome.

As we stumbled down the porch steps, three bikers on huge silver choppers roared into the front yard and gunned their motors. "Well, well, the boys are coming up in the world," one of the bikers said. He stared openly at Marty.

We looked away and quietly strolled down the broken pavement to the front of the Archer residence. Robert Archer washed and polished an ancient Jeep Cherokee in the driveway. He wiped, stood back to admire his work, took another swipe with an amazingly clean cloth, then buffed with a new chamois. Archer was a treat to look at after the twins—clean shaven, fresh haircut, cologne, pressed jeans, and a slight tan that highlighted the baby-blue eyes. He looked to be thirty-five or so.

"Are you the folks who called? Private investigators?" he said.

"Yes, I'm Kip Crandall and this is Marty Flores." We shook hands. "We're looking into the Mary Branner situation. Long time ago."

Marty said, "May we go inside and talk, Mr. Archer?"

"I wish we could but I just cleaned the house, vacuumed, and touched up the kitchen walls. So, we'll talk here, if it's satisfactory with you."

"Sure, that's fine," said Marty.

"Oops, please stand over here," he said. "The tulips are planted near where you were. Wouldn't want them hurt." Robert pointed to the single dry spot behind him on the driveway, out of range of his glistening auto. "I think that place will be fine." The military-green Jeep shone with care, scratchless and rust-free.

"We've just seen Boomer and Bubba, so here we are," I said.

Robert's back faced us so he could continue to polish and admire the Jeep. "Yes, they are a pair. Tormented me to death in junior high. There was a clique of tough guys," he said. "We've lived here our entire lives."

His clothes were dry. Strange after washing the car with detergent and a garden hose. Only his rubber gloves were damp.

"After their folks died, they inherited the house and got into low-level crime and drugs. I think Mary and Boomer used to take the same depression medication." Robert drifted off for a moment, moving his fingers as if counting something. "I had five things to do today, but I can't recall the fifth. Bothers me."

The sun brightened the cloudy sky into patches of a smoky blue that gained momentum as they swirled above. Robert gazed upward. "There'll be a slight warm breeze in a moment, so I won't have to use my wife's hair dryer on this old Jeep. There are always a few drops here and there that I miss with the cloth."

I felt like shaking the guy, throwing mud on his clothes, or messing up his hair. Seemed nice enough, especially after the terrible twins, but the need for perfection could drive someone crazy. He made me want to scratch my head and arms for some reason, or was I allergic to the fumes of the auto detergent?

"Robert, what about Mary?" I asked. "Can you help us out?"

"She was very disorganized. Very unpredictable. She called me at 3:20 a.m. once, and rather than apologize she said, 'What are you doing up at this hour?' "

"What else?" said Marty. Robert half-turned toward her as she smiled at him.

"Well, we never fought, but I didn't care for the sort of person she was—messy, confused, impulsive, and very sloppy and fat. She lived on greasy, high-cholesterol junk food and so did Tami."

"Do you know anything about her disappearance or murder?" said Marty.

"Not really. The neighborhood recovered quickly after she disappeared. I'm not sure any of the adults really missed her. Her dog was around, though."

"No one liked her, but no one stands out as wanting to harm her," I said. Now Robert actually looked at me. Our best eye contact yet.

"Right. The twins had pistols and knives and Willie was a big hunter and fisherman. There were weapons around here and still are."

"That's helpful," Marty said.

"Isn't that what you look for—motive and means in a case like Mary's disappearance? You'd have thought the cops would have tied up all the loose ends by now," Robert said. He walked around the Jeep toward the garage in back of his house. "Come on back, I've just remembered. Got to sweep out the garage—leaves, sand, and grease. Get ready for spring, almost Christmas already."

We followed Robert like baby ducks in a row behind the mother. "Willie and Mary argued a lot, especially over money. Tami didn't like Mary. But you probably know all that. The police knew it. Willie made Tami into kind of a slave. I never did trust her or him." Robert grabbed a new long-handled broom and began to sweep. The sun was more insistent and the baby-blue of his eyes nearly matched the sky. All was right with his world as he cleaned.

We thanked him and carefully walked away.

Marty said, "Robert's parents disappeared on a camping trip. Cops found a bone buried in his backyard. Blue Throat said it was from a dog." She flicked open the Suburban's doors with the remote-control button. "There's more to this guy than meets the eye, boss."

"Christ, we've got to go over our data, reassess things. They've all got alibis that satisfied the police. My gut says one of them is involved in this Mary business."

"Let's shoot some pool," said Marty. "It's close enough to noon for drinks and food." She pointed the Suburban toward Arnie's, where the trade-off of food, drink, pool, and a friendly atmosphere produced benefits that far outweighed the costs of second-hand cigarette smoke, lung cancer, and emphysema. At least until we came down with one of them. Then we'd sue Arnie's for killing us, just like everyone else does.

The weather continued to improve. Sunny, mid-sixties, bright and hopeful. Could weather be hopeful—yes, if it arrived in late December and we rose to blissful blue skies from the depths of gray clouds and dark doldrums. I always got the weather and emotions mixed up, but they did fit together—research on sunlight and depression proved it.

The Suburban knew its way without a GPS gadget. From the north side, we took 475 to the Secor turn-off, then a few blocks of heavy west side noon traffic to Arnie's. Marty parked near the front door.

We pushed past some folks waiting to use the pay phone, and grabbed our usual booth in the small non-smoking section. Looked on as pariahs, we still stood our ground. The place was cooking already, rock music, replays of old Super Bowl games, the crack of cue balls, and the clink of ice cubes luxuriating in vodka, cushioned by olives.

"Two vodkas over ice with olives. Two cheeseburgers with everything and fries. We'll be at the pool tables," I said. The waitress winked—hello, thanks; I'll get you when the burgers arrive. Marty nodded.

We jerked pool cues from the wall stand, checked the degree of warp, and said the hell with it. We really did need to buy our own cues, the ones with strips around the top made of dark cherry wood. We dipped the tips in blue chalk.

Marty broke and got two balls, the four and the twelve on the break. She looked like a pro on TV ready to run the table and win the $50,000 first prize in a tournament. Instead, she shot the one and barely missed. I ran the table on her. "Winners pay," I said. She hugged me.

"After all," I said, "we couldn't have played very much longer. The burgers would get cold and the vodka warm." I peered at our booth through the heavy blue haze and our waitress winked twice.

We pushed ourselves into it.

Marty said, "This is heaven after way too much of hell."

"Amen. Bon appétit. Enjoy, and all that stuff," I said.

Her mouth full of burger and fries and catsup, Marty's words were nearly indistinguishable. "I'm lost. All have alibis according to Blue Throat, and each has some degree of motive except maybe Robert, and he was a suspect in his parent's disappearance a long time ago. You could say that the immaculate condition of his ancestral home is a shrine to his parents. He's never left. What's a guy like that doing in a neighborhood like that? Doesn't make sense, but doesn't make him a murderer either."

I laughed. "You make damn good sense with your mouth full. Couldn't agree more." Then I pursed my lips, scrunched up my eyes, wiped my mouth with one big swipe of the paper napkin. "Let's make a rank order of them, as suspects, just for fun and see if we match up. Number one will be the most likely suspect and on down to the least. Very scientific, just like a college criminal-justice class. We don't have to say why."

"Okay, I'll have mine by the time I've eaten the fries and ordered my second drink," said Marty.

We did it. Boomer, Bubba, and Robert were near the bottom for both of us. I had Shari Lynn above Tami, Marty the reverse, but we both had Damone last and Willie marked first.

I found the waitress' gaze, held up two fingers and she winked. She looked better to me than when we'd arrived, but I was working now and couldn't play.

I said, "It's all hypothetical. We've got a confessed serial killer who's pretty damn convincing. But take Willie. He hated Mary, didn't miss her much, incest with his natural granddaughter, and fishes and hunts, so he know knives and guns."

"Don't forget that Tami was his sex slave and surrogate wife. She'd lie from fear of his temper, or maybe love. Maybe she covered up something, or they both did. My instinct says that's our best shot at the moment."

We pulled ourselves up and out of the booth, but I felt too good to leave Arnie's. "Let's make up a game. We'll call it nine-ball," I said. "It's an important number. The Chinese have a lot of ideas tied up with it. Especially in the Forbidden City."

"Okay, boss. No chow mein. Want a wild idea? Let's name the balls." Marty chalked her cue tip until blue dust surrounded it.

"What names?"

"Our people. You know, the perps and suspects and Chuck, just for good luck, since he's paying the bill." Marty pulled out her pad and gold pen. She numbered a column one through nine.

"Betty should be number one," I said. "She's the heart and soul of things we're doing."

"Okay, *muy bueno*. But Mary can be the cue ball. She's the reason we got hired; without her there's no case," said Marty. The waitress handed her a vodka and put mine on the edge of the table. Marty sipped hers; immediately, a flush hit her neck and bronze cheeks.

"What about the others?" I said. I gulped half my drink and ate the olive. I wanted chips, nuts, or dip or guacamole or salsa or something.

"Well, how about I'll write Archer at three. Oops I forgot. Chuck is two. Then we can have Boomer and Bubba at four and five." Marty took practice shots with her cue stick, apparently ready to break the balls.

"I want Willie on the nine ball," I said. "Don't know why."

"That's fine, we'll put Damone, Tami, and Shari Lynn at six, seven, and eight. Works out perfectly."

"That's it, all nine spots are used," I said. "They're all named, so what's the game?" I strolled around the table, ready to rack the balls and decide who would break them.

"They're our suspects. Mary's the cue ball. She'll guide the action, tell us what to do," said Marty.

"You don't have a game planned out do you? You just want to name the balls."

"Just wait and see. I'll break." Marty chugged the rest of her drink. She was in one of her take-charge moods. Booze brought out the tiger in her tank.

She smashed the cue ball into the rack. Crack! Balls flew around the table, bounced off of each other, hit the rails, and dove for safety. The two ball slipped into a side pocket. "Good-bye, Chuck. See you later. You didn't do anything to Mary, but you sure as hell got yourself into something with your loving Betty. Plenty to work out in therapy. A lot of men couldn't handle it."

"Shoot the one. What are you waiting for?" I said.

"I'm still thirsty. Can I have some of yours?" Marty sipped. Then she tapped the one ball into the far end pocket, leaving herself in good position to knock the three into the side. "There goes Betty. She's in a hole anyway."

I laughed, grabbed my drink, and ate the olive. "You're set up. Take the three. Easy shot."

"Okay," said Marty. Down it went, flying into the pocket so hard it almost backed out. "That was Robert Archer. He wouldn't hurt a flea unless something unwrapped him. Then he'd explode or kill himself."

"If you don't miss, I'll never get a shot, for Christ's sake," I said.

"Tough shit, boss. Here goes Boomer." The four ball was partially hidden by the seven, and Marty could just see enough of it to slide it down the rail about a foot or so into the far-end pocket. Her gentle touch and clear vision overwhelmed Boomer.

"Boomer was an asshole, but Bubba gave you trouble. You're snookered. He's hiding behind the eight ball. See it? Number five," I said.

Marty finished my drink. My AA sponsor would approve. She energetically chalked her cue until the blue dust met the cigarette smoke in a tornadic mist. She stalled. "Can't win them all." She lagged the cue ball so that it stopped about six inches in front of the eight.

"I can't do a thing except go to the rail and hope for the best," I said. I lined up a geometric shot, hit the rail, bounced into Bubba, and sent him into the oblivion of the far side pocket. "I did it. Can you believe it?" My voice was too loud, even with four TVs, rock music, and seventy-five half-drunk adults as background. Drinking, even on a full stomach, is simply risky. "That's five down, four to go."

"Kip, see if you can finish them off. We're down to Damone

and the lovely, charming, sweet, considerate Branner clan, none of whom lost much sleep over the disappearance of Mary. There's a mother, father, daughter, granddaughter, but that's where any resemblance to the American family dream stops.

I shot Damone, or rather, I shot at Damone. Number six was approximately eight inches in front of the opposite end, a very long shot under the circumstances. Maybe another drink would steady my hands. I finally let go, but the cue ball went wide of the mark, circled the pocket, and picked up speed to graze the nine ball into the side pocket furthest from me. The nine ball had to be snagged in sequence and it had to be "called," the shooter declaring which pocket it would enter. I'd lost!

"Well, Mary got her revenge on Willie. The cue ball got the nine," said Marty. "Loser pays in nine ball."

"The real question is whether Willie got Mary," I said. Damone, Shari Lynn and Tami sat on the table, undisturbed and isolated. I knocked my empty glass off the edge of the table with the cue stick accidentally. Once again, my sponsor would like it.

"Sore loser or just a cheap drunk?" said Marty.

"Look who's talking. Let's go."

I was about to suggest that a conspiracy of silence could even include Shari Lynn, but my cell phone interrupted us. I turned the speaker to low volume and Marty stood near me, so we could both hear but no one else could.

"Hi, Kip, this is Chuck. Just finished a two-hour counseling session. Said I have post-traumatic stress disorder, brought on by the shock of Betty's change of sex. I'm more hurt and upset she didn't trust me."

"Your voice is strong and you're getting the right help. You're in charge. How's Mama?" I slumped into the booth.

"She still is in a dream world. It's okay for now. She just wants Betty out of jail but they're holding her for a probable cause hearing, or the grand jury, without bail now. What have you got for me?"

"Well, Chuck, we may have something or we may not. Our instincts tell us something might be fishy about the husband, Willie Branner. Betty says she did it, but our hope is to verify this and see if someone else was involved. We haven't bothered with the other murders yet. If it is Betty, her goose is cooked." A good feeling came over me, a sense of relaxation and calm, having something to report to Chuck. I sat up.

"Please, please, Kip, let me know the second you have anything. She hasn't hurt a flea for the ten years we've been together."

"Okay, Chuck. Marty and I will do our best. Hope you know that. Bye."

Marty said, "Poor Chuck—uptight but loyal. He's standing by Betty for now." She eyed the pool table. "Should we check in with Goldbaum?"

"Yeah, you're right. I'll dial him."

A husky, female, radio-announcer voice answered after one ring, "Goldbaum and Goldberg. How may I direct your call?"

"Mr. Goldbaum please."

"Yes, this is Goldbaum."

"Hi, it's Kip Crandall. We've finished the first round of interviews on the Betty Fowler case. Maybe something, maybe not." I shrugged at Marty, fearful of promising the attorney too much.

Goldbaum said, "We need the real perp on that case, since her credibility is questionable. She's innocent until proven guilty though she's given us quite a story. Said nothing to the police and she won't."

"Good, because it's quite a story she has. A lie-detector test could show she's lying," said Kip.

"She won't." There was no room for debate.

"Too bad," said Kip. "I forgot to tell you that Butch went to some kind of a group meeting. Called it a discussion group of truck drivers that met when they were in town. They talked about common concerns, did some praying and singing. Kind of strange because it met in a local mortuary. Maybe they were all cannibals and danced around a big fire and ate truckers they hated."

"She's innocent. What else have you got?" No wasted words from Goldbaum. He'd been a company commander in Vietnam.

"Well, we've got a hunch based on a couple of ideas. Statistical probabilities back us up." I knew that sounded weak.

"Husband?"

"Maybe yes, maybe no," said Kip. "We may fudge a bit. You know, suggest we've got more than we have." This was code. Discomfort ran through my body, and the sudden uncomfortable warmth could be due to the vodka or to the exaggeration and lying ahead of us.

"Don't tell me about it." Goldbaum hung up.

CHAPTER TWELVE

We were private. We could get away with things that the police couldn't or shouldn't. They'd be brought up on charges or have to take early retirement. People dealing with us had to file written complaints with the state licensing board. That spelled money and delay.

We felt that the end, getting Betty released, justified the means. We tried to be fair, but we weren't saints. Goldbaum didn't want to know and Chuck didn't need to know about our procedures and practices. Interestingly, Goldbaum had called back to say he was sorry to be so abrupt but he was sure that I understood, and that he needed something, anything because the DA was salivating over the Betty Fowler case—probably preparing his run for governor or the U.S. Senate.

We were desperate, to be sure. Gut feelings or ex-cop instincts didn't do the job. Sooner or later Betty would give herself away, regardless of whether her story was true or not. Either facts or self-admissions of guilt or a pattern of homicidal behavior built on weak circumstantial evidence would come to light. The case, if built on Betty's truthfulness about all the murders, could eventually have national and international appeal—serial cannibal killer who was also transgender. Maybe the DA could get enough publicity for a run at the White House. It'd been done with less.

Goldbaum had enough to produce reasonable doubt at trial. Better yet, enough to force the grand jury or a judge at a preliminary hearing not to bring down an indictment and trial. The cops, having failed for a decade to solve the disappearance of these women, would have tunnel vision. If Betty ever told them what she'd confessed to us, they would dig up anything they could on her. Depending on whether they had a warrant for her medical records and the surgeries, they might already be on the trail of Butch Waddell. With luck, she'd had a good lawyer help make the scent difficult to pick up on. Goldbaum better keep the cops away from Mama, who still thought her dutiful, loving son Butch dressed up for parties and holidays.

I called Tami on her cell phone at work. It was the day before Christmas. "Hi, it's Kip Crandall. We've got a couple more questions. Pizza and soda again?"

"Okay, but not too long. My boyfriend is jealous. Just time for one medium double cheese on thin crust and one, well, maybe two quick super sodas." What a woman.

We agreed to meet at 5:00 p.m. Marty and I needed to work up a plan. How could we get Tami to roll on Willie? Was there anything to roll about? Was he involved? The FBI and every research study that I knew of instructed us to look to family members or close friends as the first line of perps in a murder or a disappearance case. Did her own family do in Mary T. Branner? More bizarre yet, could there have been any connection between the Branners and Butch at that time? Willie and Butch both drove trucks, traveled some of the same roads, and probably hung out at truck stops. And Shari Lynn packaged meat.

On the drive to the nursing home to deliver a rich, syrupy fruit cake and can of whipped cream to Herman and Susie, we deliberated. Marty was already dressed in Christmas garb. She looked like somebody's surprise present under the tree, bright green-and-red plaid jumper worn over a white turtleneck and thick white hose covered by knee-length black boots. Even straight she wouldn't have gone for me, in my water-repellent brown boots, baggy Levis, and washed-out gray sweatshirt with GO BUCKS! printed in red on the back.

She said, "Blue Throat confirmed that a guy named Waddell was stabbed to death about the time Betty said she'd done it. So, maybe the rest of it is true, too." Her eyes and mouth were pinched into a quizzical stare.

"Wait a minute. Doesn't prove Butch did any of it, including Waddell. Right?"

"Okay, I'm with you. But I keep replaying in my mind all the garbage from Betty. I remember feeling lucky to have walked out of the interviews still in one piece. She didn't chop me up." Marty chuckled, apparently to relieve the tension. Both of us were still uncertain as to what we confronted in this case.

"Don't stop me with Tami," I said. "I'm going to accuse her of lying. See if she'll crack a little. I hope she covered up for Willie boy." My left thigh felt damp, and as I leveled the cake dish, I could see the moisture dripping from it. Hurriedly, I mopped it up with my handkerchief to avoid damage to the Suburban. It worked. Marty didn't notice.

Marty said, "If we get anywhere with her, we'll bring the two of them together and let the sparks fly. Is that the game plan?" She drove too fast, staring straight ahead, back slightly arched. "Then we nail them."

"In the words of the poet Shari Lynn, bingo. I've even had the weird idea that Willie drove Mary to the ATM, then saw her kidnapped or whatever, and kept his mouth shut. So, it all could be true—Willie, Tami, and Butch."

"Too far out, boss. Way over the edge."

The late afternoon air was glorious, still warm and moist after another unseasonably sunny day. Marty parked the Suburban behind the nursing home in a lot marked 'private.' We never inquired 'private' for whom but always used it. Marty carried the whipped cream while I tightly held onto the cake. The damp spot on my jeans looked suspicious but with the nursing home's poor lighting and frequent spills, who would notice?

Herman and Susie struggled with the holidays, especially Christmas. The home decorated a huge tree, gathered high school students who caroled, and tried to create a colorful, ebullient holiday spirit. Still, it was a nursing home and no amount of forced cheer could alter that fact. Yet, as we walked past the nurses' station to their room, I felt we were entering a zone of sanity, if not justice.

Herman and Susie barely spoke as we entered. Susie mumbled, "Hi." Herman might have been dozing.

"Santa and Mrs. Claus have arrived. Come on you guys. Got something good here," I said.

Herman lifted his head. "I need a drink and about fifty years. This golden stuff is for the birds."

"Glad to see you, Kip. Hello, Marty, you look beautiful. Thanks so much for coming. We've had a slow day." Susie brushed her hand through her curly, gray wig and pulled her shoulders back.

Her soft, dark eyes widened, while the skin on her face and neck tightened; suddenly she looked ten years younger than when we arrived.

I put the cake on her end table. "Here's the kind of fruit cake you like and the whipped cream. Santa will bring more tomorrow." Susie's gift was an exquisite blue and white cashmere shawl for her shoulders, with a new red wool robe for Herman. So few gifts were right or useful for people at their point in life. No gift like life itself.

Marty said, "Should I cut it now, or do you want to wait until after supper?" She had just the right touch; her warm smile, soft voice, and twinkling eyes simply spelled 'life.' It was easy to imagine her hovering over a wood-burning fire stove in a simple hut making fresh tortillas for a big family in Mexico, decades ago.

"You smell real good," said Herman. "Let's eat it later. Just cut some pieces for us now." Marty did just that.

Susie laughed. "He meant what he said. Your cologne smells good. Of course, the cake smells good, too."

I chuckled. "The place doesn't smell too bad, either. There must be a thousand pine cones scattered around. Should be there all year."

We all laughed now. The room was full of cheerfulness from that moment. I felt fulfilled. This brief mission with Herman and Susie was obviously a success. People, visitors, volunteers, family, friends, doctors, nurses—human attention and interaction kept them going.

"We've got a tough case, but we've got ideas," said Marty. She wanted to pique their curiosity, arouse some interest, get their minds out of the room. "We'll play hardball. We think the husband may have been involved, so we're going to try to trap him and his granddaughter into some kind of admission." She spoke slowly and plenty low for Herman to understand without wearing his despised hearing aids.

"Sometimes innocent people look real guilty and the law gets them anyway. Is that the woman who disappeared?" said Herman.

"That's the one," I said. "Your memory is pretty good. The police think it's likely our client murdered a woman."

Herman said, "Didn't they used to say 'the butler did it?' I think the husband did it. He needs a good lawyer. So does your person. I wonder what we would have done to a he-she in the locker room after a basketball game." He winked at me.

They were both cooking now. The juices were flowing. I debated how much of this nightmare to reveal. "We've got two families involved. The woman who the cops think did it while a man, and her husband and her mother. Then there's the family of the woman who was the victim, her husband, daughter, granddaughter, and some neighbors. Two families that are both pretty strange."

"We've got to go," said Marty. "We're meeting one of them a little after five. Take care."

"Oh my goodness, dinner in a half hour. I'm starved," said Herman. "Cake for dessert. I sure wish they'd turn the lights up in here. It's too dark."

They thanked us again and again. We kissed them both and left quickly. "See you soon," I said. As we hurried past the dining room, the tables looked attractively set with white linen, silverware, and candles. Holiday cheer. Hell, the only thing any of us has, old or young, is today, this moment.

Marty did an emotional 180. Tears rimmed her blood-shot eyes as we jumped up into the Suburban. "My mom died in one of these joints. Her English wasn't so hot, *muy malo*, so I was never sure they understood her very well. No one spoke Spanish. She had a stroke and then a heart attack. She seemed old. Had me real late. I really miss her, she was everything."

I leaned over to dry her eyes with a tissue. I thought she might push my hand away but she didn't, so I dabbed at both eyes and flicked on the CD player. Fortunately, it was Eminem, the perfect distraction.

We drove to Gino's in a cloudless dusk, the Suburban riding slower than usual. I struggled with my own sad thoughts of life as it had been, compared with what it was now. Like an apothecary scale—up and down—Herman and Susie uplifted momentarily, then Marty and I bummed out.

Tami was in the same booth, already eating her double-cheese medium pizza with a large soda. It was only 5:10 p.m. so she hadn't wasted any time. "I knew you'd be here so I thought, why not get started early?" Upswept hair, black lipstick, and black open-necked shirt with tight black jeans. Did supermarkets hire Goths or had she changed clothes when she left work? We'd never know. She was the best-looking Goth I'd ever encountered.

We crowded into the booth on the same side. "By the way, Tami, did you tell the cops everything about Mary's disappearance? They think you lied," I said.

Tami choked on the crust and coughed several times while recovering. "Ugh, what do you mean? I had an alibi," she said. Her hands trembled and nearly dropped the next slice. She coughed again.

"We know you lied to the cops," I said.

"It's okay, Tami, we like you and we're private. Your secrets are safe with us," said Marty.

I said, "You lied didn't you, you little bitch? You were scared to death of Willie. You slept with him." It was good cop-bad cop time. Betty's life was at stake.

Tami made a move to slide out of the booth. Marty quickly blocked her exit, then sat on the aisle next to her. "Don't be afraid, Tami, we're friends, not out to get you. Everything is okay. Want your next soda?" said Marty.

"No, I want to leave," said Tami. "It was a long, long time ago. I've got a job and a boyfriend now." She sucked on the straw until it gurgled at the bottom of the super-size plastic cup. Then she plopped several ice cubes in her mouth.

"You help us and we'll help you," I said. "We know you lied. What else did you do wrong? Willie can't hurt you now. You're safe." I shifted my position further into the booth and stretched out my legs on the bench.

Marty said, "You were a kid. What were you, about twelve years old? I would have done the same thing." Her voice was a soft and soothing monotone, nearly hypnotic in its gentle persuasiveness. Maybe Marty's own sexuality created the empathy for a twelve-year-old caught up in incest and abuse.

"You won't tell, will you? Can I have another soda? Willie made me lie," said Tami. "I had a bad dream the other night that I went back to the old apartment and hid in the attic. A scary nightmare."

I signaled the waitress for another soda and coffee for us, sorry we hadn't taken a chunk of the fruit cake to go with the coffee.

"Go ahead, honey, tell us," said Marty. She put her pad and pen in her purse. "We have no notes and no tape." She didn't mention the digital recorder twirling away in her purse.

"All I know is they had a really, really big fight. Really big. Willie made me go to the attic. Mary had lost some money or something. He told me to tell the police that he'd been there with me and the little ones all night long. I did. I always did what he told me."

"What else?" I said. "We won't say anything. You won't be named or identified. Get the rest out. Now!" I leaned forward on my elbows and stared hard at her, willing to push further if necessary, even threaten her.

"That's all. In the morning we took his deer meat to the freezer in packages. He always stored his venison and fish, after he cleaned it, at the place where Shari Lynn works," Tami said.

In the words of the poet Shari Lynn, bingo. A surge of adrenaline shot through me. Marty appeared incandescent.

"Maybe I'll have another pizza. I'm more hungry than I thought," said Tami.

Marty hugged her. I threw a twenty on the table. "Eat your heart out. We're real late for our next appointment."

My cell phone trembled, the buzzer accidentally turned off. "Hello, Kip here," I said.

"Herman's hurt. He fell. I'm so scared," said Susie, her usual grace, judgment, and charm lost in the panic. "Please come help me."

"We're not far. Be there right away. Can staff help?"

"They know," she said. "They called 911. An ambulance is on the way. They're afraid to move him. It may have hurt his back."

"Herman's hurt," I said to Marty.

I drove as fast as I could. It wasn't quite like Steve McQueen in Bullitt—the landscape was flat and the demanding hills and narrow streets of San Francisco didn't plague me.

"Jesus, boss, you ran a red light. Think you're blue again," said Marty. "We don't have to go very far. Let's get there alive."

The hell with caution. It was Herman. I wheeled the corners, tires smoking and squealing. Nearly hit a parked bus. Flew by an almost invisible senior citizen slumped so low in an aged Buick that it almost looked driverless. White street lights blurred, red turn signals barely had time to blink at us—speedometer went crazy.

Their place was two blocks away. Slowed down for the approach. Landing gear down. I abruptly braked into the space marked 'For Administrator.' I didn't care. The closest spot to the building's front door. Herman was hurt. Susie was scared. Nothing else mattered.

We jumped out of the car, a momentary recognition that Tami and Shari Lynn and the whole Branner clan didn't really matter a hoot. That was business. This was love. This was family. In fact, it was a relief to be needed by Susie, a welcome pause from this crazy investigation of Mary's murder.

"It'll be fine. Don't sweat too much," said Marty. She was slightly ahead of me as we ran through the wide slippery hallway.

The dining room windows were lit up like July 4th. At the rear of the building, directly outside the huge dining room, rested an EMS van and a small fire engine, a light show of blinking reds and yellows, sirens off, out of respect for the elderly occupants of the center.

The goal line, Herman and Susie's door, suddenly loomed before us. Hushed voices. Crowded room. Two paramedics and two firefighters in full uniform and hats. A stretcher, BP cuff, a drip already started and a portable EKG.

Susie sat upright in her chair now parked near the door. I walked to her, held both hands and kissed the top of her head. Her palms were drenched and she'd been crying. "Thanks, Kip."

Marty had a nodding friendship with one of the paramedics. She smiled at him. He peered up at her over his glasses. "Know him?"

"Yes, close friend. What's up?"

"Fell. Probably a broken hip. We'll strap him on the stretcher in case his back is involved. Vitals not bad." The EMS technician spoke just loud enough so that we all understood the report.

I rubbed Susie's shoulders. "He'll be okay. They do hips all the time. He'll be fine."

A sudden torrent of hot tears and sobs racked her body. "He's all I've got. He's all I've got."

One nurse planted herself in the hallway. Had anyone been at the unit desk when we ran by it? Major accidents, falls, broken bones, and injuries belonged to physicians, EMS and police and firefighters. The extreme liability for treatment of accidents insured that regular nursing-home staff would call 911 and take steps to protect other residents as needed in case of fire or accidents or other acts of God, but otherwise not play the Good Samaritan or provide more than temporary palliative care. In Herman's case, that meant a pillow and a blanket for him, and a glass of water and a tranquilizer for Susie.

I stood over Herman. Eyes closed, his right hand clutched a large silver cross. "You'll be fine," I said. No reply. He was either unconscious or so weak he couldn't answer me.

"Oh, hello, it's the two of you. Thanks for that pizza," the tall, taciturn nurse said. "How's Herman doing? He fell getting into bed. I called 911 and treated for shock." She'd covered her butt all the way around.

The EMT said, "We're going to move him now. He's secured into the stretcher. Take him to St. Vincent's ER. Please sign this travel confirmation."

The four EMTs carried Herman out the door. Marty stayed with Susie. I led the way to the ambulance, clearing the path of imaginary impediments. The stretcher slid gently into the waiting tracks. Then the ambulance wheeled off with flashing lights, but no siren. The team was fast, efficient, and empathetic.

When I tiptoed back to the room, all was quiet. Marty was

in a yoga-like trance lying down on Susie's bed, holding Susie's hand while she dozed in the adjacent wheelchair. I slid into the recliner and closed my eyes. We'd take Susie to the hospital in the morning. They would probably immobilize his hip and take X-rays or do an MRI. If required, hip surgery would take several hours and she probably couldn't visit him until then. Herman's prospects for living more than one year after suffering a broken hip were not very good. Goddammit! I loved the guy.

Out the door in warp speed, Suburban fired up, ready for take off like a jet on a carrier. Marty said, "Him or her?"

"Her."

I called Shari Lynn on my cell phone, double-checked her address, and she agreed we could come by her house for a follow-up question or two. She said, "As I always say, take your time, but hurry back."

The six blocks whizzed by as we came to a racing stop at a nondescript white-frame house on a street where every house was identical except for the entrance way and the siding. No rust buckets in sight; rather there were three-and-four year old Neons, Sentras, and an occasional older Grand Prix or Oldsmobile. The builders had saved money on this post-war subdivision by eliminating garages.

The pleasure and excitement of the chase and kill to an ex-cop is hard to describe. The main problem is to keep emotions and feelings under control. It had been a gut-wrenching day. We sensed we were really on to something, something Goldbaum could use to help Betty. Hell, maybe something that could promote justice, whatever that elusive lady may be.

Shari Lynn answered the door in a slightly stained pink and yellow kimono. She wore her hair in curlers with tiny Elvis designs on them. A cigarette in one hand and a chocolate-covered cherry in the other. The kimono had NASCAR emblems sewn into it, which I hadn't noticed in the half-light of the doorway.

"What a surprise. Take me as you find me." She laughed and motioned us into the tiny living room, feigning embarrassment by smoothing chair fabrics and plumping small pillows.

A black leather couch was cracked and old, but still held us rather comfortably, indeed, too deeply. To raise oneself from it could be difficult unless you did several hundred sit-ups or crunches each morning. We shook our heads to the offer of chocolate.

Marty was bad cop. She said, "Shari Lynn, thank you for seeing us. You're in big trouble. Tami has confessed. She told us everything."

Shari Lynn choked on the cherry, tried several times to clear her throat. The candy popped out onto her robe. "That little shithead. I love her, but she talks too much. I didn't do anything. I have a perfect alibi. Ask the cops." She puffed on the acrid handmade cigarette.

"You'd better do as Marty tells you," I said. "You're not in trouble. That is all confidential. There's no record." Unless of course, Marty's digital recorder fell out of her purse.

"Give it to us dammit, Shari Lynn. Give us the fucking truth," said Marty. Her voice was loud and demanding, her dark eyes hinted at unspeakable threats.

"It's all okay, Shari Lynn. We know you didn't hurt anyone. No matter how much you felt about Mary, you'd never hurt her. We know that," I said. I felt cheap, sensing she was in it up to her ears. Our job was Betty and Chuck and Mama.

"I have seizures when I'm stressed," said Shari Lynn.

"It's all going to be fine. Don't worry. We're private investigators, not cops. We just want to clear our client of any wrongdoing. That's all." Now a shadow of shame, pity for the general human condition, came close to the surface. I grabbed a piece of Shari Lynn's cheap, cherry chocolates.

Shari Lynn's double chin quivered and her freckles stood out. "Willie fucked me a lot. It was his thing. The way he did Tami. I blamed Mary for all of it."

Marty jumped in. "Quit the bullshit. What really happened?"

Shari Lynn brushed at some stains on her kimono. Her smallish, nondescript eyes narrowed even further, as if squinting, but they appeared vacant. Were her suspicions overtaking her? "Why should I trust you two? Just met you both. I get upset—but you know that." With that Shari Lynn plopped into a ragged black-and-white tufted armchair. Her eyes had that distant look, then they closed. She trembled. "Hold my hand," she whispered.

I sat on the floor next to the chair and did as asked; Shari Lynn breathed heavily, actually panted for a moment or so. Then she was silent.

I turned my head to Mary. She threw her palms into the air. The she said, "Should I call 911? Is this real? She said she gets upset and sometimes has seizures. Is that what this is?"

I was plain scared. I'd never had a client or suspect die in my presence, on or off of the force. I prayed it would pass quickly. I said, "Her hand is chilly and damp."

Marty was frightened but not much showed. I know her pretty well.

"Better call in for an ambulance," I said.

She pulled out her cell phone and flipped it open. "She's opening her eyes. She's conscious. I think she's coming out of it," said Marty. Her voice was stronger and a half-smile crossed her lips. She closed her cell phone.

Shari Lynn's eyelids fluttered. She took several deep breaths and then sighed. "Jesus H. Christ. That's the way it happens. I don't remember a goddamn thing. Felt like God held my hand. Did I fall?"

"No, no you're fine," I said. "Do you want anything?"

"Yes, give me some water or a beer. I'm thirsty as well. I've had these things since I was a kid. Scares the shit out of people when they see me the first time. Think I'm going to croak."

I ran for the water. "We were a little shook up," I said, "but knew you'd be okay." I lied through my teeth. Marty looked up at me and arched her eyebrows. I didn't take her advice. I played bad cop now. "You see that you can trust us, Shari Lynn. We just want to help our client, not hurt you in any way. Cops won't know a thing."

"I don't know." She gulped the water. "Can I have another?" She pulled herself up and sat upright in the chair. "I don't think so."

I said, "Willie will get you, Shari Lynn. I'll tell him you ratted him out. He'll get you if you don't help us. We're your only chance."

She bolted out of the chair and trotted into the kitchen. Opened the fridge and grabbed a cold quart of cheap American vodka from the freezer. She gulped it like a bone-dry actor in a desert movie who'd been searching for water for days. This woman was something. "Bingo," she said as she wiped her mouth and chin with the kimono sleeve.

"Does bingo mean yes?" I said.

"Bingo," she said. "You protect me. I don't want Willie after me. I've had more of him than I can take. You know, I didn't have anything to do with Mary's death or what happened to her."

"We understand perfectly," said Marty. Her sincere gaze was steady, directed at Shari Lynn.

"You won't be in any trouble, Shari Lynn. The police aren't interested in you. Willie won't know. We just want to clear up any confusion about our client, a Mrs. Betty Fowler." God would judge me some day. I knew that. In the meantime, my conscience waxed and waned. If Shari Lynn did it, she deserved punishment and was not above the law. If she didn't do it, what I said didn't matter a hoot.

"It was the middle of the night. He told me to come over, that Mary had stabbed herself, to come over to their place. Mary was dead and he said it was suicide. If I didn't help him, he'd say we'd killed her and I'd get the electric chair."

"Go ahead, finish it, for Christ's sake," I said.

"I packaged her up after Willie skinned and dressed her. She stole my only child. We cleaned up and in the morning Willie brought the packages labeled 'venison-Branner' to my place and we froze them. One of them is close to me every day. Willie thinks he moved them all. It's a safety valve for me." Her suddenly placid demeanor matched those dull, filmy eyes.

Marty raised her eyebrow to me. Cool it. We didn't want another seizure or volatile explosion from her, not now. Marty said, "Thanks, Shari Lynn. I'm sure you were very frightened and intimidated by Willie and that part of you had positive feelings for him."

"Bingo," she said.

We cleared out with muffled good-byes and thanks. We'd had enough of her and the rest of Branners, and we had plenty for the cops. Betty would walk. There was every chance that Tami, Shari Lynn, and Willie would all be charged with murdering Mary—or at least, with cutting up and storing a dead body.

We high-fived as we marched out to the Suburban. Marty said, "I wouldn't be surprised if Willie ate her heart after he skinned and dressed her. That fucking animal."

I called lawyer Goldbaum on my cell phone. He was at a cocktail party for the mayor. All I said was, "The husband did it, assisted by his daughter and granddaughter. You and the cops can mop up. Betty may or may not have stolen $200 and been nipped by Mary's little doggie in the process, or else just grabbed its collar. Tell the cops to get a search warrant for the cooler at the place Shari Lynn works. A chunk of the lady is there in a package marked 'venison-Branner.' The DNA should match the DNA from Mary's lock of hair the police found in her scrapbook." I didn't wait for his response.

Marty and I headed straight for Arnie's post-haste to celebrate with burgers, pool and vodka.

We were quiet, both of us pleased but decompressing, until we luckily found our usual booth. The place was packed, foggy smoke, surprising for a Christmas Eve. We ordered drinks. After they arrived I said, "Here's your present. Hope you like it. Merry Christmas."

Marty opened the slim maroon velvet box. "Wow, these are beautiful, really stunning earrings." She slipped them on.

I said, "Matched pair of Mabe pearls. Got them on the Internet from a company in Honolulu. Glad you like them. They look terrific on you."

Not to be outdone, Marty reached into her purse and out came a small box tightly wrapped in thick gold paper. I opened it, feeling bad about tearing special paper. "Oh, no, you shouldn't have." Nestled in velvet was a magnificent eighteen-carat gold Corvette anniversary watch. I slid it on my wrist instantly, replacing my trusted ten dollar beauty from the flea market. "Thank you, so much. It's perfect." We leaned across the table and pecked on the lips. "You're wonderful to work with, in case I haven't mentioned it."

"Bingo," said Marty. "Bingo. Bango. Bongo. Wasn't that a song?"

I pulled out the cell phone, took a sip of vodka, and dialed Chuck. "'I refuse to leave the Congo' is the next line."

"Hello," said Chuck. The new speaker attachment was working.

"Hey, Chuck, it's Kip. Marty and I have good news. We have reason to believe someone else killed Mary T. Branner. Betty's lawyer has been notified. He'll follow up. My strong hunch is that Betty will be freed soon." Despite some of our methods, I was happy to give him this news. Marty and I had done much worse stuff while interrogating suspects in the old days as cops.

"Oh my God, how wonderful. Mama will be so pleased. I'm ecstatic. I knew it. Betty wouldn't hurt a soul, no matter what she said." I heard a tear, a crack in his voice.

"We're pleased, too. You'll get a full written report from us. Maybe we could all have lunch next week."

"I can never thank you enough. We'll have plenty to thank God for tonight. We're going to Mass if I can get Mama to budge from this place. Now she'll feel so much better. Bye for now."

Christmas Eve, Mass, the holy sacraments. The flesh and blood of the Son of God. God is family, the Father, the Son, and the Holy Spirit. God is love. Only in God's loving hands would there be forgiveness and redemption for the Branner family and the Fowlers. Me too, I hoped.

CHAPTER THIRTEEN

Marty and I did higher math over dark roast coffee early Monday morning in my living room. We multiplied the number of workdays times our daily fee for Betty and then added our expenses to that for the total charge. Lawyers often kept retainers in addition to the other fees. We didn't, at least not yet, but our total charges greatly exceeded the retainer. Marty was adding up our expenses for a second time on the calculator when my cell phone rang. She said, "We're rich, boss, very rich."

It was Goldbaum, and I immediately punched the speaker phone button so Marty would be involved.

"I need you," he said abruptly.

"I thought Betty was going free." Marty and I high-fived.

Goldbaum's voice lost a bit of its edge. "She will but when I'm finished with Betty, Willie wants to retain me to defend him against whatever charges the DA comes up with later—murder, conspiracy, manslaughter, cutting up a dead body, perjury—you name it."

"Isn't there a potential conflict of interest?" I demanded. "Would any upstanding criminal defense attorney do what you're planning to do?"

"There's no confession, no eyewitnesses," Goldbaum retorted. "Shouldn't be too difficult to plead him out to manslaughter or simply cutting up Mary. Shari Lynn has an axe to grind, so she's not a perfect witness against him. Who the hell's the lawyer here, you or me?"

I smiled at Marty, pleased that I'd gotten to him. "If you want to hire us to build Willie's case, it's the usual retainer, fees and expenses. Both of us?"

"Yes, God, you're expensive, but Willie will pay. I'll put it in the agreement."

"What's the deal? Why us?" Marty gave me the thumbs up sign.

"This is in confidence. My contact at the coroner's office just called. There were several packages of Branner venison. One of them is not Mary Branner. It's part of a missing prostitute, Es Martinez, not seen for more than ten years and presumed dead. Hung out at truck stops. They found her hand and arm near the highway one night and ID'd the fingerprints from their files, since she'd been arrested so many times." Even unflappable Goldbaum had his personal limit. He sounded flappable.

"We'll see what we can do. Fax me what you have and we'll get on it right away. If Betty's fingerprints were on that hand, it makes sense since she claimed Butch had sex with the prostitute. Blue Throat also told us that there was key forensic material found under the Martinez fingernails and kept on file." No answer from Goldbaum. He hadn't lost his memory.

Several minutes later the following arrived: Esmeralda Martinez, Hispanic female, single, age forty-one, needle scars on arms and ankles, disappeared thirteen years ago, twenty priors for prostitution, shoplifting, and drug-related offenses. Addicted to meth, tequila, and heroin. Severed hand and arm with rings and watch found near Highway 75 linked to her through prints. Known to frequent truck stops wearing trademark large gold-hoop earrings.

Marty and I both eyeballed the fax several times.

Marty said, "The cops found a partial print of Betty's on a watch or ring on this woman's hand. Now a body part turns up in Shari Lynn's frozen food locker."

"Looks like it. How in the hell? Unless Willie put it there. Betty couldn't have been involved, could she? There's no connection between Butch and Willie is there?" Marty didn't answer.

We were glad for the work. Full pay, no discount. Goldbaum could be a goldmine for us. Tough cases. Good pay. Very little conversation. Goof up, and we wouldn't hear from him again. "No explain, no complain," was the motto with Goldbaum. Give him what he wanted and needed and the check was in the mail. Our Christmas Club savings account at the bank would be very full this year.

"All we have to do is cast reasonable doubt on Willie as the kidnapper and killer of Ms. Martinez," I said.

Marty said, "Goldbaum has a huge mess on his hands if Willie killed them both. He fries. Maybe Shari Lynn, too. Who knows?" She gulped her coffee and poured us both another steaming cup. Fresh chocolate Italian cookies with macadamia nuts were perfect with the coffee. We'd try the vanilla biscotti next time. Or maybe we should just go directly to Rome or Venice and have the real thing.

My fax bubbled again and out came several photos of Es, one black and white from a police line-up; the other a color shot of her standing between two truckers, an arm around each one, filed by the cops. Very attractive woman, with high cheekbones, dark eyes, aquiline nose, and the large hoop earrings. Slightly over five feet tall and 125 pounds if I had to guess. She had the appearance and clothes—print blouse and fluffy skirt—of a flamenco dancer. In the background was the cab of an eighteen-wheeler under a sign reading Easy Over Motel—Vacancy. I made copies of the pictures in case we needed them.

"Heads the Corvette, tails the Suburban," I said. Tails, so Marty drove to Flint, about ninety miles north of Toledo. Another faded Midwestern factory city, its premier waterfront development had suffered the same sad fate as Toledo's Portside.

Marty kept the pedal to the metal. We hurried past a microcosm of Americana—burger and taco joints, cheap motels, used car lots. And so on. And so on.

Marty was ravishing in tight beige hip-huggers and a black cotton turtleneck. I tried to avoid staring, but failed.

"This thing gets weirder and weirder, doesn't it?" she said. "First, this Betty and now Willie with parts of two women in his frozen locker for game and fish. Makes you wonder about these coincidences. Seems so unlikely." Her gaze held the road tightly, as the speedometer settled on eighty-five miles per hour.

"I know. One minute I think Betty's honest, the next I think she's totally fucking unbelievable." I settled into the leather lounge seat, comfortable and safe.

"And Willie, too, with his bullshit story and now parts of two women in his freezer. Maybe he killed them both. Maybe he was set up with the prostitute. The fat drunk must have paid plenty for

Es. There are attractive truckers who don't belch and fart in your face."

"What about me?" I'd jumped off of the high diving board.

"What about you?" said Marty. Her gaze didn't move from the road.

"Am I attractive? I don't belch or fart—well, I do, but privately."

"Boss, you're not coming on to me, are you? I'll have to go to a truck stop to get you laid." Marty's gaze turned to me for just a moment. Then she smiled, "I feel good about you. But you know about me and my professor. I'm loyal to her. I love her and she loves me. You'll be Uncle Kip to our kids."

"You drive me nuts. It isn't just the way you look either. It's more than that." My jaw sagged. I wanted Marty so much that I closed my eyes, hoping the feeling and need would disappear somehow.

"I know, Kip. I think I know. I'm loving. I love kids. I've survived anything you can imagine. I treasure my partner, the idea of family. You're a wonderful person. You know that I think that. I think I'm bi as much as anything." Marty's skin was alive with bronze tones, her lips trembling, her dark eyes misty with honest emotion.

"Let's stop at Micky D's for a value meal. I'm hungry," I said.

"Why not tacos in my honor?" Marty sent me a sly sideways glance and laughed out loud.

"Okay. They'll arrange the meat, beans, tomatoes, onions, tortillas, sour cream, and cheese, then re-arrange it, and give it different names. You'll love to help a gringo figure it out."

"You got it boss." She wheeled off at the next turn and braked quickly in a parking lot of a Mexican restaurant.

It was cold outside, probably about fifteen degrees with a brisk wind, heavy cloud cover, but fortunately, no rain or snow. Into such a dreary, gray, cold day we stepped, leaving the comfort and warmth of the Suburban. We walked into the restaurant holding hands, some kind of secret bond that said we had great affection, respect, and concern for each other—maybe love—but it could not be acted on now.

Several tacos and burritos later we were back on the road to Flint. No talk at lunch. Quiet in the car, too. Time to think, to evaluate, to process. I felt like crying and saying how much I hurt, how alone I was. I wanted to talk endlessly about Wendy, but thought better of it. You just don't talk about a lost love, even one who died, to a current love whom you can't even put your arm around. Or do you?

We blasted into the Easy Over Motel parking lot to begin the search for something. I wasn't sure just what. It was about Willie and a thirteen-year-old unsolved murder case of a local prostitute. Can't imagine that the police busted their butts to solve it, but you never know who's banging who, and maybe she was a department favorite.

We'd been lucky digging into the past of the Mary T. Branner murder, just following a more-or-less obvious possibility. This was different. The cops had a hand, and according to Blue Throat, fingerprint evidence from Betty, I mean Butch, and DNA evidence from Willie boy obtained with a warrant.

Blue Throat also told Marty that Es was popular, paid her drug bills on time, gave good service, but only talked vaguely about family in Mexico and growing up in the states. No one knew much about her. No one hated her. No one wanted to kill her. She didn't appear depressed, so no one figured she'd kill herself. I guess the question was whether Willie had anything to do with it or was just one of her regular johns. Did he even know her? We couldn't assume anything just because a package containing her body parts had been discovered in Willie's freezer. We had to keep an open mind. I'd rather think about Marty and me than Willie and Es, but I had to regain a modicum of professionalism.

The Easy Over's 1940s authentic retro look featured a white latticed stone façade above tan brickwork. An inner courtyard with an untended, decrepit center fountain area was horseshoe-shaped with about thirty single rooms. Driving into the courtyard meant passing a corner window with a huge sign, still blinking purple neon, marked "office." We parked and walked in, transported into the late forties. The cracked and stained walls relived the past with framed photos of a few notables and celebrities, mostly truckers in pairs or trios, usually with a woman between them. The men uniformly wore jeans, cowboy boots, T-shirts, and baseball caps, setting the stage for a Ralph Lauren design revolution of the late 20th century.

Thousands of hours of thousands of smokers of tens of thousands of cigarettes left their mark in the office. A thin film of brown grease covered everything, fused with the dust and grime of years of heavy and unrepentant use. At the helm sat an elderly gentleman positioned below desk height in an ancient wooden wheelchair. He wore a heavy black sweater and white turtleneck, long white beard covering rough, leathery skin, and a Greek shipping captain's hat.

"Lost one outside Paris in WW II, or was it WW I? I can't remember." Laughter triggered his cough, which scared me with its depth and the leftover gurgling sounds. "Twenty-five bucks cash for a half-hour. Forty for the whole hour. You two look like hour people to me."

I flipped open my wallet to show a PI identification card. I added a picture of Es. "We're private from Toledo. Just need some information and we'll be gone. Do you remember her from about thirteen years ago? Were you here then?" Marty and I adopted a professional stance, serious, no smiles, but no threat or bribes, either.

"Been here since the war. Owner promises me a piece of the action some day. And I don't mean the kind of piece you're thinking of." He tipped his hat in mock salute.

I put a fifty dollar bill in front of him on the ledge. Marty placed her hand on it.

"She was a beauty," he said. "A real beauty. Like a Spanish movie star. The guys loved her. She brought a lot of them back here. She'd do it in the trucks if they didn't have enough money." He reached his hand for the fifty and Marty released it.

"Got any pictures of her?" Marty said.

"Well, everything here is arranged by year. I started hanging them back of the desk and now they're out there by the chairs. Let's see, ten or fifteen years ago. Try the area to the left of the magazine rack." The cough doubled him up in the chair and sputum erupted, which he caught in a mottled, huge handkerchief, maybe a small towel.

"Did you know a guy named Willie Branner from Toledo?" Marty said.

"They never used their right names. You know how it is. They'd just give me cash. Go ahead and look at the pictures if you like."

Marty was good at this. In barely a moment, she found it. "He's with Es and two other guys. A lot thinner with more hair and no glasses. But that's dear Willie. He's got one hand inside Es's backside. Can we have this one, sir?"

"Don't call me 'sir.' I was a corporal. It'll cost you."

I laid out another fifty dollar bill. Gone in a flash. My cell phone rang. Guess who?

Goldbaum commanded, "Get back here pronto. See Willie. The shit's going to hit the fan. I need a full report of his story and his background."

"Okay," I said.

Marty grabbed the photo. "Thanks."

We arrived back in town, so I had a quick drink and called Willie. Told him that Goldbaum asked me to see him again when he was sober. He said he hadn't been drinking, to come out and talk if I wanted to.

Here's my account of two hours with Willie. Instead of drinks after my time with him, I had three chocolate bars.

E-mail
From: Kip
To: Marty
Subject: Willie Branner Interview

William Bendix Branner was born in Beaufort, Mississippi, then grew up and attended high school in Toledo, Ohio. He graduated, married Mary the same month that Shari Lynn was born. He was eighteen, she fifteen.

His mother and father divorced when he was sixteen, and he had three siblings, all younger sisters. Willie's father drove truck and until the time of Mary's disappearance, Willie drove semis for the Atlas Trucking Company, usually moving homes or offices throughout the U.S. and Canada.

The divorce of his parents didn't have much effect on him, since he hardly knew his father. When the man was home he was drunk, asleep, or violently abusive, according to Willie.

He loved his mother, who worked as a waitress in a strip-tease club where she also danced in a G-string and pasties. She danced for Willie at home occasionally, when his sisters were at weeknight prayer service. It was something that Willie recalls very clearly.

Willie loved to eat. With a full stomach, he felt all was right with the world, that he could endure his father's wrath and the perpetual stimulation of his mother's activities. Around age ten or eleven, he started eating raw meat and raw fish—raw rabbit or squirrel, a chunk of walleye fresh from Lake Erie.

Twice a year, Willie went hunting and fishing with his father, and he loved it. They went deer hunting with a group of truckers yearly into southern Michigan. And they fished Lake Erie for a weekend aboard a party boat owned by the head of the trucking firm. Willie learned to gut, skin, and dress a deer and also rabbits, squirrels, and ducks. He could gut, scale, and clean a five-pound walleye with the best of them.

Willie turned eighteen, married, and got his commercial license so he could drive truck himself. There were a lot of sexy women around the truck stops. Willie had Mary and Shari Lynn at home, but he liked the women of the night; the sexier the better. He had a favorite at each of the major stops, and for the very special ones he'd even rent a motel room for an hour, shower first, share a pizza and a six pack, then do his thing with them; otherwise, it was wham-bam-thank-you-ma'am in the back of the truck cab.

Occasionally, Willie got rough with the women. He would bite a woman he had sex with, not hard enough to break the skin, but with enough pressure to leave teeth marks. He'd growl and pretend to be a bear or a pit bull.

When Mary was in her late twenties, before their two younger children were born, Willie's interest in Shari Lynn perked up. In her early teens by then, Shari Lynn was easy prey for Willie, who couldn't quite understand his sexual needs. He stated that he didn't plan an ongoing intimate relationship with Shari Lynn but it just "sort of happened." Willie continued sex with Shari Lynn until she had her baby at age fifteen and moved out of the house. Willie often wondered if her child was his, but kept his speculations to himself. He doesn't think Mary knew of their relationship, as she was so preoccupied with her own needs and so often absent from home. He states that Shari Lynn harbors resentment against both parents.

Then he basically repeated the same relationship with his granddaughter, Tami, beginning when she was around twelve and he was in his mid-forties. Willie said Tami was the best "wife" he'd had, and that she was the "best in bed ever and when she was just a kid." She helped with the younger kids after Mary disappeared.

Willie feels that Shari Lynn tolerated his advances, though they never spoke during or after the encounters, but feels she'd have welcomed Mary stopping them from happening. He isn't sure she loved him the way Tami did. Tami was expressive, made endearing remarks, reassured Willie and told him repeatedly how wonderful he was and how much she loved him, "not as Grandpa but as a damn strong man."

He has literally no awareness that both of these women were very frightened of him, hated him, resented Mary's passivity, and couldn't wait to get away from him.

Willie remembers many of the prostitutes that hung out in the Flint area and he was especially fond of Esmeralda. He liked his women like his coffee, he said, dark, hot, and sweet. They liked his money. Es preferred the motel to the back of his truck cab, so he'd pay a few extra dollars for a half-hour at the Easy Over Motel.

One night, short of cash, he had Es do her thing in his truck just before he gassed up for the empty haul back to Toledo. She asked to ride with him, and against all company rules and his own better judgment, he agreed. It was a dark and wet night. Es wanted to use a restroom, so he pulled up to a rest stop and waited for her while she went to the women's room. She stumbled off in the dark in her high-heeled shoes; fifteen minutes went by and he became concerned, then found her slumped over a washbasin with a syringe in her hand. She was dead.

Willie panicked; fearful he'd be implicated in her death, maybe blamed for it. She was riding in his truck, her purse full of his money, and he had no alibi. He thought the police might blame him for the drugs or think that he deliberately gave her an overdose. He threw her body over his shoulder, dumped the syringe in a garbage can nearby, and drove off. No one saw them.

Willie drove aimlessly until dawn. He parked at a campsite. He cut up her body after skinning it, like he'd done with a deer or elk so many times. Then he used some of the freezer paper he kept in the cab, just in case he ran into road kill while driving, a deer that mistakenly came onto the highway. He packaged Es's body into seven or eight meat-freezer-ready packages, cleaned up the mess at the campsite, burned her clothes, and said to himself that he hadn't hurt her or killed her. She was dead and she had no kin, so the state would bury her in some lousy grave near a factory or a highway.

Willie had been careful, but not quite thorough enough. Es's arm and hand with her rings and a large, costume-jewelry watch had either fallen out of the truck or been left behind by mistake at the campsite. It was moved or blown or rolled to the edge of the highway and found by passersby. Eventually, Willie removed all of the packages from the freezer and put them in landfills in the area, but he either forgot one, or it had been moved when the owner fixed the air conditioning system.

So, there you are. The best laid plans. Willie's DNA found under Es's nails and on her hands—they'd had an intense sexual encounter that night. Willie will say, of course, that he didn't kill her, just cut her up. She either OD'd or committed suicide, or a bit of both. Didn't Mary supposedly commit suicide, too? I suppose that you're like me, wondering if dear old Willie has developed a taste for human flesh or blood.

Finally, we'd better check out Betty's story. If sex with Es is really all there is to it, fine. Otherwise, could be trouble for her later on.

CHAPTER FOURTEEN

Marty and I were tanked on cups of icy beer and hot tortilla chips. Chilled on the hayrack ride, we'd bundled up in warm blankets and an old fur wrap. Six or seven couples, with a few singles, comprised the bodies half-hidden in the cold, nearly dry hay. The draft horses snorted steam as they lumbered down bumpy, hard country roads near the Cap's spread.

I snuggled close to Marty, who wore red long-johns under jeans and a black-and-red checkered lumberjack coat, with a fleece vest. She still shivered. Near the rear of the rack we had a private space for the moment. A silk shirt underneath my new parka wasn't enough layering to ward off the winter night.

Marty's hand found its way between my legs. Stunned, I fell still, yet trembled inwardly with excitement. Had she lost her marbles? I'd come on to her endlessly but to no avail. She was so beautiful. So smart. So sexy. Such a partner for me. Now she had made a move. I lifted myself with both hands, a push-up in order to catch her gaze in the moonlight. Eyes were closed. A smile on her lips. Was it my imagination?

"You'd like to fuck me, wouldn't you?" she said.

"Excuse me."

"I said you'd like to fuck me wouldn't you?" Her hand squeezed me. I almost lost it.

"Are you conscious of what you're doing and saying?" The thrill of the moment sent powerful chemicals racing through me. Was I in heaven? There was no white light beckoning me at the end of a tunnel, simply Marty's lascivious smile speaking to my lust.

"Yes, I am, boss. Very conscious. Guys still like to have their dicks pawed and sucked, don't they?" She did not let go.

"You're drunk as hell. Stop it. I'll get you coffee when we get back to the barn. No more booze," I said. I pulled away and rolled over.

Marty moved, too. Then her hand was underneath me in that same spot. Luckily, she was quite persistent and goal-oriented.

"What's going on? The stars and moon get into you, on top of a lot of beer. Better not start something you can't finish."

"The professor and I want a baby. We need you."

"The sperm-male?"

"Yes, but I want the real thing. Not just test tubes or syringes. You fuck me until I'm pregnant." Her hand unzipped my cold corduroy pants. Hidden from the others, her beautiful, soft, moist warm mouth encased me. I tried to pull away but she held tight. It had been a long time. This was so unexpected, so brief and explosive, a momentary headache hit like cold ice cream does to you on a hot summer afternoon. She chuckled. A throaty whisper. "What's your answer?"

"My what? Oh. Yes, is my answer. I'll be ready again in about twenty minutes. I love the country air."

I hadn't had much fun lately. Almost forgotten what it was, laughter, enjoyment, feeling good, even high, sharing something, or someone, playfully with other people; no need to investigate, interrogate, or report back to Goldbaum. Herman and Susie were after me to date, find a good woman, get a new life. The first step, I guess, was to rehab myself, have some fun again, simply enjoy life. Live in the present, forget the past, go forward. Get a life!

So the answer had been easy when the guys from our old precinct invited both Marty and me to their annual shindig. Sometimes they got drunk and took a bus to a gambling casino, or had a drunken, obscene golf outing; once they rented a bowling alley and a movie theater for the night with strippers in between games and shows.

This time it was a hayrack ride, a bonfire, horseshoes, volleyball, cards and dice games—inside the captain's pole barn on a farm no one was quite sure he could afford on his salary, even counting his soon-to-come retirement pay. Had his wife come into an inheritance recently? Well, who's counting anyway?

Captain Miles called with the New Year's Eve invitation. He said, "I've got a new in-ground pool and exercise gym in addition to the old farm house."

"You've got us, Cap. Marty has other plans but we'll be there for a few hours at least. It's been a long time for both of us."

Miles' voice was full of holiday cheer. "I know, I know. Can't wait to see you both. Hayrack ride, if no snow. It's New Year's. Keg of beer on the ride, bourbon to warm up afterward, then hot toddies to stay warm the whole evening."

"Sounds great, Cap. Just great. Looking forward to it. We'll sing that Bud commercial song."

Cap's voice changed to his gruff, no-nonsense, 'don't cross me' style. "The hell we will. It'll be better beer than that," he said.

I hoped he wasn't offended. Cap always had a touch of class. He was only about fifty but looked older, paunchy with shaved head and a thin gray mustache. He'd been there for me when Wendy died. Told me to take whatever time I needed, got me extra medical leave and money, and went ballistic when I quit, well, really gradually faded off of the force. He should have been a priest but he wasn't even Catholic.

The night had been glorious so far. Bright sky with occasional drifting clouds hiding a full moon, toasty inside the largest pole barn I'd ever seen, horseshoe pit along one wall, badminton net set up in the rear, and a blazing fire pit just outside the main door. The rhythmic thuds of the two draft horses pulling the hayrack still rolled around my brain, merged with the dusty, moldy odor of half-frozen hay, and Marty's magnificent scents. Cold and warm, dark and light, sober and drunk, loneliness and sex, night and day, man and woman; what contrasts. I felt alive.

Somebody had pulled the fur right off of us when the rack parked. What a joke. We were shamed into going into the pole barn with the others, having duly noted that another smaller horse barn was just a few paces away. Full of horse and hay and stalls, it was a perfect hideaway from the group. The layout was really impressive and we hadn't toured the house, pool or gym yet. Half-barrels propped up on metal tripods beckoned us, full of aromatic barbecuing chicken, thick hot dogs, T-bone steaks and baby-back ribs. Cap sure could throw a shindig. Sex, booze, and rock-n-roll, just like the old days.

Vince Johnson said, "Come on, Kip, you used to play horse-shoes. Bet you a cold one." He was very drunk and a surefire mark for me.

"Bet you ten bucks," I said. "The booze is free here."

I winked at Marty. Vince and I strolled back to the pit. He put his arm around my shoulder, part camaraderie, but largely for support.

"Been a long time, old buddy. Good to see you again. You're still a legend at the precinct. You never gave up on a case," said Vince.

I had a terrible premonition he'd regurgitate on my new, navy blue, down parka. He didn't. He simply plopped himself down in the middle of the pit, holding a horseshoe in each hand. "They don't feel the same. Cap has loaded the dice on us." He swung his arms wildly. "Me Tarzan, me Governor Schwarzenegger."

"You're drunk, Vince. Give me the shoes." He gave them up easily and I squatted a few feet away. My head hurt and I couldn't really get Marty off of my mind. What had happened? What did it mean? I knew there would be conditions attached to our hastily arranged agreement. Hell, I'd agree to anything.

"My wife's sick, Kip. Real sick." Tears replaced bravado. Chest heaving, jaw sagging, it appeared that Vince would either pass out or cry himself to sleep. He did neither. He grabbed one of the shoes, jumped up, and threw it as hard as he could at the back wall of the barn. The horseshoe fell harmlessly to the floor. "Goddammit. She's dying. First night I've been away in weeks." Then he fell in his tracks, a victim of alcohol, sadness, and that desperate anger fueled by the futility of wanting to help a loved one, but being unable to do so.

I knelt near his face, sure he was still conscious. "Don't do like I do, do like I say. Her pain and your helplessness are real, so do everything you can for her now. She'll be at peace. Without Wendy, I felt so much self-pity and so sad that I've never really recovered. Lost the job, drank to forget, really shut down. After this case we're on is over, I'm going to honor Wendy's memory. No more booze, and back to five AA meetings a week. Volunteer for the American Cancer Society. The most important thing she'd want is for me to find somebody else. Not fall in love with an impossible dream, like Marty. There's always counseling if you need it, but you can't make a good thing out of something bad, no matter how hard you try."

Vince's eyes were shut. He mumbled, "Why have you waited three years?"

Cap said, "He's grieving. He'll be okay. Come out here and get some chow and a drink. Don't relive it all."

The chill of the night air startled me, and I knew some barbecue would help with the hangover ahead in the morning. Drinking too much on any kind of stomach, empty or full, created a hangover, but full was better. Cap handed me a plate of chicken and ribs, crisp with dark sweet sauce on the outside, delicate and tender close to the bone.

Cap said, "You don't want to come back, do you?" Marty, warming her hands near the fire pit, must have overheard him.

"No thanks, Cap. Marty and I have a PI business. Getting rich legally." I was drunk, too, so I belly-laughed to cover up any indiscretion.

Cap laughed, finally. "Okay, glad to hear it. You could always get re-instated. Maybe Marty, too. Who knows?"

Somebody turned on the digital sound system. There was a deafening drum roll, then complete silence. Several flashlights pin-pointed a wide paper banner with hand-painted lettering: "Happy New Year! Welcome back Kip and Marty." I put down my plate. One after the other, guys came over, shook hands, hugged us, kissed our cheeks, expressed their pleasure at seeing us. It was overwhelming. Marty and I embraced briefly. She cried. I choked back my tears. We were still a part of their scene, and they would never leave our memories or souls.

"Enough bullshit," said Cap. "Time for volleyball. Separates the men from the boys. Sorry girls. Separates the men from the boys and the girls. Oh, Christ, let's play. Losing team cleans up the campsite later. I'm glad the wives are in the house."

The barn must have been designed by Cap's wife. Rugged old gray distressed siding had obviously been carefully cleaned, repainted, and probably made termite proof. The vaulted ceiling was topped off by a green metal slatted roof which sang in the rain. Really more of a huge play pen, it was planned for parties, family gatherings, or maybe a YMCA summer camp.

The fire pit itself was a six-foot, iron, wok-like affair settled into a hole so that it was flush with ground level. I stood admiring the sparks flying up in the fire pit while I wolfed down the last few bites of chow. Delicious and filling, I realized that I wasn't as drunk as many of the guys and that I'd had an incredible, yet puzzling encounter with Marty. Better talk to her as soon as I could.

Marty was already serving on the volleyball court. She'd been a pretty fair high school player, as it turned out, so her team insisted that she do all of the serving. I joined the opposition. Vince was on my team, Cap on hers. Vince appeared to be reconstituted sufficiently to run and jump, that is as well as one could play volleyball with a sixteen-ounce plastic cup of cold beer in one hand. Vince needed AA badly, but he'd have to come to that decision and commitment on his own. He obviously had not bottomed out yet, still working and trying to help his wife survive. Maybe a sponsor could help at a later point.

Cap said, "Give it to them, Marty. The old high hard one down the gut."

Marty served a beauty, indeed, fast down the middle and we all missed. "What was that, Cap, about high and hard?"

"It's a baseball expression that means a high, hard pitch to the batter," said Cap.

"Oh, okay," said Marty. She laughed, a smart tough woman who could banter with the best of them. "Thanks for sharing."

"And thank you for caring," said Cap. He tried to protect himself from my kill shot, set up surprisingly well by Vince, but it caught him squarely in the face. Blood shot out of his nose.

"Oh, shit, Cap, sorry," I said. I crossed under the net and pressed my handkerchief tightly on his nose.

"Halftime," said Vince. "Score is tied at two-all."

We set Cap up in a comfortable chair, head back, nose pinched, ice bag on his face, and half a glass of bourbon down his gullet. "For medicinal purposes only," he said. "I'll be fine. Run along and have fun. No pain, no gain. I've learned. I'm ready for the rocking chair. My volleyball days should end."

Vince said, "Baloney, Cap, you played great. We'll finish it next time. Score is tied. Game is called."

Marty and I strolled nonchalantly through the main door. I felt great about the party. Marty apparently did, too. We had to talk. The evening's events, the future of our relationship, the professor and any offspring required a preliminary plan, at the very least.

"I'd been waiting to ask you," said Marty. "I knew you'd agree but I wanted it to be a very pleasurable and memorable experience."

The night air failed to reduce my body heat. I wanted her now, so beautiful, so warm, so appealing. I knew that there would be rules for now, for later. We stood side by side between the two barns, a breeze at our backs. "You guys want me to father your child, naturally, so to speak."

"Yes, when and where I say, and it stops when I'm pregnant. You're the best, but the professor is my love and my life, my family."

"I'll be Uncle Kip?" It sounded good to me as I said it. "Yes, I'll be Uncle Kip."

"Of course, we want you to be involved with our family. At the right time, we can decide if and how to tell the kid. Lawyers can draw up an agreement now. You'd have no parental rights," said Marty.

I sighed. "Why me?" I shivered and felt goose bumps on my arms and legs, fearful of the answer but more than willing to live with it.

"We both care for you. You're smart, single, clean, cute, healthy, and Wendy was terrific, too. So, it's logical."

"And I'm hot for you?"

"Yes, that too. Remember it's only sex, not love. But it can be great sex," said Marty. She smiled, gazed at the moon, not at me, then arched her eyebrows in a warning.

"You know I love you." Standing in the dark near her without holding hands or kissing became uncomfortable, given the earlier intimacies and the future possibilities.

"Don't do that. I call the shots. I'll take my temp and keep a chart, so we pick the right time to try, I mean to do the nasty deed."

Marty turned toward me but our bodies did not touch. She had exquisite control in this contractual negotiation.

"I've been such a mess. I suppose I'd accept your offer under almost any circumstance, but this has appeal. Part of a family, always wanted to father a child. Opportunities come one at a time." Marty squirmed away from me as my arm circled her waist.

"My eggs come several at a time," said Marty. She leaned toward me now as we kissed briefly. The deal was cemented. She turned and walked back into the pole barn.

I probably should have thought about all of this for a few days. Maybe talked to a lawyer to make sure I knew what I was getting into. But here was a lonely widower, horny as hell most of the time, presented with sex with someone I cared for who was gay, yet wanted me to father her child.

I felt like baying at the moon. Wendy would understand. She'd approve. She was a realist. She'd say something like, "It's okay, Kip. Marty's a good friend and colleague. She thinks the world of you. It's a special situation. She wants you, you as a person, not just you as a guy who could gratify her. She's got plenty of that at home with the professor. This is really all about you, your brains, your personality, your looks, your charm. She wants a kid like you."

And I wanted Wendy. We could have had a family, children of our own. I would have been a complete father. I felt like crying but I held back, more emotional control than I had a year ago. I zipped up my parka resolutely, pulled up the hood, and decided to walk in the fields for a half hour. I was flattered by Marty; still, I felt like ramming my fist into the closest tree.

As I crossed over the rough ground behind the horse barn, Marty ran to me. I stopped. "Here's the rest of it. I was married to Luis Flores for two years when I was a kid. He drank a lot. We had fun. He worked for the railroad, gone a lot. I was very lonely. A neighbor was gay. She helped me realize that I was, too. We had no kids. I divorced him and followed my true self—the life of a lesbian. Professor Ruth is my wife, my one true love. I'd never do anything to wreck it. But I do have a lot of feeling for you, Kip.

I don't hate men, not by a long shot." She put her fingers to my lips, then tried to run away again. I blocked her path.

"These earrings are beautiful on you," I said. "Moonlight bounces off of the gold and the little stones. Catches your eyes, too."

Marty said, "I got them at the art museum shop. They're copies of something about Ptolemy, serpentine shaped gold with tiny emerald beads on the outside."

"Who was Ptolemy?"

She said, "Typical man's question. Just bought them."

Then I impulsively grabbed her arms and held on for dear life. We embraced. A long and fierce hug, cheek to cheek, with faces pointed over each other's shoulders. Then we kissed, slowly, warmly, lips and tongues lost in the pent-up passion I had felt for so long. I'll never really know the extent to which it was reciprocated, but you could have fooled me at that moment. The wind picked up and blew around the altos cumulus clouds now darkened by the on-coming rain. I felt drops.

"Let's go inside the horse barn. It's raining," I said.

"Okay, but remember—sex not love."

We ran inside. Wall lamps shone weakly outside each of six immaculate stalls. Horses whinnied softly and stood at the half door in three of them. That left three stalls for us.

"Door number two," I said. My breathing was uneven. Glints of silver moonlight flitted around the barn, filtering through the wide-open double doors. I could hear one of the horses chewing loudly and then drinking water, finally slurping it all down together.

The warm fresh hay smelled aromatic, less pungent than the bed of cold straw from the ride. Marty's cologne was even better. I'm sure it was something like 'Nights of Paris.' We stumbled over a small water bucket, falling into a mound of hay. I spied a huge, heavy wool blanket thrown over the side of the stall and covered us with it. Then I yanked it off. Next came Marty's lumberjack shirt, then the long johns slid down her legs. Her beautiful womanhood was wet with desire. My parka and silk shirt flew to the ground. In the shadows, I ran my fingers slowly over the outlines of her perfectly rounded breasts, hard, firm nipples, and those luscious lips. She moaned and sighed. Such ecstasy. We kissed, long and passionately. Her skin had the sheen and feel of satin, yet was electric to the touch.

In a moment, I was inside her. I couldn't wait. So deep. So tight. That magical feeling of uniting with someone so dear, so wonderful, so close. It was truly New Year's Eve, everything I'd dreamed of for months. We pulsed together in a way I'll never forget, nearly rivaled by the experience with her in the hayrack. One of the horses bumped against the side of the wall in its stall, and the dull thuds matched our mating rhythm.

I gulped short breaths. My mind raced, and a pure white heat flooded my senses.

We reached a climax. Heavy, labored breathing, panting, and actually a soft scream from Marty, then total cessation. Spent pleasures. Complete relaxation. A light sleep. Clothes back on, capped with a deep, soul kiss.

"Thanks, Uncle Kip. You're a wonderful guy."

"I was good wasn't I? I never told you how great you are, how much I like being with you, or how much I love you."

Marty clutched my hand as we walked out. "Yes, you were very, very good. Thank you. I thank you. My family thanks you. That was my first really authentic roll in the hay."

"Will you see Dr. Murchison soon?" she continued. "He's the fertility specialist. You give him your sperm and he'll put it in me." Her grip tightened.

"Of course. Very soon. First thing this week," I said. "I'll help any way I can."

"That will be for Ruth and me. I'm not saying no to the syringe or test tube, or whatever. Going both ways, so to speak."

"Me, too."

"I want the natural way, too. Professor Ruth doesn't need to know this part. She doesn't want it. I do. You do. This is the way I want to remember it." She loosened her hand.

"You'll lie to her?"

Marty whispered, "A simple white lie of omission. She knows about Dr. Murchison. She approves of that."

I tensed slightly. Blood returned to my brain. The throbbing diminished. I withdrew from the precipice for a moment. "Am I lying, too? I will if you want me to."

"No, you're doing what I've asked. Fucking me and also going to Dr. Murchison. The issue is between Ruth and me. We both want you to help us create our child. Got it. Our child. We're the parents of our child. Ruth couldn't understand, or wouldn't understand, this part of it. I'm not sure I do myself."

"You're an old-fashioned girl at heart. Aren't you feeling guilty?"

"No more talk. We've got a deal. Shake on it."

"Why me?"

"Already told you."

CHAPTER FIFTEEN

Herman's new red robe was casually draped cape-like across his shoulders, an Italian movie star cavorting in a cashmere topcoat. He'd survived the hip surgery in tip-top shape, his upbeat mood and the boost provided by Susie the perfect accompaniment to the surgeon's skills. The trauma of the injury had long since passed and fortunately, no complications came from a slightly strained back. We were all feeling a huge sense of relief and gratitude for his speedy recovery. I fretted to myself about the longer-term implications of a broken hip at his age, but said nothing.

The room itself was sparsely furnished; several chairs, two beds, a bathroom, and a table and TV. No monitoring equipment or IV stands were visible. The monotonous pale gray of the walls increased the urgency of recovering quickly and leaving. Hospitals were dangerous places.

Marty lounged in a recliner, clutching Susie's hand loosely as she slept in her adjacent wheelchair. Marty and I had run out of supportive, positive, forward-looking statements and observations, but it didn't appear to matter. Our presence spoke to Herman and Susie; our cards and joke gifts meant as much as the more lavish Christmas presents. Their occasional crabbiness or fatigue was more than matched by pleasant and happy memories of by-gone days.

Susie had been a pillar of strength during Herman's ordeal. What a woman. She kept repeating that she'd known the guy for decades, he'd broken bones before, he recovered quickly, and the Lord wasn't quite ready for him. She truly felt that they'd both know when their time had arrived, and, absent that, she would only consider the beneficial alternatives in her life. Down with the negative. What the hell was wrong with me? Of course, at appropriate times, like Herman's fall and injury, Susie got scared. She was human.

Susie opened her eyes and smiled. "I love this shawl, Kip. It's beautiful and it keeps these old bones warm. I can't wait until next Christmas."

I moved closer to her and pulled the shawl higher over her shoulder. "I can't wait either. I've got something even better in mind for you. Wish I could spill the beans now but it's only the second week of January."

"I get out in a few days," said Herman. "Back to the assisted-living center. Ho! Ho!"

"Oh, Herman," said Susie, "go ahead and call it a nursing home if that makes you happy. Food's better there, anyway. It has no taste here."

Marty said, "We've got to leave soon for court. There's a hearing on that case of the guy who became a girl." She slowly slid her hand away from Susie, and ran it across her hair, slicked back into a ponytail today. Her warmth and understanding of the Webbers meant a lot to me, further support for my attraction to her.

"I've never felt right about that one. God made men and women, mothers and fathers, no in-betweens. Just because some he-she is real strange doesn't mean that person is a killer. I still vote for the husband," said Herman. He rumbled back toward the bed having completed ten round trips in his wheelchair. Only eight were prescribed now. "You know, like in books and movies."

"Oh, Herman, these people are detectives. They know family members or close friends are the killers, not butlers. Nobody even has a butler these days," said Susie. "You always want to think of unpleasant things like a husband killing his wife." She sat upright, eyes alert, and pulled the shawl tightly over her shoulders. Then she laughed, strong and deep for a change. "Never a wife killing her husband."

"I think we'll get our client off this time," I said. "She didn't do it."

"What about those others? You said there were a lot of them. I forget what you call that," said Susie.

"Serial murder," said Marty. "Same person does more than one." She smiled to cover up any discomfort at this kind of discussion with the Webbers.

Susie pushed it. "Did she do the others? Did this Betty kill the others?"

"We wonder the same thing," I said. "No answer to that one. The police aren't sure." I got up from the straight-backed chair in the corner of the room and put on my parka, still damp from the snow. "There is something gory about the case that surprised us. Body parts of two women were found frozen in the husband's game locker."

Marty's eyebrows shot up in warning. "Oh, Kip, really!" she said.

Herman pounded his fist on the metal edge of his chair. "I just changed my vote. That husband ain't that stupid. Don't make no sense. If he killed two women, he wouldn't leave them around like that. Unless he's a real fool. It must be the sinner, the queer one."

I stood near the window. "Do you remember when I got suspended from school for a day? My parents went ballistic."

Herman smiled. "Yes, you stayed with us for a night, or was it the weekend?"

I pulled up the blinds. The snow had stopped. "And you didn't preach to me. In fact, all I remember is eating good food."

Susie put her hands together prayerfully. She said, "You went straight home and made up with your folks. That's all we wanted for you."

Marty reached for her coat, then slid on her faux fur snow boots. "We're off," she said. "Keep it up. You guys are amazing."

I leaned over to whisper in Herman's ear as he slumped slightly. "I'll bring you a pint of the good stuff as soon as you're back at the assisted-living. Okay?"

"We love you both," said Susie.

We walked fast down the empty hall into an agonizingly slow elevator and zipped through the front lobby to the Corvette. Wendy had been inordinately fond of Herman and Susie, comfortable with them the instant they met and engaged in a mutual teasing with them, me the usual object of scorn. I turned the key and gunned the engine.

Marty rubbed my shoulders. "Wendy?"

"Yes, how did you know?"

"Herman's doing pretty well, so I just figured it's her."

"You're really something, you know that. Thanks." She rubbed harder. I drove more carefully.

The hard ground still held three inches of fluffy, white flakes. Marty and I were very late for court. The roads were slippery as hell with ice and snow, even for the imported tires, which grabbed on almost anything. Salt trucks slid around mercilessly, too.

Like criminals, we tip-toed into the back row of the visitor's section. Yet, we were happy to be snug inside, protected by the paneled walls of Court No. Four in the Hall of Justice.

Willie Branner was being interrogated by a prosecutor from the DA's office. The lawyer was impeccably dressed, while somebody, or something, had cleaned up Willie's act, a genuine make-over. His brown, poly suit was too tight but with white shirt and tan polka dot tie he looked quite presentable, hair slicked back and a pair of gold-rimmed glasses snaking down his bulbous nose. We couldn't hear or smell anything this far back in the room anyway, should he decide to let go with one of his real stinkers.

The assistant DA strode quickly and directly to Willie's chair in the witness box. "You've taken an oath on the Bible, Mr. Branner. Do you know what that means sir?"

"Yes, I do. I will tell the truth."

The assistant DA peered directly at the judge as he spoke. "Did you kill your wife?"

"No, I didn't. I loved her very much," said Willie. His face was bland, a tiny innocent smile at the corner of his thick lips, slight perspiration beads at his hairline.

"How did she die, sir?"

"She killed herself. She stabbed herself to death," said Willie.

"You've changed your story now. Why didn't you tell the police thirteen years ago when you were interviewed?" The assistant DA, a guy named Robinson, was no more than thirty, long sideburns with curly, yellow, surfer hair hanging over the collar.

"I was scared the police would think I done it."

"Your daughter, Shari Lynn, testified that you cut up your wife's body and froze it where she works."

"That's true. She was dead, but I didn't kill her. I dressed her body like a deer or elk, then cut it up so nobody would know what happened. I'd never hurt Mary, no way," said Willie. His hands trembled as he reached down to tie a shoelace. As he bent over, a button popped at the neck of his shirt and rough, red skin shone where he'd cut himself shaving.

"What did you think when Mrs. Betty Fowler was arrested for Mary's murder?"

"I didn't pay much attention. It wasn't my job to be no policeman."

"She didn't do it, did she?" Now Robinson ran his hands through his hair, straightened his striped tie and stood smugly close to Willie's clean-shaven, flushed face.

"I don't think so. Mary had a real bad knife wound in her chest—full of blood—when she stumbled out of the bedroom. Unless this Betty woman had been in the bedroom. I'd been in front of the TV having a beer or two." Willie tugged at the shirt collar out of habit.

"Did you kill your wife, Mr. Branner? I ask you directly: did you kill Mary T. Branner?"

"Nope, she killed herself. I only cut her up after she committed suicide." Willie had the look of a stuffed goose, fat and oiled and seasoned, proudly ready to help others solve a problem.

The judge said, "That's plenty, Mr. Robinson. I've heard enough. This preliminary hearing is to determine if there is probable cause to hold Mrs. Fowler for trial. The testimony of your witness has clearly answered that question. You may step down, Mr. Branner. The testimony of you and your daughter has been very helpful to the court."

Willie stood grudgingly. He said, "Your honor, I couldn't lie after what Shari Lynn told you. If I lied, it wouldn't have made no sense to you." He hitched up his pants, unaware that one side of his suspenders had snapped and dragged along the floor next to his left leg.

The schedule called for a hearing into the case of the State of Ohio vs. Mrs. Betty Fowler, #10273274, the kidnapping and murder of Mary T. Branner. The police low-keyed the whole affair, hoping to bring serial-murder charges later against Betty but unable to do so at this point. So they went ahead with an evidentiary hearing while the defense moved to throw out the charges altogether. The digital photographs of the frozen packages marked "Branner—venison," the coroner's report on their contents, and the testimony of the Branners led to the judge's saying, "All charges against the defendant Mrs. Fowler are hereby dismissed, with the court's apologies. Our system of justice is imperfect, being man-made, but it has worked here. You are free to go, Mrs. Fowler, subject to charges being re-filed. The DA's office and I will discuss any charges to be filed against Mr. Willie Branner."

Goldbaum, smug and circumspect as ever, walked out quickly without so much as a "see you later," or "thank you," or "glad you're free," to anyone. Mama didn't have much left of her estate after Goldbaum got his fees. His grey pinstripe $1,000 suit still couldn't cover up his saddlebags; in fact, the fitted English-style jacket actually highlighted them.

The visitors were silent as they shuffled out, still numbed from the testimony of the Branners. Shari Lynn and Tami held hands. We'd missed much of the hearing, which had lasted less than thirty minutes. Faces in the crowd were uniformly flat, eyes dulled, shock apparent at the notion of a husband calmly admitting that he cut up his wife's body, had it freezer wrapped, then froze the separate packages at his daughter's employer.

Willie didn't know that Shari Lynn had kept back several packages containing the stab wound near the heart and Willie's knife, which he had definitely employed to dress the body. Shari Lynn called it her safety valve, an insurance policy. Someone had probably told Willie that he wasn't in much trouble for cutting up a dead body.

Marty finally spoke. "Pinch me. Is this real?"

I pinched her upper arm. It gave me a jolt. Then I rubbed the spot. "Sorry, didn't mean to be so rough."

The courtroom cleared quickly. Mostly the regulars had peeked in at the proceedings, bored with life while waiting for some kind of a bombshell. They'd gotten their money's worth.

We slipped into the front row with Betty, Chuck, and Mama.

Mama continued to cry, thin tears dripping slowly over her heavily lined parchment skin. Betty hugged her first, unaware that the tears created an obvious wet streak in the pink velvet high-necked dress Betty chose for her court appearance. Chuck swallowed both of them in his arms, his dress wool dark blue uniform still full of sharp creases and shiny brass buttons. He cried, too, but said nothing to either woman, simply held on to them for dear life. Mama sat awkwardly. Chuck and Betty then embraced more fully, arms tightly around each other, lips close, words quiet but audible.

Chuck whispered, "I love you so very much. You're everything to me. I couldn't stand the thought of losing you. It's worse than any other thought I had."

"I know, my sweet. I've missed you so. Every thought has been of you and our life. And our children and family life." No giggles from Betty.

Now they both cried and sobbed and hugged. I wanted to hold Marty's hand, so close to mine on the wooden courtroom bench, but I knew better. Accidentally on purpose, I brushed her knuckles with my fingertips. She didn't budge.

Mama swam in her white floor-length dress decorated with pale blue sky and tiny, yellow, sunflowers. Goldbaum told her to smile and dress optimistically. She'd done her best under the circumstances. By contrast, Marty and I both wore black slacks. I sported a black cashmere blazer while Marty, quietly elegant in a black-and-white wool checkered jacket, commanded attention.

Mama said, "Butch, you're dressed up so funny. You always liked costumes and pretend. I'm so relieved. I can sleep again. You're free."

"I'm not sure this is the time, Mama. We should celebrate, not ask a lot of questions," said Chuck. He held Betty by her shoulders.

Betty said, "It's okay, dearest. I've waited too long for the truth. Mama deserves the truth. So do you."

"Oh, no, don't worry," said Chuck. "I'll never leave you. No matter what happened. We'll work it out. We're a family. I love you." He clutched her close to him again.

Marty and I listened without comment. This part was theirs and theirs alone. We'd done our part. Betty was free. Counseling or not, Betty's lies to each, encased in so much love and concern, had surfaced. Chuck and Mama now knew each other, understood to some extent why Betty had lied—to protect herself from hurt and anger, to preserve her marriage without bringing painful confusion and disappointment to her elderly mother. At least, Chuck understood to some extent. Betty had been the ever-loyal Butch, then a supportive son, while now a devoted, loving wife, though these family relationships sat shakily on shifting sands.

"Mama, I had surgery. I'm not pretending. I'm not going to a party. I'm no ghost or goblin. It's not Halloween." Betty moved out of Chuck's arms to sit next to Mama, holding both of her hands gently. Eyes brimmed with tears, they appealed to Mama for understanding. "It's real, Mama, I'm your son Butch but I'm also Chuck's wife Betty. I'm a woman now. I'll always be yours."

Mama didn't behave like she might have. No wild screams, no verbal threats, no self-pity, no wailing, no self-punishing feelings about her mistakes as a mother. She sat stone-faced and stared straight ahead, fumbling with her hands as if trying to fit her tiny dog Butchie on her lap. Finally, a single, long sigh. "I'm an old woman. I don't understand."

Chuck said, "I didn't know either, Mama. I'm still in shock. I didn't know of the change. I never knew Butch, only Betty. She's a very wonderful person. Mama, we're a family now. We'll have grandchildren for you soon. We'll adopt."

"Why? Why? Why?" said Mama. "Why, Butch, did you do this thing to yourself? You fooled me all these years. You always liked to dress up." Lids heavy, lips pursed, she finally closed her eyes.

"She almost killed me," said Betty. She moved a few feet from Mama, straightened her skirt as she crossed her legs and let go of Mama's hands.

Marty and I turned in our pew to look more closely at Betty. This was it. I was about to offer them the option of Marty and me leaving but held back. Curiosity kept us there.

"You know, Mama, I didn't know much about sex as a young boy. I learned a little bit in school. I never dated. I had sex with a woman who was killed. No, not Mary T. Branner, but another one. That's why they found fingerprints or something to link me to her. I met her and then there was sex. I was always cutting my hand or finger in my butchering, so they found blood of mine on Mary's dog after I robbed her. But I never hurt nobody. You know I'd never do that." Betty had recovered her composure. She dried her eyes daintily with a perfumed white handkerchief. She sniffed, giggling slightly, continued to hold it to her nose.

"Oh, Butch, I never knew. I knew you'd never hurt any woman. I prayed you hadn't," said Mama.

"I felt horrible about it. I didn't enjoy the sex part. It never lasted. Only once. It was almost like she picked me."

Chuck said, "Which one almost killed you? I'd die if anything happened to you." He slid closer to Betty as he curled his arm around her shoulders.

Chuck loosened his tie and slipped off his jacket. He was holding Betty's hand tightly as they walked back to us. He was too good to be true. Didn't anything Betty had done turn him off, maybe piss him off? Marty hugged Betty. I shook Chuck's hand. Then I put my arm around Mama while Marty gave her a gentle half-hug. She was so frail we had to be careful. I couldn't help wondering what the world would think of Betty's confession. A jury, a judge. Some of it might be verified factually, yet parts of it, most of it, were strictly Betty's interpretation and memory of events. She hadn't sworn on the Bible to tell the truth, the whole truth, and nothing but the truth.

We slithered out of the room unnoticed, leaving the family to its difficult process of trying to ferret out truth, justice, and honesty from the tortured scars of lies, deception, and denial. They would find some way to celebrate Betty's release. What about drinking the blood and eating the flesh? Wasn't she the cannibal she'd claimed she'd been as Butch?

We meandered slowly to the car, dazed and silenced by recent events. I wanted to hold Marty's hand, but felt too vulnerable to rejection to try. By the time we'd reach Arnie's, the post-mortem could begin. I fired up the Corvette, melted the icy frost on the windows, and pushed the FM button for the oldie station. It was the old Johnny Ray tune: 'If your sweetheart sends a letter of goodbye, it's no secret you'll feel better if you cry' in that unmistakable tenor of his. "It fits, doesn't it?" I said.

"Sure does, boss."

The windshield wipers kept time with the music drumbeat, so I pushed the fluid button two or three times for syncopation.

"Arnie's?" I said.

"Yes, hurry."

The new tires hugged the road perfectly, though I didn't have the energy to drive very fast. The strain of the courtroom seeped through my body.

"What do you think?"

"I need a drink," said Marty. "I feel drained, as if some kind of emotional heart-lung machine had put me through the ringer, disgorging feelings and sensations then returning them purged." Her hand slid over my shoulder as she tried to make herself more comfortable. Privately, secretly, without much self-awareness, we needed some kind of strength and sanity from each other. More zaniness lay ahead if we tried to reconcile Betty's confession today with the hours of interview material we'd gathered initially.

Could Betty be a self-confessed serial-killer, a lying transsexual cannibal named Butch who had one-night stands with several women, all ostensibly kidnapped, murdered, and never seen again before he went on to gender reassignment surgery?

I parked in the spot labeled "Manager Only." It was next to the door, quickest way to a table, a drink, smoke, and noise to blot out the courtroom experience. Our waitress stood near the bar, held two fingers, and I winked back twice. Two Navy destroyers in an old World War II movie sending signals only we understood. She had a damn good memory—or was it the huge tips?

The drinks arrived within seconds, perfect vodka martinis, olives stuffed with blue cheese, floating in the clear cubes. "Burgers and fries?" said the waitress.

"Thanks. A bit later," I said. "For once, the noise in this joint is a relief. We don't have to make sense of Betty, do we? We did our job."

Marty sipped. "You're right. Spot on. Judge let her go. They'll hang Willie for the Branner case. Conscience got you, boss?"

"You?"

Marty said, "I asked you first."

Saved by the bell. My cell phone rang before I could respond to Marty. I held it and said, "Yes." Then, the phone at arm's length, I looked across at Marty. "Yes, to him and yes to you, too."

"It's Goldbaum here. Wanted to thank you and Marty. Good job so far on Willie's story."

"Thanks. Do you think Betty did the others?"

"Just the facts, ma'am. Just the facts," said Goldbaum.

"Betty said some pretty weird stuff after the hearing. Admitted to her family that she had sex with one of them, but didn't harm anyone."

Goldbaum paused. His voice deeper and softer now. "I never ask about guilt."

"What if they admit it?"

"I'm not God," said Goldbaum. His voice regained that crisp edge. "I'm not even a judge or a jury, just a simple criminal-defense attorney."

"We may have put a serial killer back on the streets." My free hand over one ear, as the noise reached a deafening roar.

Goldbaum said, "What? What did you say?"

This time I literally screamed, much too loud, fearful that my tiny cell phone would explode in my face. "She may be a killer!" Several patrons stared us down, so I collapsed the phone and put it away. Goldbaum would understand.

Marty reached across the table and held my hand for just a moment. Her eyes, soft and dewy, spoke concern and sympathy. "We're not lawyers. They draw the line easily. A lot of cops do, too. I don't feel right about this thing, either."

"Could she be a liar for a reason? Maybe in her mind it makes her strong and powerful, able to intimidate people. You know, just in her mind."

Marty said, "I need another drink. Remember what Professor Aggie said. You can't always trust cannibalism reports. They're usually anecdotal, sometimes false, a way to control people in your own tribe, even your enemies in a nearby clan."

I looked for the waitress. For drinks, I winked twice. Then I mouthed the words, "Two burgers, everything, crisp fries."

"I hope that's it. I really do," I said. Marty was very special to me. Lucky for me she was with me on this case. "Maybe it's as simple as Butch was crazy as shit and almost brought Betty down. Now she's covering for him, but it might not work."

CHAPTER SIXTEEN

"The Group" met in the eye-blinking, neon-lit back room of the Harley-Indian Memorial Mortuary. This depressing space, alive with a long, glistening, stainless steel, embalming table, empty now, featured a spotted drip jar and several IV stands. Streaked gray floor tiles emptied liquids into the stained drainage area, the black-brown color of dried, clotted drops of human blood. Shelves of an ancient imitation wood sideboard, sloppily layered with antique instruments reflecting the history of mortuary science, held scimitars, curved knives, needles and syringes, some huge and astonishingly filthy. These contrasted strangely with an intriguing array of shining clean and wholesome-looking tubes.

Marty and I stood resolute, hands firmly at our sides, reluctant to touch anything, even each other. I thought that we might have worn latex gloves, perhaps a surgical mask, too, though the only true safety, the full-body condom, was yet to be invented. Stay away from the blood and other human fluids. That should do it.

Mr. Jeremy Isaacs, a balding, fiftyish small man, sported a tiny ponytail done up with a rubber band, dirty jeans, a tight black Harley T-shirt, and oiled biker black boots that matched a black studded belt when we met him briefly yesterday. Can't tell a book by its cover. Today, invited back to discuss "The Group" with him and tour the mortuary, he was impeccable in a navy blue pinstripe suit, white spread collar shirt and silver striped tie. No ponytail, hair now smoothed over the sides to the collar, still an empty crown.

The oil from the boots and belt slid seamlessly into his personality. The empathetic—make that psuedo-empathetic—funeral director greeted us. Real concern for the families and friends of the deceased, strangers in life, died slowly day after day, week after week, year after year. Immunity built up naturally. "So glad you've come back. Most people are only here when they're in need. Seldom do others care to learn about us as people, our jobs, what motivates us. We're human beings, too." His eyes blinked with intended sincerity and honesty, almost a coquettishness in this little man with the carefully manicured hands locked behind his back as he strutted.

I rubbed my hands together. Death was neither a friend nor foe to me. I'd seen my share, but I was never completely at ease in a morgue or mortuary, nor talking to coroners, medical examiners, or morticians. Death couldn't rub off from them, but still. They were the untouchables in the caste society of India, those who arranged the elaborate burning ritual for the deceased.

Goldbaum was 'concerned' as he put it, not scared, anxious, worried, fearful, or frightened, merely 'concerned'. His defense of Willie Branner was flimsy now with the discovery of a piece of Es's body. Willie was shocked by his carelessness, couldn't quite figure out how a package of Es had survived all of these years. Shari Lynn's treachery horrified him, yet it still might only be evidence of crimes much less serious than murder or manslaughter. Es's body and his relationship with her unbalanced the equation. Willie swore on his mother's grave that he didn't kill either woman, but his credibility shrunk by the minute. Parts of two missing women, one your wife and the other your whore, found frozen in your game locker.

Goldbaum knew how to mix the carrot and the stick. He said, "Get your two overpriced asses back to Flint and clear this thing up. I'm concerned about Willie's case. A bonus of five grand if you do it."

"We're on our way."

Back up to Flint in the Corvette, flying at low altitude. We reviewed the case file on Willie, studied the photos of Es and the Easy Over Motel, Willie and the others. We noted the rest stop where Willie said she'd OD'd. Time permitting, we'd visit it later. The only other information that we could follow up was a photo of a gang of truckers and bikers in which one of those tough-looking guys held a piece of paper with "The Group" written in script. He looked like Willie. The guy next to him held his hand behind the other man's head, with index and little finger upright—it means "hook 'em horns" at the University of Texas, but it was a sign for "bullshit" in our high school. Who were in "The Group?" Did it mean anything? The old geezer at the motel remembered it was some kind of gang of guys that met, strangely, in a room at a local mortuary.

We'd tracked down the mortuary. We'd found Mr. Isaacs who'd been at this mortuary for a "life that the Lord had wanted me to live for the last twenty years."

I handed the photo to Mr. Isaacs. He studied it. Stopped prancing. Pulled out half-glasses. Moved closer to the embalming table to be directly under a long neon bulb. "Yes, yes," he said. "That's maybe a dozen years ago. I recall them. Some pretty tough customers—drank a lot, used drugs, had rather inordinate sexual appetites. By the way, I've made copies of my poem, *Love and Life* for both of you." He placed the photo gingerly on the table and handed us each a copy. I glanced at the poem while he studied the photo again. It read as follows:

> *Love and Life by Jeremy Isaacs*
> *Where have you gone*
> *After the dawn?*
> *Why did you leave*
> *Afraid to believe?*
> *You were for me*
> *Struggling to be free.*
> *Heat over and done*
> *Gone with the sun.*
> *Peace and quiet ahead*
> *Cool darkness of the dead.*

Marty and I padded to the wall opposite the sideboard. We opened gray metal chairs and sat stiffly. Isaacs pulled his glasses off and replaced them in his handkerchief pocket.

Marty folded her hands and gazed at the floor, almost prayerfully. She said, "That's a beautiful statement of life, Mr. Isaacs. Very beautiful."

"Thank you. It gives perspective for our families. Dust to dust. Dawn to dusk. We're all part of the process," he said. A white linen handkerchief appeared from nowhere for him to dab at his high forehead.

"Mr. Isaacs, what about 'The Group'?" I said.

"Yes, yes, indeed," he said. "They used to meet here, maybe a dozen years ago. I think it was drug or alcohol problems, maybe it was AA. We let them use a room here at no charge. Sometimes there were six or eight men, sometimes more. They talked and prayed together." No eye contact with either of us.

"Anything else you can remember?"

"Well, they were always very well behaved even though they looked like hell-raisers and ruffians. They were very appreciative of us letting them use this space for their meetings. We have very expensively decorated air conditioned spaces, sitting rooms with soft couches, luxurious chairs and tables and wall-to-wall carpet framed by heavy damask drapes. They liked it in here, where they could smoke and light candles. Their-excuse me-dirty work clothes and lack of hygiene weren't a problem in here. Called themselves "The Group." Yes, they broke up some time ago." Mr. Isaacs now crossed his arms over his chest and tilted his head to his right side.

I tried a long shot. I felt juiced up, excited by the prospect of this group leading us somewhere in the investigation. An old, cold trail is very smooth, tracks obliterated by acts of God. I asked, "Did they leave any materials or pictures here?"

Marty came alive, overcoming the obvious discomfort behind her reticence in this place. She didn't raise her eyebrow to me, appeared inattentive, when suddenly her eyes flashed the alert signal, opened wide, and her facial muscles tensed. "Yes, that would help us, Mr. Isaacs. We're trying to find info on a member of "The Group." Willie Branner, a truck driver who came through this area. We represent someone who wants to help him."

"It might be here," Mr. Isaacs said. He strutted again. Walked to us, then away, hands behind his back. The photo lay still and alone on the embalming table. "Yes, it just might be." At the sideboard, he yanked at a bottom drawer. It stuck and he pulled harder. Finally open, he stretched his arm into the rear. Out popped a perfectly square black velvet box, maybe a foot long, wide and deep. He brushed off the arm of his suit. Some kind of symbol was imprinted on the top of the box in red leaf. "Here it is. They used this at their meetings and it's been here all these years—maybe five years since they stopped coming here. I'm a saver, thank God."

"What's in it?" I said. Immediately, I realized that comment was an insult to a mortician. He'd never pry. If he did, he'd lie.

"What Kip meant is, he wonders what's inside," said Marty. Now her eyebrow arched menacingly.

"Yes, that's exactly what I meant."

Isaacs gripped the box lightly, reverently, both hands underneath it so that they did not leave marks or soil it.

I said, "As private investigators, we're officers of the court, part of the legal system. We could get a judge to subpoena the box, or we can simply sign a requisition for it now, then return it after the case is completed. Everything would remain the same, nothing would be taken. It would be evidence." My over-the-edge bullshit suited an ex-cop turned PI.

"If you think it's proper. They never came back here for the box. It's years ago. Just return it," said Mr. Isaacs.

Any honest, professional mortician would tell you that possible criminal evidence really belonged in the hands of the police or the FBI. It was all show here.

"Thank you, Mr. Isaacs. This will help our client and the attorney representing him," said Marty. She arose, folded her chair, and returned it to its place against the wall. She walked confidently with strong strides to the table, plucked the picture from it and turned to face the slightly hunched Mr. Isaacs.

Inside a wide smile, her teeth glistened under the bright neon lights. "Very helpful, Mr. Isaacs. Very helpful." She cradled the velvet box as he had done.

"Are you quite sure it's legal?" he said.

"Oh, my yes, quite legal. We'll be very careful to return it to you in perfect condition, should "The Group" ever need it again," I said. My body had a mind of its own, raw nerves, limbs restless, twitching, feet pointed toward the door and ready to leave.

Marty looked like I felt, drummed her fingers on the box. Her body language, as she faced the door, spoke to flight not fight. Something about a mortuary. Something about morticians.

Maybe it finally got to the the truckers, too. Nobody wants his nose rubbed in it, death and dying that is, not even habitual drunks and druggies or worse.

Mr. Isaacs said, "Would you like to tour the rest of our home? It's quite peaceful and restful. We have coffee and homemade cookies in the lobby." He resumed a professional manner, clearly in charge once again, straightening his tie and rubbing his hands.

"That's kind of you. You've been so hospitable. We'll take a rain check, if that's okay," I said. Happily, no one cracked some old joke like 'remember I'll be the last one to let you down.'

We had our treasure. We'd been successful in our quest. We had something, a bit of information and description of "The Group," confirmation of the photograph, and the box that they had used in their meetings. For all I knew, the box contained chocolate bars from AA meetings, melted beyond recognition or petrified after so many years of storage. The imprint was confusing, too. It reminded me of the boxes and bags given free today with department store purchases of cologne, perfume, or jewelry. Maybe that was the designer-du-jour years ago, since passed into the oblivion of cutthroat competition. Heaven forbid, the box could be empty, or simply contain a key to a bank vault or a stub for a package being held at the bus station. Too many old late night film noir movies with Edmund O'Brien seeped into my fantasies.

"Goodbye, Mr. Isaacs. Thanks again," I said.

We fled to the parking lot in a flash. I pinched my nose and glanced at Marty to acknowledge the acrid odor of the embalming room. Was it the embalming fluid? Could it be formaldehyde, or something like it? Dried blood? The outside chill flushed out our nostrils, the slight breeze blowing the dry January air into us. The odor inside was actually more noticeable once we left the mortuary back room. We'd wait a while to have lunch.

Tucked inside the car, motor running and warm, Marty peeked. Christmas Eve excitement was hard to fight. "Jesus Christ, look at this shit." She lifted the top, held by a pair of small hinges, to reveal the inside, lined with cracked brown leather. "Holy shit, the inside appears to be caked with dried blood. What the hell is this shit?" She slammed the lid tight and shoved the box on to my lap.

I turned off the motor. "Let's go back to see Mr. Isaacs. The little prick is lying through his teeth. Some AA group—into blood and weird shit, not booze, their Higher Power or the Big Book."

"I think I'll retch," said Marty.

"I know what you mean. Let's go back and grill the little fucker." My scar raged thicker and hotter than it had in a long time.

Her voice suddenly calm and her demeanor bland, Marty sighed. "Let's wait. I want to know what this symbol means. Maybe he didn't know."

"He must have known," I said.

"Screw him for now. We've got the box. We need a book on vampires or cults, or blood rituals." Lids slightly closed, her eyes were serious with confusing hints of humor and angst. The frown spoke more of the angst.

I said, "Makes sense now doesn't it? A group meeting in a mortuary embalming room. Willie could be some sort of fucking cannibal or satanic worshipper. Probably a murderer, too. This photograph isn't clear, but if it weren't so faded I'd bet Butch was there."

Marty said, "What about Betty? I mean Butch. He was a trucker. He at least thinks of himself, or herself, or whatever as a cannibal. Was he in "The Group," too?" She touched up her make-up, preparing for action again.

I sat straight-backed, pleasantly alert, mind clicking a million miles an hour. "Butch and Willie knew each other. Is that the connection to Mary and Es? Both of them were involved in some way, maybe others, too."

"Are you thinking what I'm thinking? We try to clear Willie by providing evidence that it was pure coincidence. Some other trucker really did do these two women and covered it up." Marty sucked in a deep breath, closed her eyes, and curved her back into the leather as she exhaled.

"But we just got Betty released," I said. I held on to the steering wheel for support. The zigging and zagging left me both sweating and chilled.

"I need a drink," said Marty. Her hands covered her face, obviously not sure whether to laugh or cry or scream.

I said, "After the library. Let's go online with Satan." I turned the Corvette's heater down a notch.

If we were on the right track, these cases were even more bizarre and confusing than we realized. And that was going some. What general conclusion could we reach at this point?

A quick cell phone call to the main library for directions. We found our way easily. Driving was smooth and easy without ice, snow or rain. My car ran better when sailing ahead of a cold breeze.

"Do you know anything about cults or vampires?" said Marty.

"Not much. Professor Aggie told us when we started on this case that primitive societies and ancient cultures or religions sacrificed animals or humans to the gods. Sometimes they drank blood or splattered it on objects or themselves or animals. Remember?"

"What about devil worship? I'd bet the symbol on that box is a substitute for Satan." Marty winced as she said this, her mouth pinched against her teeth. The word Satan could bring horrific fantasies and feelings to anyone's mind.

"I remember terrifying movies as a kid—much scarier than the current versions. Vincent Price types wore black capes and tortured young women. Drank blood."

Marty's body lunged forward with excitement, contained only by seat belts. Her voice was over-powering. She said, "No, no, it's not a Satanic symbol. I'm wrong. It's a peace symbol, like they used in the 1960s during the Vietnam War. The hippies used it at anti-war protests."

"You're right. I love you. You're so smart. Maybe it's a peace group of some kind," I said.

"Piece of tail," Marty said.

I slipped into an open spot at the curb in front of the library. It was a beauty. Ultra-modern, sleek, long glass walls with thin aluminum braces—rooms and halls immersed in light and high-tech features that forced the surrounding red-brick, shuttered two-story office buildings to beg for the wrecking ball. Probably tore down some historical landmarks to rebuild the library, since it's usually either-or; either save the old or build the new. Paris did both. So did Scandinavia. Why couldn't Ohio or Michigan?

These scattered thoughts about urban renewal dissolved quickly as we entered an atrium fit for a downtown Marriott, sans concierge and designer furniture. What the hell did an aging ex-cop know about renewal anyway? I couldn't do very much for myself, so what did I know about downtown or the inner city? One day at a time. Do the right thing.

PIs like us don't hang out very often in urban libraries. Bulletin boards crammed with announcements of classes on taxes, horticulture, and political action side-by-side with glass-covered display cases of reproductions of ancient jewelry and glassware. The technology was overwhelming. Long tables chock full of computers marked "Internet Here" and "Local Entertainment" and "High Speed." To the rear, printers hummed, fax machines whirred, and speedy e-mails flew everywhere. Mostly, down-on-their luck folks pressed the mouse and pounded the keys. Hackers my ass! They looked for jobs, stayed warm, and maintained the distant camaraderie of the dispossessed, willing to help each other but unable to do much for themselves.

One of six librarians at a round kiosk, Danish, neo-modern, grainy brown wood, smiled at Marty. I said, "We're not computer wizards. We need some quick info on cults, Satanic worship, and that kind of stuff."

He openly admired Marty again. "Use machine twenty-two which features online annotated bibliographies. Short paragraphs about books and articles. Click on cult, Satan, the devil, whatever turns you on." Obviously pleased with his own pun, he couldn't flirt successfully.

Marty avoided his gaze.

I said, "Thanks."

We sat crammed together in front of a new PC with a small brass emblem "Friends of the Flint Library" bolted into its top. I said, "Let's try 'Satan' and 'Demons.' I'm afraid 'blood' will open up too much for us to handle." The bibliographies were perfect, a short paragraph or two providing a superficial, quick eye into the material.

"Here's an old book from 1894 by a missionary to China. He says there are demons who possess people, always have been. Not just crazy or sick people, either. Real demons." Marty bent forward and slipped off her parka. I fit it to the back of her chair.

"Yeah, really real," I said.

"There's all these other theories, but he calls it demonic possession. Sounds a little like Butch and Betty. New personality, new knowledge, and bad morals. But the demons and the person don't relate to each other. They're separate."

"Maybe Butch was possessed by a demon," I said. The screen blurred, so I slipped on my reading glasses.

Marty's sarcastic tone prevailed. "I didn't say that. Hold on. Just thinking out loud. Butch didn't have fits or go crazy and flail around on the floor, did he?" Her fingers flicked the keyboard.

My chair moved inches at a time. Closer to Marty. Our knees touched. What a wonderful library, twenty-two was perfect for me. She didn't budge. "And Butch and Betty are on speaking terms so there go your demons," I said.

"Oh, I love this one," said Marty. "Here's a book of chants. 'One and one they always make two, Yet two become one, in an act old and true'. At last some romance in the supernatural."

"This text says that witchcraft is tied to pagan religion and rituals. They worshipped nature way before Christ came." My back and legs stiffened uncomfortably, and I felt restless yet unwilling to budge from this library chair.

"Colors are important in this stuff," she said. "This one says that red is blood or the life force and black is evil or Satan. We knew that?"

Marty tapped her left foot. The movement jiggled my right calf. Could I survive this delicious torture? "Here's a definition," I said. "A coven is a group of thirteen who practice the occult. The male leader of a coven is named the magister. I'll bet you that's Mr. Isaacs, your loyal humble mortician."

She said, "You're probably on target. By the way, here's

a picture. The peace symbol on the box is called the Cross of Nero. The Christian cross is broken so it means the defeat of Christ. Guess I was more right about that imprint on the box than I realized. Would have expected a pentagram, with all that blood involved."

At that moment the hair on the back of my neck stood up. I felt a presence, no gust of wind or howling wolves, just a human presence. It was the seductive, unctuous librarian standing much too close behind us. He'd crept up quietly.

"Did you satisfy your needs?" he said.

I jerked my chair into his leg. "Yes, thanks so much." He limped away.

"Let's go see Isaacs," said Marty. "Then we can have some fun. We'll have coffee and cookies with the little dick. Give him truth serum." Her unblinking eyes and tight jaw were fixed with determination and resentment. She hated being lied to.

We spotted a small Coney Island truck across from the library, standing frozen in cold isolation. We trundled over and each wolfed down a foot-long hot dog with mustard, onion, and pickle relish. No catsup! It was red.

I hardly chewed at all. I did choke and cough. "I've got a surprise for the little fucker first."

Marty daintily wiped away the mustard. "Midnight auto supply?"

I said, "Exactly. Let's see what we can dig up. Then we can nail him to the cross."

Marty nodded with her mouth full.

Poirot's subtle elegance, Charlie Chan's Oriental wisdom, or James Bond's sexual energy—none of that was required for our next step. An empty box, yet the insignia suggested demons not angels. Isaacs thought he could blow us off. The old, 'Gee, I wonder where the contents are' gambit. Or was it, the game of 'Give them a little and they'll eat and leave,' or was it the 'Get out of my face or the cult will get you?' He had mentioned a rough trade membership in "The Group." Were we supposed to run back to the safety of Toledo and hide behind Goldbaum?

After lunch, Marty and I took our sports bags to the World

Wide Athletic Club in Flint, jogged three miles, cleaned up with a healthy steam and sauna. Pores wide open, hearts beating perfectly, hundreds of hot dog calories burned off, we headed for steak and salad, holding off on the drinks, just for tonight.

The steak and salad, tough and warm respectively, were undeservedly costly. The steak house featured awful, stringy meat and yellowed lettuce topped by squishy tomatoes; it should have been free. We ate in silence, storing energy for the evening's activity. I mused to myself about the Watergate burglars' last meal before their arrest, even the last death row guy electrocuted in Texas—he'd had a cheeseburger with everything, fries with catsup, and two sodas. After a restroom break, we headed back to the Corvette.

Marty's voice was low and conspiratorial. "Should we wear black tights and a black turtleneck?"

"Yes, we should. We should also have those deadly metal stars Ninjas throw at people," I said. I fingered my holster quickly.

Marty noticed. "What's the plan, boss?" She closed her door and nested. "We've done some peeping in divorces and some picture-taking lately, but no break-ins for at least a year. They're still illegal, aren't they?"

I turned the key. Turned on the cabin light. Turned half around. Frowned at Marty. Turned myself on unintentionally. Then I did my best Halloween pumpkin horror face. I said, "Ugh. Ugh. Ugh."

Marty criss-crossed her arms over her face and peeked at me as she pulled away. "Oh, no, master, please don't hurt me. Please, kind sir." She swept her hands together prayerfully.

"You're safe," I said.

She bowed her head several times. "Oh, thank you, kind sir. I'll do anything you say."

"Really?"

"No," she said.

A seductive smirk apparently concealed her underlying control. She called the shots in our relationship. All of this 'what's the plan?' and 'what shall we do, boss?' only applied to work.

I parked a block from the mortuary, hidden from the streetlights.

Real cops and robbers stuff. Who in their right mind would want to break into a mortuary at night? What is there to steal? Some furniture. Maybe a bad check? Someone else's dead uncle or one's own? I could think of a hundred places with more worth or value, diamonds, cash or gold to rob without confronting one's mortality directly. And that odor.

A slight breeze, plenty of low, thick clouds covered the slim new moon, and most of the stars were hiding. Several tall lamps in the parking lot behind the Harley-Indian were in full view, but their light failed to reach the rear entrance or the French doors which welcomed the caskets, in or out, take your choice. An ancient Victorian refurbished into a mortuary, it was perfect for our purposes. Nothing much happened after 9:00 p.m., the conclusion of the so-called viewing hours. It was now 9:30 p.m. I didn't even feel like a Ninja.

I squeezed Marty's hand. She responded with, "Way dong. Gon shee."

"Yo tang," I said.

Now Ninjas of the night, speaking Chinese, though precious little, ready for combat. But the dead don't fight back, and Mr. Isaacs wouldn't have guard dogs or even much security. Normal people just didn't invade a mortuary after dark, too creepy, too morbid.

Remaining in the shadows, we circled the parking lot perimeter. The pale blue diffused lights of family TVs shone in several large nearby homes, but there was no street traffic or barking dogs. Surprisingly quiet neighborhood, but on second thought, it would be expected after dark; residential gave way to light commercial. The mortuary set the pace, followed by small insurance agencies, podiatrists, and financial planners—closed in the evenings.

We had stalled long enough. No one in sight. Parking lot empty. Weak light bulbs over the French doors easily unscrewed. Still no sound. No security system sign, and no evidence of it on the doors or windows. Must be counting on a combination of fear and loathing, avoidance of death, some measure of genuine respect for the deceased, a dose of luck and plenty of fire insurance. Death benefits for a mortuary could only mean the fires of hell and damnation.

I slid in my credit card and opened the rear door in about two seconds. Marty held it for me.

"Shouldn't we have a black bag with a bunch of tools?" she said.

"No more jokes. Deal with your eventual demise another way. We've got two flashlights and we're breaking the law." I flashed my pencil-thin light around the room quickly. Everything seemed the same as on our previous visit.

Marty raised her light to the table. "Oh, shit. You won't believe it. There's a goddamn body under the sheet. I hated this shit when I was a cop. I puked every time I went to the coroner's office. You know, I'd say 'get me a report by morning,' run out and throw up all over the women's room. That horrible smell, too."

"Forget it." I put my arm around her, crowded out other thoughts which instantly percolated in my brain when I touched her. "We're here to steal stuff, not examine bodies. We're not Dr. Frankenstein and his trusted hunchback. Hell, he didn't even have a female assistant."

The play of light and shadow in this back room, the heart and soul of embalming and body preparation, spelled dizziness for me. I almost welcomed the notion of getting caught and how we'd lie our way out of it. Here to see a dead relative, came all the way from Toledo, found the place closed—hence, our own private viewing.

A helicopter thudded close overhead, so we must be on a flight path to a local hospital. Couldn't be a SWAT team after us, searchlight on this place while they encircled us. Ready for a screaming voice from a bullhorn, "Come out with your hands up. You're completely surrounded. This is Clint Eastwood speaking." The silence of the dust surrounded us, nothing else. I had to maintain sanity and some degree of calm, faking it to help Marty.

"Now, where's that sideboard? The little fucker got the box from a bottom section where he reached way into the back," I said.

Marty moved close to the table, light beam on the sheet, her voice tremulous. "I'm going to look. I can't help myself. You know me."

"Better not, they'll know we were here."

"They'll know anyway. We'll steal any evidence we find. We broke in," she said. "Maybe it's Mr. Isaacs."

"I don't like him either, but we're better off if he's alive and gives us information," I said.

Her hand jerked so much that the intense light beam danced over the corpse. "Okay, I won't look. There's a painted toenail sticking out so I know it's not Isaacs. On the other hand—or other foot—it could just be him."

"Let's search the sideboard and the drawers. If no luck, we can go into the office inside," I said. "My intuition says it's here. I'll bet he just took out papers or whatever and left the empty box in case someone like us or the police ever inquired. He's no rocket scientist."

Both of us now on our knees, reaching and peering into the bottom drawers of the sideboard. As far back as we could. Flashlight showing the way. I had the drawer open where Isaacs pulled out the box. Marty worked the opposite end, pulling out a size ten wide, man's shoe box.

"Well, well, well," she said. She opened the box. A single sheet of paper fluttered to the floor. It was labeled "Magister's Tools." I flashed my light on it.

Black candles
Black bread
Red-black blood
Black velvet drapes
Chants
Symbols
Rituals
Spells
Ashes
Arthame
Goat and wolf flesh/skin
Trinkets

Spells and exercises

She turned the paper over and this time we read it out loud in unison:

> *Opening Ritual*
> *Power and spirits of fire who*
> *reside in the south, we ask that*
> *you burn brightly in this circle.*
> *Bless us with your transformative*
> *powers. We ask you here to join*
> *in our celebration and magick.*
> *Welcome and merry*
> *meet again.*

"Holy shit," I said.

"Amen."

Next, out came several knives, a rusty scalpel and what appeared to be a shot glass caked with dark blood. Long hatpins with twisted handles were at the bottom.

I slid my hand across my unintentional Al Capone face-lift, which felt raised, thick, and irregular, probably as hot and bright as a setting sun over Key West. Scars supposedly became tight at times, pulling on the underlying and surrounding skin. Mine got sore and hurt. Maybe it was all in my mind. I was afraid we'd get caught, breaking and entering or burglary would fit, but we weren't going to steal anything of value to anyone else. Who the hell would want an old shoebox crammed with junk you couldn't give away at a household garage sale? Still, what self-respecting pair of PIs hired by Goldbaum wants to get picked up for a crime? We'd need a good lawyer, more importantly, an honest lawyer. I suppose our boss could always refer us to one.

"We've struck gold, old timer," said Marty. "If we weren't in this fucking place, I'd do a Walter Huston, *Treasure of the Sierra Madre* dance." She put the paper and objects back in the box, covered it, and stood up. Then she closed all of the open drawers. "Let's go. We've got him by the short hairs."

CHAPTER SEVENTEEN

"I thought you might return. How do you like your coffee?" said Mr. Isaacs. Dressed in a black suit with a slight sheen to it, white shirt and solid black silk tie, he looked every bit the somber, tortured funeral director praying for a better day.

We found him lingering in the hallway, having just rearranged the hands on a body to be shown in an hour according to the sign on the door of the so-called 'east chapel.'

"Thanks," I said. "We both take it black, unless you've got cappuccino." I smiled. Nothing wrong with some goodwill in a place like this.

Marty dove into a navy blue velvet striped sofa near the coffee urn. Face expressionless, an outward appearance that usually meant that the wheels were turning fast, not quite sure where to stop them and begin the action. For some strange reason, she took out her sunglasses, wiped them slowly with a towelette, and put them on. A Jackie Kennedy look. I decided to follow her lead. Not sunglasses, just not say much.

Mr. Isaacs handed us each our coffee, an expensive crystal cup with tiny chocolate cookies seated on the saucer's edge. We sipped. The coffee was delicious, hot, dark, nearly as thick as Greek or Turkish.

He chatted. "An investment banker keeled over last weekend on the golf course. Too heavy. Only forty-six. Cholesterol and high blood pressure. The showing will be here and the service at St. Luke's. Devoted family man and a big philanthropist. 'You know who' sure works His will in strange ways, doesn't he?"

I sank into a black-and-blue patterned armchair close to Marty's couch, smiled benignly, and feigned comfort by rolling my shoulders and sighing. Mr. Isaacs stood not more than five feet away. Marty remained silent. The tension built. The pale blue plush carpet, thick and soft, was intended to produce a calming effect on us. Still, the tension grew, palpable as they say. If this kept up, a world-shaking event might occur: a nervous, edgy mortician, finally at a loss for words.

Marty said, "We found the shoe box, dickhead." Gaze hidden behind the glasses magnified her sentiment.

"Excuse me, miss. I don't like to be talked to that way. Please have more respect for the dead, if not for me."

Voice strong, yet modulated, Marty said, "We opened the shoe box last night, fuck brain. Don't play with us. We used to be city cops." She placed the coffee cup delicately on the table and admired the cookies. Then she nibbled. "Really delicious, thanks."

If only a mortician could blush openly and honestly. The crimson abruptly stopped at the edge of his shirt by sheer force of will. "Whatever is the problem? Whatever it is, we can solve it— I'm sure. This is a place where problems are solved and feelings resolved." Mr. Isaacs pleaded with his eyes as he looked down at me—help me, please, help me.

I said, "We opened the shoe box, scumbag. We paid you a visit but you weren't here."

How will Mr. Isaacs handle this? He can't run. He can't yell and scream. He'd never call the police and report a break-in or robbery. He might try to invite us into his private office or for a return visit to the embalming room. Hell, he probably had more bodies in there by now. We'd been gone for hours.

"Confession is good for the soul," said Marty.

Before he could answer, I spoke. "You dumb buttfuck. Did you think you could blow us off like that?" I could really let go with a couple of left jabs and a right cross at this SOB.

Now, Mr. Isaacs showed some emotion. His hands, gripped tightly behind his back, couldn't stop the trembling up to his elbows. Then he grabbed a small antique chair, twirled it back to front, and squatted. When a prancer sits, you know he's in trouble.

Face immobile, loud-voiced, eyes hidden, Marty was impenetrable. "Look, shithead, you'd better trust us with the truth or we'll bring state inspectors and FBI galore all over you. Start talking—or should we report this place? Pretty strange stuff going on here, wouldn't you say?"

Isaacs spoke slowly in hushed tones, eyes darting back and

forth from us to the coffin, barely visible in the east chapel. "We had meetings. "The Group" met here like I told you."

"Tell us all about it," I said. "It's all confidential. We're private. No one will know but us and one lawyer." Where was my Oscar?

Marty slipped off her shades. "Sorry, Mr. Isaacs, we just need the truth."

He leaned forward, spoke in a whisper. "We had a group of thirteen guys. We were into some spiritual stuff. People wanted things. They wanted to change. They were active men, drove trucks for a living, liked to ride motorcycles. It was like a prayer meeting, so the mortuary was a natural home for it. We met every couple of weeks. That's about it. Okay." His eyes closed as if to gain strength through prayer and communicate with his higher power.

After a pause of a minute or two, head now tilted downward, eyes still closed, voice a monotone, Isaacs spoke very slowly. "I'll recite a prayer called the *Circle*."

> *Those we avoid we protect ourselves.*
> *We keep the energy*
> *contained until it goes toward a goal.*
> *Here we have our own place, our*
> *circle of union with the dark one.*
> *We circle in power and energy.*
> *The fever breaks, the headache flees,*
> *the ears are clean, the pain is gone.*
> *Blessed be our efforts to consume*
> *and transform our desires. May our*
> *will be rewarded.*

The body in the coffin could hear me now. "Look, Mr. Isaacs you bullshit artist, that sounds like a sweet little men's church group. We don't buy it. We opened the shoe box, asshole—knives, blood, the works."

Isaacs hesitated while his voice morphed into a hurt little boy. "We had a fire here. Really a fire-bombing of the west chapel area. About five or six years ago. Had it rebuilt. They spray-painted a huge white cross on the wall of the east chapel. Decent Christian folks burned us out. We rebuilt."

"I'm not surprised," Marty said.

An elderly couple harmoniously dressed in white polyester pleated slacks and pea-green T-shirts with white belts and shoes slipped past us into the chapel. Red-faced and teary, they were the first mourners, at least thirty minutes ahead of the viewing and family support time.

Isaacs said, "I don't have much time left. Can't you come back?"

"No chance," said Marty. "It's now or we call the cops. Your choice."

"Nothing we did was illegal or a violation of the law." He stood, then sat again, moved even closer to us. The words shot out quickly, without much emotion. "We were a coven of thirteen. I was the magister, the head of it. We believed in the life of the spirit. We were not Christians. We believed in living life to the fullest, truly enjoying ourselves and satisfying our needs, even the baser needs. We had our own rituals."

Marty slipped on her shades and let them slide down her nose. "You little fuck. You were Satanists who drank blood and worshipped the devil and demons. You probably dressed in black. The evil odor is still in that back room of yours." She dropped her glasses. Isaacs picked them up and handed them to her obediently.

"So what if we were?" he said. "We didn't hurt anyone. We were the victims. They hurt us with their fire. We drank blood from a goat or wolf, never a human being. Red is the life-force. Our group wanted to develop themselves through rituals and beliefs."

"And the box?" I said.

"The athame is the curved knife used in rituals. The vial of ashes was left over accidentally from a cremation of a child long ago. We were into aggressive assertiveness, not destruction or violence, with one possible exception. We felt strongly about revenge—never turn the other cheek, like they say, don't get mad, get even."

"A real tough guy," said Marty.

"I can prove it to you. There's a false bottom on the box. It contains the *Book of Shadows* for our coven. Notes on our meetings and goals. Read it if you don't believe me."

"Oh, we will, we certainly will," said Marty. She sat up on the edge of the couch, leaned toward Isaacs.

I said, "Did you know Willie Branner?"

"Yes."

"How about a little guy named Butch, drove a meat locker truck?"

"Oh, my yes. Two of my best and most loyal. They were close, what we call a coven of two; but then something happened. Willie teased Butch unmercifully, called him pussy and faggot and other names, questioning his manhood. Why do you ask about those two in particular?"

Marty's matter-of-fact tone now surprised me. She had Isaacs' number, big time. "One night over a decade ago they fucked the same whore."

Isaacs said, "You know pagan rituals go back to the Greeks and Romans. They're not necessarily anti-Christ. They're just continued into today."

"How did the coven stop?" I said.

Isaacs appeared to relax. His face softened, the intensity of his fearful gaze diminished and he stopped rubbing his hands. "Well, the firebombing by those religious people. We were afraid that it might somehow all get out of control and ruin my mortuary business. Most of them joined a group up in Detroit with Canadian truckers. I'm on the Internet now as a consultant on witchcraft, spells, sorcery and the Black Mass with black bread, red-black blood, and black candles. Of course, it's really dark red wine from Hungary."

"You make me puke," said Marty.

I said, "Thanks so much, Mr. Isaacs. We'll keep your dirty little secret. Trust us."

He arose slowly, straightened his tie, brushed off his cuffs and walked resolutely toward the chapel to support the bereaved.

Then he turned to us again as we were ready to leave, parkas zipped up. "There's something else. I've never told anybody. I got suspicious and very worried. Willie's wife disappeared and then later that local whore disappeared and was thought to be murdered. I couldn't help thinking that maybe the coven had something to do with it. Maybe more."

Marty said, "You're no fool, Mr. Isaacs. Maybe you should have gone to the police."

"I couldn't," he said. "The coven was mine. I made it. I dissolved it. I just couldn't do it. I never preached crime, just revenge and aggressiveness. Not murder. Believe me, I never directly encouraged murder."

Back in the Corvette, Marty pushed the empty black box on to my lap, not so gently I noticed. The false bottom was weakened by time, so that the dark brown cardboard shredded when I touched it. Crumbled pieces stuck to my fingers. The *Book of Shadows* was not sinister in appearance, merely a thin gray-and-black streaked book that small business owners use to keep track of purchases and expenditures. No marking on the outside except the word "Group" in black marker pen. I felt a tiny twinge of guilt looking into someone else's secrets, but that is the job of a private investigator. They couldn't cast some kind of a spell on Marty and me for looking, could they?

The first page contained several thick, dark red spots encircled in black marker pen. At the top, printed in black, was a kind of title which read "Heresy is witchcraft." The same peace symbol from the top of the box appeared again in black marker.

The inside pages were disorganized and confusing. Words or phrases written on a page, then a blank page, next a list, then what would pass for a prayer. I thumbed through the pages, some printed in black, several in red cursive writing.

Marty leaned back comfortably in the deep leather and closed her eyes. At least she didn't need her sunglasses. In my deepest radio announcer basso I read the *Chant* about love out loud to her.

Chant
We walk the left path
We worship the dark one
We love the demons
We are thirteen around nine
We love our own Yule,
We love red for sexuality
We love black to forget.

Marty curled up into a warm, tight ball. Next came a beautiful little *Prayer* to Satan.

Prayer
In the name of Satan, our king,
we ask that the forces of darkness
give us power and strength and
purpose. We seek revenge upon those
who would harm us. Let Hell open
up to bring us our king and leader,
the ruler of all. We command
the weak and unbelievers to fall
before us, in pain and torment.
Hail Satan, Hail Satan, Hail Satan
We say so mote it be.

Marty said nothing. She stretched and sighed. I knew she was awake. Then it got more interesting with a prayer for revenge called *Get Even*.

Get Even
God of darkness, of cold,
of night, we pray you
instruct us in revenge.
We praise your power, we bless you,
and thank you for everything.

"Listen to this instruction here in parentheses," I said.

"(Magister instructs all coven members:
Revenge items put in a bag
and then burned in a camp
stove in center of the circle.)"

"Read me the *Get Even* again," said Marty.

I handed her the book. "You read it. I'm sick of this shit."

Marty said, "I get the flavor here. Even this old book stinks of putrification. Knives, candles, blood, ashes—some kind of fucking AA group. Then the revenge stuff. They invoked prayers for whatever they wanted, whatever they desired—sex, money, revenge. Then they used the power of "The Group" under the magister to ask Satan for help to accomplish it." She coiled in her seat like a snake poised to strike.

"I wonder if Willie just taunted Butch verbally, or if he hurt him, beat him up. Butch could have developed a real hate for dear old Willie."

"And they'd been two for one, butthole buddies originally. Then they broke apart. I smell motive amidst this horseshit, don't you?" said Marty. She wore her glasses again.

I slammed the lid on the box. Peace symbol my ass. This was a blood-sucking, homicidal group of maniacs who worshipped the devil and could justify just about anything in the process. Goldbaum should be concerned.

CHAPTER EIGHTEEN

Who or what should we believe? Mama and Chuck? For that matter, what did Betty believe to be true? Did she continue to tell people what she thought they wanted or needed to hear? Was she capable of distinguishing truth from fiction, reality from fantasy, honesty from delusion? Was she a congenital liar, a clever manipulator, perhaps some kind of genetically-based, dissociative freak of nature who, medically speaking, at least, was not responsible for what Butch had done? If it ever came to a jury trial, any right-minded judge would get her a psych evaluation, possibly several of them.

Yes, I was increasingly bewildered when I drove to Mama's place to meet the family again. Marty and I didn't evaluate the uncertainties or come to a decision when we left Flint and Mr. Isaacs, and all of that behind us. Still confused, Marty preferred to visit Willie alone, while I tackled Mama and the gang. Marty felt that I provoked Willie and she was sick and tired of raising her eyebrows at me. Although I played bad cop with Isaacs, she'd also been bad but so brilliant.

We lounged in chairs arranged around a new coffee table in Mama's living room. I wasn't sure if it was an authentic antique or a reproduction of an Italian or Spanish ship's hatch cover, with a tiny circular window in the center. The notion of ship of fools came to mind ever so briefly.

Mama and Chuck appeared stone-faced and rigid, parts of a puzzle fixed in place. Betty was the missing puzzle piece. They had all agreed, perhaps too quickly, to see me again. I'd simply told Chuck there were a few follow-up queries and a brief update on new information. Mama soothed Butchie on her lap, Chuck toyed with his ribbons and sharpshooter medals, though Betty appeared delightfully fresh and rested in a pale green corduroy jumper, long white hose, and black granny boots.

I smiled, said how glad I was to see them again, and gave a Ben Franklin type warning. My personal version of the Miranda rule: Three may keep a secret if two of them are dead. Mama and Chuck managed smiles. Then I reassured them again that this was a private, personal, confidential interview and that nothing said here was to ever leave the room. Three heads bobbed with reassurance and seriousness. Maybe Betty and Chuck felt half-dead anyway, so my warning from Ben didn't add much of a threat.

Chuck served coffee. Mama mumbled something like let's not beat around the bush. I had delayed, not sure of where to begin, but Chuck abruptly raised himself and stood at attention at Mama's side, while Betty toyed with a small red pimple near her hairline.

I told them that Goldbaum now represented Willie Branner, jailed without bond, in connection with the discovery of body parts of two missing women in his frozen meat locker. I wasn't sure whether he'd be charged with manslaughter, murder, kidnapping, or a lesser crime. Further, that Marty and I had Betty's best interests at heart, but that we were now employed on the Branner case by Goldbaum. We saw no conflict of interest, nor did Goldbaum, unless new information developed which suggested that there was a conflict between what was best for a former client and one that was current in the same case.

Betty had been cleared and released from custody; Willie had been arrested and jailed. They nodded. Betty mumbled a quiet thank you. Chuck agreed that we'd done a good job on Betty's behalf. Mama blew a kiss at Butchie, who whined softly.

Next I reviewed our last trip to Flint. I told them that Butch and Willie had been friends but had experienced some kind of rupture in the relationship. It appeared to Marty and me that Butch and Willie participated in a Satanic coven which celebrated the Black Mass, drank blood, ate goat or fox flesh and human ashes, performed prayers and chants to the anti-Christ, and specifically sought spiritual power in issues of revenge. That the timing of these meetings of the coven coincided with some kind of relationship between Willie and Butch, and that disappearances, violence, or even homicides were possibly traceable to "The Group."

I said that this was the third time around for questioning Betty. She'd told us of multiple murders, then only sex with several women such as Es, so now what was the story? What was the truth? Was she connected to the disappearance or murder of these women? Would she want an innocent Willie Branner to die for murders he did not commit? Would she like to see Willie in prison for the rest of his life, leaving his two younger children in need of both mother and father?

I ran out of words for the moment. It had all spilled out of me. I didn't even ask if Betty wanted to talk to me alone or with Mama in the room. I just blurted out most of what we had unraveled, without any direct accusations of Butch's involvement. Marty and I had our pet theory: even if Willie had murdered his wife, somehow, some way, evidence connected Betty to Es's disappearance and death. Betty was on the spot here. They were probably still in the process of adjustment, becoming familiar with the last story Betty told us in the courtroom—sex with Es, theft from Mary.

Betty stood to face Mama and Chuck. She brushed off her skirt and straightened it. She pushed her bangs lower and smoothed her hair. She held her hands at arm's length and studied carefully manicured nails. She gazed directly at them. "It was a long, long time ago. I was a mixed-up kid. Always on the move and lonesome at times. I went to church with you, Mama, but never believed all of it. Mr. Isaacs was like a priest, but more real. He'd come to the truck stop, take over a big table in the back room near the toilets. Well, he was real nice to us. He'd buy us burgers or donuts. He talked about how cruel the world could be. He'd have one of the truck-fuck girls in the men's john if you wanted a quickie. Usually, he'd pay."

I felt uncomfortable with Betty's preamble, a sickening feeling in the pit of my stomach, the area of my brain still consumed with "truth" put out a neurochemical signal. I didn't want to sit through another half-hour one act play. "Betty, I've heard a lot of different things from you. You have lied so many times. Is this the truth?"

She walked to me. Her sad, weepy gaze did not flinch from mine. "Yes, this is the truth. I swear Kip, it's the truth."

Chuck's voice ached with pain and desperation from Betty's

conflicting accounts, obviously choking back disappointment and tears. "Oh, God, Betty, there's so much I never knew. You spared me knowing you as Butch. I don't know if I could have stood it." He stood stiffly. At parade rest, chest thrust out, hands frozen behind him.

Mama listened to Betty, but concentrated her attention on Butchie. She still heard what she wanted, or needed, to hear. "That dress is sure pretty on you, honey. You always liked pretty costumes."

Betty said, "There were meetings of what we called "The Group" in the mortuary. Isaacs ran them. He wore black clothes and a black cape. We stood in a circle and we'd chant different things. We drank blood and ate black crackers. It was all men but we hugged and kissed each other's cheeks. I belonged to something." She lowered her face to the floor, and her hands cupped in supplication. She said,

We love the cypress tree
for death rituals.
We love the mulberry tree
for protection.
We love the oak tree
for personal power.

"It felt good?" I said.

After Betty sighed deeply, her breathing became more shallow. "And very exciting to me and powerful. It gave me a thrill to be in a coven. We were all in the same boat, drove truck, loved motorcycles, worked with our hands, took an oath to each other. We tried to see the world as it is, not some fairy tale. It's not a nice place. Our coven taught us that that's the truth, there is violence, so many nasty people."

"An eye for an eye?" I said.

"Yes, an eye for an eye. Don't ever turn the other cheek. Strike back when you have to." Betty touched her face, her left hand appearing to feel for the missing roughness of Butch's beard. "Get even."

Mama and Chuck did not speak. They appeared to hang on Betty's every word, as if hoping and praying for a final truth, closure on these legal matters. Willie was a stranger to them and must be the killer of his wife and Es. Butch, lonely and overworked while driving and selling meats, actually made friends and joined some kind of group, sought fellowship when he traveled away from home so often.

Betty stepped over to Mama and held her free hand. "Not now, Mama, it's all different. I'm Betty. I see the world in a different way. I feel different. All I want is a family with Chuck. Satan is a long way from us. We'll have our kids baptized and you'll be there to see it. I promise." Betty kissed the top of Mama's head. Then she crossed herself.

Mama appeared overwhelmed, her face pale and bony, lips trembling. Eyes misty, she stroked her little dog Butchie very gently. She said, "I'll always love you Butchie. I mean Butch. I mean Betty. You know what I mean. I get mixed up."

Chuck said, "What's the rest of it, Betty? Let's get all of the dirty laundry hung out today. Isn't the truth supposed to set us free? I'm sure glad we weren't together in those days. Don't know if I could have stood still while you became yourself." He remained standing at Mama's side.

Butchie squirmed and squealed. Mama set him in Chuck's cupped hand for a moment. He cradled the tiny dog in one hand with his other still stiff behind his back. Mama recognized Chuck as one of the family if she'd trust him to calm Butchie. Noticeably, Chuck did not say any of those lovey-dovey things to Betty, did not hug her or hold her hand. His overt behavior spoke volumes to me, and I'm no social worker or therapist. The cold shoulder if I'd ever seen one.

Betty said, "I don't like to think about it. Willie treated me badly He called me swishy and said I was a pussy because I didn't like to fight. He'd say things during the group, taunt me to hurt somebody or get revenge. He always talked about revenge. He hated his wife. Really hated her."

She eye-balled Mama and Chuck closely, then me. "This is the God's honest truth. I knew him in court. That's the same

Willie Branner. Our friendship turned to hatred. I got scared he'd kill me or drive me off the road." Betty's poise slipped slightly as she plunked herself into the chair, not very ladylike.

"Do you think he killed them, honey?" said Mama. "He sounds mean."

Chuck said, "Yes, it fits, Betty. He's violent and they found pieces of several women connected to him." He returned Butchie, now half-asleep, to Mama's lap. "They've finally got him. He'll fry." Chuck walked briskly into the kitchen and returned with a decanter of red wine. "It's kind of sweet Hungarian wine. Mama likes it." He poured a glass for each of us. Then he proposed a toast. "To Betty. Let this nightmare finally be over with." We all clinked glasses and sipped.

"Thanks, sweetheart, but I'm not finished. Here's the final part. My whole truth." She gulped her drink, quite unusual given Betty's social demeanor. She sucked in a deep breath and gathered strength. "I decided to get even with Willie. I still liked him a lot, we'd been buddies, so I couldn't let myself do anything directly to him to hurt him. I decided to set him up. I'd do something bad and they'd blame him. That would be my revenge. I'd get even."

"That's understandable. He'd treated you like crap and you didn't like it," I said. I thought I knew what was coming next from Betty, but I didn't want to accuse her. She could always clam up, and then where would we be?

Betty dashed into the bedroom. Strong emotion must be getting to her, so she needed to compose herself. This was her moment of truth, and I supposed the red wine was her truth serum. It seemed but a moment or two, then out walked Butch, tight white jeans, pink golf shirt, slip-ons; he could have been headed for the beach, with dark shades on and hair slicked back from his forehead.

"Oh, Butch, my sweet Butch. You liked to dress up and pretend," said Mama.

"It felt better to me, more real, that's all Mama. I killed Mary Branner and I killed Esmeralda, the prostitute. That's it. I did it so it would be blamed on Willie. That was my way. They finally got him, after all these years. I should have just killed him."

Chuck's face was flushed. His knees buckled. His hands shook noticeably. He literally threw himself, protectively, into the soft cushions of a huge round chair. "Is this the truth, for God's sake, Betty, or are you Butch again?"

Voice strong, hands punching the air. "I'm your Betty. Just wanted to be Butch for a moment. I followed Mary home, snuck into her bedroom and stabbed her. While her dog nipped at my heels, I got away. Willie thought she'd stabbed herself. Then he cut up her body and stored it. I followed him when he had Es in his truck. I stabbed her with a hypodermic needle full of drugs to cause an overdose. I forgot my gloves. Willie thought she killed herself and he sliced her up. He'll finally get his due. He treated Butch very, very badly. He actually tried to do it to Butch one night, like faggot priests do to young boys." At that, Betty tore off Butch's clothes and leaped into the bedroom, her pink panties and bra and slip showing as she ran off. We could hear her dressing and sliding into her granny shoes.

Although I was nearly immune to Betty's revelations of sex, cannibalism, and death, this time it did have a ring of truth. The story of sexual encounters only, purely coincidental encounters with some of the women was a stretch. This version had motive, opportunity, and means. Very clever choice of place, timing and methods. Both Mama and Chuck held their heads in their hands and sobbed.

A proud Betty came back dressed, with her head up as she took firm steps. Maybe she was relieved of the burden of lies and deceit. Her hair was primped, fresh make-up and glasses in place. "I'm so sorry, feel so bad for everything, but Butch needed revenge. The coven said so. Willie deserved it. I stole the money from Mary and I did have sex with Es. Those things were true, too."

The tension coated us like the thin ice of flash-frozen vegetables. I wasn't surprised and, for the moment at least, believed this story more than Betty's earlier versions. She would later amend this one with plenty of mea culpas, "I'm so ashamed," "So very sorry," "Hate myself," "Betty would never have done this kind of thing," and so on. Bottom line, Betty said Butch murdered two women in cold blood, intentionally, deliberately, in order to arrange for Willie to be arrested, charged, and convicted of murder. After doing it once and failing with Mary, Butch did it again. Same MO, same purpose—set up Willie and see him swing from the yardarm.

"Oh, Butch, you should have stayed here, lived with Mama. Then those things couldn't have happened. I wouldn't let them happen," said Mama. The parchment skin, near the point of cracking under the strain, now softened under the cascade of tears. Butchie jumped out of her arms and ran to Chuck. Both hands still covered his face, sobbing uncontrollably behind his huge meat hooks.

Chuck jumped up. He screamed and raged, sweaty face beet-red and eyes burning, the career military sergeant furiously upbraiding his underlings. "You dumb fucking bitch, or whatever you are or were. You really are a murderer. You got away with it. You stopped killing by becoming Betty, but you still did it. I married a double-murderer. You weren't satisfied with killing one woman. You did it twice. And you failed. Willie hasn't been given the electric chair. How can I stand this? I can marry a man but, holy shit, I never even killed anybody in combat. How can I live with a confessed fucking murderer? I'm sorry Mama, I can't do it. You're good, but Betty is evil. She's plain evil. You can have her back." Chuck grabbed his hat, his olive green overnight bag, saluted smartly and stormed to the door. He turned on his heel. "I used to think you were just a horny truck driver or maybe sort of crazy. But now, you're a killer. Sayonara." He ripped off his sergeant stripes and threw them at Betty. Butchie found them and chewed contentedly.

Chuck planted himself near the door. His feet dug in firmly, knees slightly bent, eyes scanning the room, sweaty face taut and red with vigilant anger. A tiny pearl-handled revolver stuck in his right fist, nearly encased in his broad, thick hand.

I said, "Chuck, give me the gun. You don't want to hurt any of us or yourself."

His nostrils flared. He gazed into space, vacantly, no eye

contact with any of us. Lost in a crowd. "I can't live this way. Too much pain. I love her. I can't go on. I love you, Betty. I've pretended I can handle it. I can't." Tears streamed down his cheeks.

I said, "You're upset, Chuck. We'll talk. Please give me the gun. We can work it out." This guy was more than my match with a weapon, a drill instructor enraged, confused, and not sure if he wanted to live or die. Would he kill someone else in the process, too? You didn't have to be a rocket scientist to know he could shoot any of us before I could get to the automatic in my belt holster. Breathe slowly. Try to talk him down and protect the likely targets—Betty and Mama.

Betty cried out as she fell to the floor at Chuck's feet. "Chuck, I've lost you. I love you. Don't leave. It's all my fault." Her fingers scratched the carpet, tears hidden and sobs muffled by flattening her face into the floor.

"Don't cry, honey. Men get upset. They come back," said Mama. It was possible she couldn't see the gun, or maybe couldn't believe it was there in his hand.

I thought of Marty. If only she were with me. I could be the good cop and try to talk him down. She could be the bad cop and have the .38 in her purse, pointed directly at Chuck, ready to fire if it appeared he was going to shoot any one of us. I couldn't even call for back-up.

"Chuck, please give me the gun. There's a way out of this. If you can't deal with it anymore, you and Betty can split up."

"No," he screamed. "I'll never divorce. Never. Never. Never."

"Chuck, let Mama and Betty go to the bedroom. We can talk it out. Please do that. You don't want to hurt them."

"I can't think. I'm overwhelmed. I hate everyone."

His gun hand flared straight up and he pointed at the ceiling. No loud crack of a bullet. His hand flew back to his side. Butchie whimpered and raced to the bedroom.

"Come back Butchie. Everything is fine," said Mama.

Chuck continued to cry and sob at once, tears flowing down his uniform. Mumbled words were indistinguishable at first.

The wailing pain made any clear-cut understanding of them unnecessary. "Stay away. Can't stand it." Shoulders slumped, he appeared ready to fall or simply dissolve into nothingness. The life force drained from him.

Chuck suddenly pitched the gun at the wall to his left, hit an antique framed mirror which cracked in large shards as it hit the floor.

"That's smart, Chuck. Thanks for getting rid of the gun," I said.

He did a military right-face and stumbled out of the door.

Mama said, "He'll be back. He's upset." She plopped down in her chair as Butchie jumped into her lap.

Betty still lay prostrate on the floor. Her lips were in the carpet. She mumbled, "I've ruined it all."

My heart stopped racing. I thought of what might have been. He'd have killed himself. He'd shoot Betty and I'd kill him. We'd been lucky as hell. I reached to pat my automatic and my hand was soaked with sweat from the back of my shirt.

"It's okay, ladies. We're fine now. We're safe. Chuck will get over it. He just freaked out for a moment. We're all safe and secure."

Betty lifted herself and put her head in Mama's lap. She shared it with Butchie. Mama patted them both.

I picked the gun up. "I'll take care of it," I said. "Should I call the police, or do you want to file a domestic violence complaint? You could get a restraining order."

"Oh, no, no, not that," said Betty. "We'll be fine. We love each other."

Betty now appeared strangely self-contained, no tears or screams, yet pain obviously inside her somewhere, almost as if the scenario played out just as she had composed it earlier in her brain. "I wish he'd have hit me, beat me up, but stayed. I love him. I need him. Now what will happen?"

Moments later Betty's limp body slowly slumped to the carpet. She had fainted without hitting her head on anything. There was no blood. No sound of cracking bone. Just a thirty-five-year-old housewife who had fainted in the aftermath of a tense, angry family confrontation. Her husband had bolted.

"Call 911," said Mama. "She must be dead."

"I know CPR and first aid for shock. I'll put a pillow under her feet and a blanket over her," I said.

Betty's eyes fluttered immediately. More swoon than faint. Real or imagined? Driven by shock and surprise, or by a larger plan to gain our sympathy?

"You stay there," said Mama. "Just rest, honey. Just rest a moment."

"Okay, Mama, I will. I must have passed out. I'm so ashamed of everything. I don't deserve to live." She lay on her back, closed her eyes and folded her arms neatly across her breasts. Ready for Mr. Isaacs.

"Oh, Butch, you always did the darndest things," said Mama.

I told the ladies to call me if they needed me as I opened the door to leave.

By the time I arrived at my apartment, I was really beat. Time with Betty and her family drained me at some subterranean level of my soul, in addition to which I was constantly saying, "Is this credible?" to myself. So many stories, so much violence, so much death and blood, so much bullshit. Maybe we were zeroing in on the truth. I'd have to tell Goldbaum what Betty said.

I sunk into the couch and must have dozed off. The dream jolted me awake with joy and love—our honeymoon at sunset near the beach in Maui. Perched on a craggy ledge of rock, the sun still moving while we held hands to protect each other from the strong salty spray. The day left us with a beautiful sexy night, but first a romantic dinner of broiled fresh tuna and chilled white wine. Any young cop would go crazy from this experience. With my new wife Wendy, it was a moment of ecstasy frozen in time—all but forgotten for several years.

I felt much better and looked forward to a toasted cheese sandwich, a small bag of spicy crackers and a cold beer. First, I wanted to read the e-mail from Marty. The computer hutch and the kitchen were a mess. I cleared a space to sit down and scan the screen.

E-Mail
To: Kip
From: Marty
Subject: Interview of Willie Branner in county jail

Hey, boss, Willie looked great. Clean-shaven, fresh haircut, some overpowering cologne, so I hardly noticed the orange jump suit and the shackles on his legs. They let me see him right away. He actually smiled when he saw me, glad for the chat. He's not given much freedom because he's an alleged killer.

When I mentioned the name of Isaacs, I thought he'd explode like "The Hulk," burst his chains and devour me. He said he knew Isaacs. He reported that he was in "The Group," which met at the mortuary; it helped a lot, as he made some nice friends and learned a lot about religion and the spiritual world.

Willie said he got involved with the coven through sex. Mr. Isaacs provided girl and boy sex toys in the back room at the truck stop.

He stated that the ideas of the coven fit his views. He emphasized that the stories of Satan and his disciples were true, and that Christianity was all about war and intolerance, that it was fake, stuff like turning the other cheek and forgiveness.

Willie remembered Butch very well and stressed that friendship was a big part of the coven. Says they were pals, drank coffee together, fucked the same whores and so on. He noted that Butch was slender and weak, while Willie was big and strong. He admits that he teased Butch, called him names like Butch the Butt-fuck, or simply Butt-fuck. Said he was "swishy," that's his word not mine. Once or twice he tried to give it to Butch in the rear-end but it didn't work out.

After the episode with Es, he stopped attending the coven. Said he didn't want to draw any attention to himself. Willie had no idea that Betty Fowler had been Butch. Apparently he forgot about Butch long ago. He bragged that he had his hands full with Tami and all the truck-fucks.

Willie sticks by his story that he didn't kill anyone, though it may look that way. His version is that Mary got robbed at the

ATM. She came home, they argued, she got into bed with her dog, closed the door and then later stumbled out of the bedroom with a gushing stab wound in her heart.

He admits that he had sex with Es, gave her a ride, and she either deliberately or accidentally overdosed in the restroom with a drug-filled syringe.

He got scared both times, feared the police, knew how it would look, decided to cut up the bodies and dispose of them once they were frozen packages. Somehow, parts of Es and Mary were left in the food locker and Es's arm and hand most likely, accidentally fell out of Willie's truck. He repeated several times that he cut up the bodies of two women who had committed suicide but did nothing to harm either of them.

Willie knows how bad it looks for him. That body parts must be more than a coincidence. He figures there would be plenty of evidence like hair, prints, and DNA against him. He hated Mary and he might have had a reason to hurt Es, or at least he's afraid the police will assume that he did. His record of domestic abuse and incest doesn't help him

Forgive me, boss, but I believe him. He's not very nice, a lousy husband, abusive father, and a sloppy beer-head, but I don't think he's a killer. He's full of hate and has so little insight into himself that he's really disgusting. If he'd played it straight, cops might have caught the real murderer of both women. Better yet, Es might still be alive if Butch had been hung out to dry for killing Mary. As it is, police will search for murder weapons, eye witnesses, use fancy chemical tests to search for blood evidence at Willie's original apartment and possibly re-do the forensic tests on Es's remaining body parts for drugs she'd OD'd on.

With limited crime scene evidence, there may not be enough to pin more on Willie than cutting up dead bodies. There's probable cause, we can't undo that, but that's different from guilty beyond a reasonable doubt.

If Willie's telling me the truth, then Butch was very clever, but quite careless with his prints and blood. He followed Mary home after robbing her. Somehow he got into her bedroom, stabbed her and escaped. He must have done something like that with Es, when the Mary murder didn't put Willie in prison for life. Willie and Butch deserve each other.

I replied to her e-mail immediately. "Great work with Willie. His story fits with Betty's. Come over for dinner. I'll cook. I've got wine. Is it a good time for you know what? I hope so."

Marty's reply excited me. She said, "Thanks. Be there at 7:30 p.m. Yes, it is a perfect time."

Any remaining fatigue dwindled away quickly in a frenzy of cleaning, dusting, straightening and hiding things like old newspapers and dirty clothes. The hell with the toasted cheese. I defrosted two T-bone steaks, whipped up a lettuce and tomato salad with Italian virgin olive oil and balsamic vinegar dressing, heated a box of home fries and finally pried the broken cork from a medium-grade bottle of Chianti. I showered, soaping and shampooing twice. Fresh pressed chinos, old blue button-down, and a pair of Nikes. I was ready a half-hour before Marty arrived. Was I the same guy who'd looked forward to sleep, a sandwich and a beer?

The doorbell rang. I opened it to view a dream.

Marty held her faux fur coat over her arm, dressed in a sexy school-girl outfit—dark blue and green, very short, plaid skirt, high white stockings, white blouse and a thick long-sleeved cardigan sweater. "Excuse me, kind sir, am I too early?"

"Yes, ma'am, I'm the dean of students and classes don't start for at least an hour or so. Please come in. You can wait in here." I pointed to the bedroom. She followed my directions.

"Oh, sir, you won't hurt me will you? I'm such a young inexperienced girl. I just want to graduate and get a good job as a secretary in some nice office." A demure smile creased her lips, gaze lowered, hands fidgety with a tiny leather purse.

The phone rang. I gave it four rings. Then Goldbaum's irritated voice barked at me. "Pick up, Kip, pick it up for God's sake."

I finally lifted the receiver. "Yes, sir. What's up?"

He was voluble tonight, usually just a word or short phrase from him. "You two forget about me? What's the story? I'm the guy who pays the bills, you know. And they're pretty damn high."

"We just completed interviews with Willie and Betty, trying to verify the information we gave you from Isaacs and our other discoveries in Flint," I said.

Marty perched on the edge of the bed. She slid the long stockings down slowly until they bunched up at her ankles, then pulled the short skirt above her waist, covering up her blouse. The red thong across bronze skin overpowered me. She smiled as innocently as she could, sighed and moaned softly, then slowly rubbed the smooth skin of her inner thighs.

Speaker phone on. I wanted Marty to hear all of this, so she knew how hard I was trying to keep it brief. If she touched me, I'd lose it and probably drop the phone or disconnect it. "They confirm the coven. They confirm friendship and then a split. Willie says he just cut up both bodies out of fear of police. Betty says Butch killed both in order to set up Willie, revenge for Willie's mistreatment of him."

"Believe them?"

"Yes, we do. It fits. Isaacs recalled they'd had a quarrel."

Marty unbuttoned my shirt and yanked it off. The sleeve tore slightly. She untied the Nikes and jerked my feet out. She pulled at the zipper on the chinos. Fortunately, it caught on something. I backed away a foot or two. I only had so much control.

"So," I said. "What do you think?"

Goldbaum's charm was overwhelming, but I appreciated his gruff brevity this once. "I'll let you know." He hung up. I was grateful for small favors.

What happened next is still hazy in my mind, a delicious delirium bordering on shock, like lottery winners describe when they first matched their tickets with the winning numbers. My jackpot.

A surprisingly edible thong, red cotton candy that contained something to solidify it. Then the passionate, intense embrace, a fierce entrance with Marty screaming that I was so big and so hard and so deep that she didn't know if she could stand it. A mutual demolition derby. Then we got into new cars, smashed into each other, and wrecked them again.

Finally, mouths sucking air while breathing rates slowed a bit. I said, "God, Marty, you are so wonderful."

"Quiet, boss." She held several fingers to my lips to hush me. I pulled my head up a few inches and sucked on them. If I couldn't talk at least I could stay busy.

No romantic chatter. No holding each other. No cuddling. This was fulfilling as agreement, a contract, promises to be kept. It was tantalizing water torture, more difficult than I'd imagined. In a typical one-night stand, people say things they don't mean, express affection, even love, when they can't even recall their partner's name a week later. Here, I was overcome with feeling for Marty but had to restrain myself.

"Thanks, boss. Just what I wanted. You were perfect," Marty said. "Absolutely perfect." She rolled off of the bed, stood up, dressed in a flash and disappeared into the bathroom. She yelled loud enough to be heard over the sound of running water. "Did you mention dinner? I'm starved."

I tossed the salad again and added some shredded Parmigiano Reggiano cheese, my hands still shaking. The steaks slid under the broiler. I couldn't remember if I'd turned them or not. I reheated the potatoes. Marty and I each gulped two glasses of Chianti while I cooked. We toasted the pirates of old; to a merry life and a short one. She'd brought a chocolate something or other for dessert—a second dessert for me. We ate and drank the rest of the bottle, sipped espresso with the chocolate something.

We tried to have a conversation about the case, Willie and Butch, Betty and Chuck, but it fell flat. We agreed that Goldbaum faced a difficult challenge with Willie, especially given the strong possibility that Butch set him up. How could he prove it? Or at least get one potential juror to believe that someone else had killed those women, that Willie had only done what any frightened and confused outdoorsman would do: skin, butcher, package and freeze another hunter's fallen prey.

My earlier exhaustion returned. Marty appeared edgy as she sat, then stood, cleared the table, and shook the tablecloth over the sink. She slipped on her coat after she helped wash and dry the dishes, gave me a peck on the cheek, and headed for the door.

"Thanks, boss."

I said, "I hope you don't order peanut butter or pickles very soon."

Her right hand descended in a half moon in front of her stomach. Then she blew me a kiss.

I was headed somewhere new. I needed more. I wanted more. I felt better inside. A shrink might say I was ready for a real relationship. Then I did the unimaginable—clicked on to a new matchmaking service called "Dates for Cops." They wouldn't mind a PI, would they?

CHAPTER NINETEEN

Marty and I drained cups of African roast at my place in late January. Betty shared Mama's apartment, Chuck even considered a divorce, Goldbaum worried over a potential conflict of interest over Willie's case and when Betty's statements should be reported to the police. We were deciding how to spend the $5,000 bonus.

The snow of January was outrageously beautiful, but for only a moment. Five inches of while powder covered us quickly, melted in three days into dirty slush and huge mounds of tarry eye-sores in malls, parking lots, and street corners. The final meltdown would clog the sewers and flash flood low-lying areas and many of the popular intersections. Here and there a stalled car, overwhelmed by tire-high rising waters, would dot the landscape in the next few days. Who said you couldn't predict the weather, or at least its consequences?

I fingered the check for five grand. Marty grabbed it as she bent at the waist in supplication. She said, "All hail MacBeth, I mean Goldbaum." She plopped her feet on the coffee table and brushed a few drops of moisture from brown corduroy riding pants. "He's got a problem. We don't. Even though Betty had been released by the judge, he should have thought ahead. Both perps for the same crimes. You never know where the evidence leads you. One day it's Willie, the next it's Betty."

I poured us each another steaming cup. Two donuts remained, one chocolate-filled and the other with white creamy gelatin. Marty got the chocolate. "What the hell do you think Goldbaum will do? He gave me his famous non-committal line 'I'll let you know'," I said.

Marty sighed. She grinned. Then nibbled. I wanted to wipe the chocolate filling from her lip but better judgment prevailed. "We didn't do anything wrong, did we?"

I said, "Of course not. We just did what we were asked to do—gather information on Goldbaum's clients that could assist in their defense. I'm sure Goldbaum would say that he terminated Betty as a client before he accepted Willie's $15,000 retainer. He doesn't have a crystal ball. He didn't know where this would lead." I felt slightly uncomfortable and too warm in my blue cashmere turtleneck. Marty said it matched my eyes.

"You're right," said Marty. "Hell, we should have asked for half of Willie's money. You know the old saw, 'feel for others, in your pocket.' This is not the welfare department we're running, boss."

"Would you like to—you know?"

"Boss, don't give it a thought. I'll let you know all you need to know. Good Boy Scouts just prepare themselves," she said.

"I'm prepared."

"I can see that," she said.

Saved by the cell. It was Mama. She'd never called me, so I knew it was important. Her weak voice was hollow but quivered with fear. "Kip. Is this Kip? Please come over. Chuck's here. It's bad."

"Okay, Mama. We'll be there in a few minutes. Do you want the police now, or fire department?"

"Oh, no, just you. Hurry," she said.

We flew out of the apartment. The sun peeked through some low-lying patchy clouds here and there, a bit of blue sky. I should have asked Marty if it matched my eyes. The Corvette knew the way to Mama's.

Marty said, "Must be something big. Love birds at each other's throats. Maybe Chuck wants her back and she won't go."

"Or Mama has had enough of both of them. You know, take the fight outside, don't mess up my life."

Marty was right. We found a spot in front of the building and ran up to the apartment. Betty was no longer Goldbaum's client, so we were not working for him on this run. We were just there as friends of the family, or something like that. Visiting an ex-client, her husband and mother at the mother's invitation. I hated to think of human beings in these categories but I did. I automatically felt for my gun, safely tucked into the tiny belt holster.

"Go slow, boss, could be trouble."

Shoes wet, parka dry, I pushed the apartment door open as I knocked. It was already slightly ajar.

"Over here, I'm here," said Mama. Blinds pulled, she sat in semi-darkness, adding to the mystery. "They're in there."

Marty said, "You mean Betty and Chuck are in the bed-room?"

"Yes," she said.

"Well, Mama," I said, "They're still married." Butchie licked my wet boots.

"They were yelling and screaming like the end of the world. Now it's real quiet," Mama said. "Chuck called it the end."

Marty said, "Don't worry too much, Mama. Divorce only feels like it's the end. It's also a beginning, maybe something better. I know. I've done it, too." She walked to Mama and held both her hands. Then she turned on the lamp next to Mama's chair.

Mama's half-open red eyes, deep in dark-rimmed sockets, pleaded with us. She'd spilled cereal on the front of her dress. Butchie wouldn't come to her. "See what's wrong. Please. Please."

I strolled to the bedroom door. Ear to the door, no sound from inside. Probably asleep after making love for all I knew. I knocked softly. "Hi guys, Kip and Marty to see you." No response.

"Butchie, go to Mama," I said. The dog wouldn't let go of my boot. I must have stepped in something he liked.

Marty scooped him up, then laid him in Mama's lap. She said, "They're probably asleep, Mama. We'll come back later."

"No, no, they're not asleep. Something's wrong," said Mama.

I knocked much harder this time. "Please, would one of you talk to us? Mama is very worried. Probably better to have your love spats somewhere else." Still no reaction. The door was locked. I jiggled the handle several times. Then I really pounded until my knuckles were sore and slightly swollen.

Marty raised her eyebrow at me, the usual warning not to go too fast or too heavy. "I'm going to kick the door open, Mama."

"Good."

Marty said, "Wouldn't it be better to call 911 or have the police check it out?"

"No," said Mama. "Break it open."

I kicked the lock, and the wood crushed easily as the door flew open. The room was dark, shades drawn, only a tiny lamp on the bedside table provided light. It was enough. Both bodies lay spread out in the shadows on the bed covers. Betty, fully dressed in dark sweater, white blouse and plaid skirt, had a small bullet hole in her forehead, satin pillow underneath her skull drenched in bright red blood. Chuck, in a V-neck maroon sweater and a pair of jeans, lay near her, with what appeared to be a long barrel .38 with a silencer in his right hand near the middle of his chest. He'd shot himself in the mouth and the back of his head was blown off; most of the blood, bones and brains now covered the curved headboard and the wall. They'd settled it somehow, a domestic murder-suicide if I ever saw one.

I held the note on the table up to the lamp-light. "I couldn't stand it. Married to a guy, a two-time murderer, whom I love more than life. We leave together. I've dishonored my country, shamed the Army and abandoned my sense of loyalty and dignity. Sorry, Mama. Your loving Chuck."

It had been some years since I'd been the first responder at a murder scene. I wasn't a police detective anymore, hell, I wasn't even a cop on the beat. The shock and horror of unexpected death never gets easy, especially here with Mama in the next room dying to know what I'd found. I thought of telling her they were asleep and buying some time. She'd see through it, ask me to wake them, or else come in here herself. "Be right there, Mama. Just a moment," I said.

I waved Marty to the door. My voice was a hoarse whisper. "They're both dead. It's a crime scene. Please call 911 and Vince on your cell phone, away from Mama." She nodded.

I stumbled out to Mama, pulled a chair up to her, cradled her cold, gnarled hands inside mine. Butchie jumped down again and ran toward Marty standing outside the apartment door in the hallway. "I'm very sorry, Mama, but they're both gone. A gun. It had a silencer so you didn't hear it. You couldn't have done anything to stop it."

She said, "Butchie, you come right back here to Mama. I

need you, right now." She gazed beyond me, to the bedroom door. "Where did they go? They're gone?"

My mind whirred into a personal orbit. Betty, such a fascinating and horrifying creature, dead; very convincing and persuasive in her stories, though I never could be sure of her honesty. As far as we knew, she'd had an exemplary life with Chuck since her gender change. If only Butch had never been. Here they were, all three of them gone. Chuck had coped with one surprise after another, his love for Betty stretched thin by her recent admissions. He'd stood by her and their marriage, been a rock-hard support through a challenging set of legal and criminal circumstances. He'd reached his limit, snapped, and killed himself and Betty.

"Yes, they're gone Mama. They're both dead. Chuck killed himself and it looks like he's killed Betty, too." I stopped short of telling her that neither was breathing and that I'd felt for a pulse on both and there was none. "Ambulance will be here in a moment. And the police. They have to come and talk to us. I'm so sorry."

Mama said, "I'll bet Butch is pretending. He always likes to dress up and pretend to be someone else. You saw that."

"They're gone, Mama."

"Butchie," she said. "Will you please hush and let Mama think?" The dog trembled, jittery and restless, testing her patience now. He jumped down again, so Mama replaced him with my left hand in both of hers, stroked it instead of Butchie. "They can't be dead. No one screamed. I didn't hear any gun. I've been here the whole time. You know that."

"I know. I know you were."

You may delay but time will not stop. It was gradually dawning on her that what I'd said was a grim reality. "Maybe they're alive. I've got to see Butch." She tried to pull herself out of her chair, using my hand and arm as a crutch, but her strength was sapped. I didn't push her down, but I didn't pull her up either.

"Better wait a little bit. You may not want to see it all right away," I said.

Mama's dam broke wide open. High-pitched wails followed by forlorn screams of sadness and pain, her love for Butch, her need for Butch, wishing she were dead, not Butch. The tears soaked her green-and-yellow patterned housedress. She tore at the tufted chair cushion. Her shaking hands punched her temples. "Butch, oh my little Butch, you're all I have, all I had. You're my life. Butch, come right out here and talk to Mama. Don't go away. Stop pretending. Stop fooling Mama."

Marty appeared at the door with two husky paramedics, pulling and carrying several pieces of portable equipment. She pointed them to the bedroom. The larger of the two EMTs came out momentarily, "I'm sorry folks, they're both deceased. We'll call the hospital and the coroner's office. A doctor has to make it official. No chance to save them. Sorry. The police will be here shortly. Since there are gunshot wounds, it will be a crime scene. Very sorry to tell you folks the bad news."

Mama edged herself out of the chair and inched her way into the bedroom. No one interfered even though it was a crime scene. She had a right, a need, to view the bodies of her dead child and son-in-law. "Get up now, Butch. Stop it. Quit joking with me. Stop funning." She kissed them both and rubbed blood from each body on her dress and face and hair. Then she lay down on the bed with them and closed her eyes. "Take me, too, Lord."

The two EMTs witnessing the scene placed their right hands briefly over their hearts, a salute to Mama in her grief. Wordlessly, with no wasted movement, they treated her for shock, raising her legs, covering her with a blanket, taking her blood pressure and starting an IV.

They'd need a stretcher for Mama. For now, she simply lay prostrate near the departed, her tiny, withered frame slumped at the foot of the blood-splattered bed. Cops would move her soon enough. I thought of rearranging Chuck's note so she wouldn't see it near the night table. She'd had enough. She appeared even more peaceful than Chuck and Betty, if people shot to death can be said to appear peaceful. Chances are, she'd wish for the rest of her time that she'd been physically included in their demise. Spiritually and psychologically, she had been.

Marty stood on the left side of the bed peering at the three of them. The skin on her cheeks sagged and a trembling hand wiped away the hot tears. She'd never get desensitized to such carnage, and I loved that about her. "My God, oh my God," she said. She ran out of the room, her hand now over her mouth.

It felt like a few moments before Vince walked in, slipping on his white latex gloves. His tired green eyes were rimmed with dark, baggy circles, probably no sleep for the last twenty-four hours.

"What happened, Kip?" he said. He paused at the head of the bed to review the crime scene.

"This is Betty Fowler and her husband, Chuck, both dead of gunshot wounds. Mama is Betty's mother. She's alive."

The EMTs cautiously brought in a stretcher for Mama and then eased her on to it very slowly. The IV was maintained. "She's doing okay. Pulse up a bit. BP not too bad. In shock. We'll take her to St. Vincent. The coroner's office and forensic folks are in the hallway waiting for the green light to get started, Lieutenant."

"Thanks, guys, good job," said Vince. "On your way out, please tell them to lay out the crime scene tape and keep everyone out of here. So, Kip, tell me the story." He bent over Betty and Chuck in order to closely examine the gunshot wounds.

"We got a call to come over here pronto from Mama. Been here before to see them because Betty Fowler had been a client of Goldbaum's and Marty and I had interviewed her, her husband Chuck, and her mother on several occasions. Mama told us they'd argued and yelled, and then it was real quiet. I broke the door open and we found them like this. Both dead. A note here from Chuck."

"Is she the one?" said Vince.

I breathed a sigh of relief, turning this whole crazy mess over to the police. "Yes, she was arrested in connection with those murders. Then released. Willie Branner was then arrested for them, but you know that."

"I thought so. Knew she looked familiar. She's the wacky one who never would talk to us. I thought we had her on some forensics, but evidently hubby Willie did his wife. She's the he-she, right?"

"You got it," I said.

"So, why did Chuck kill her?" He read the note slowly, gazed at me, then slipped it into a plastic bag. "We've all got a personal limit on this kind of shit. Loved her, hated her, didn't want to live without her. His buddies would have a hey-day with this gender shit."

I said, "To tell you the truth, I doubt Betty's mother ever did believe it." I walked to the door.

The smaller EMT knocked, then hurried by me. "Tiny dog hiding inside the old lady's shawl. What should we do?"

I said, "Let it go with her. All she's got. Named Butchie."

Vince nodded. "They can decide at the hospital. Maybe they'll put her in a nursing home or somewhere else so she can keep it."

"Anything else?" I said. I mentally reviewed the apartment layout, now very anxious to leave.

"The usual," he said. "You and Marty come down to my office in the morning and make a complete statement. If I understand you, Mama had nothing to do with the deaths. A domestic quarrel, Chuck wanted a divorce, he came over here, they argued, he shot her once, then killed himself." He leaned over the bodies again and sniffed the gun several times.

"That's the way we've got it. Except, Mama's been through a lot. More than most people her age can stand. If they release her back here to the apartment, maybe a police woman or a social worker or home health, or somebody professional and sensitive should be here to help her until she gets on her feet. She loved her son more than he probably deserved."

"Take care. Thanks for calling me right away," said Vince. He stood, slid the gloves off and padded into the living room. We shook hands.

"By the way, how's your wife doing?"

The rehearsed emptiness in Vince's voice validated his words. "It's gone faster than the doctors thought. Hospice comes to the house every day. They've explained it to the kids. Just a matter of time. We're birds of a feather in several ways, you and me. I've taken your advice."

I felt for him, the long, lonely path ahead for a fellow young widower. At least he had kids.

Marty and I barely made it to the car, nothing left to say, completely drained. Seated in my car, warm even before the heater blasted us, I realized that we'd never taken off our parkas. Everything had happened so fast. Cold outside, warm and dry inside, wet sidewalks, melted snow—what a difference in a life-and-death situation like this. I meandered in my mind over the possibility that Betty would have somehow been convicted, that the police would come up with more evidence, or else she might have confessed to save Willie and punish herself. They'd kill her or rape her in prison. Chuck would have been forever lonely and miserable without her. Mama would have suffered lifelong grief for her Butch, maybe believing the gender and murder stories, maybe not. She'd lost her Butch no matter what.

Marty said, "What were we going to do? What if they hung Willie out to dry, maybe murder one times two? Our job was to clear Willie or get evidence to help his case. We did just that. Would we blow the whistle on Betty? She's no longer our client, no longer Goldbaum's client. Goldbaum had to rat out an ex-client to save a current client?" Eye-lids half shut, cheeks sagging, her head fell to her chest.

I said, "Good questions, but would anybody be able to prove anything about Betty without her confession? It was a long time ago. There are still no eyewitnesses and a lot of stuff that can be explained away. You know, despite everything, there was something about her."

"I know what you mean."

"Two down and two to go," I said.

Marty said, "What's that mean?"

"Betty's two murders down—Mary and Es. Two disappearances or murders, or whatever to go. Ice-cold cases of Kerry and Sheila for Vince and our brothers and sisters in blue."

This conversation served its purpose, which was obviously not a moral crusade. It simply filled space. We didn't cry for the human race. We didn't bemoan our inevitable fate, we didn't carp about the unfairness or craziness of life, or that even trained observers like us can be fooled repeatedly. We didn't bitch about the fact that there are just about as many versions of the truth as there are people on the planet. And we didn't make plans for lunch or drinks at Arnie's either. Tomorrow after our deposition was soon enough for lunch. We just went home.

CHAPTER TWENTY

We were in Vince's office by 11:00 a.m. the next morning. Statements dictated to a rookie were typed up and we signed them. The rookie seemed impressed—"wow" and "no kidding"—but didn't say much else. Vince must have been getting some much-needed rest. Cap wasn't around either. A few "Hi, how you doing" were sprinkled around as we walked out of the station.

I was wearing a pair of old jeans and a nondescript wool shirt, while Marty was in jeans and fleece boots, hair tied up in a bun with no make-up. We weren't much to look at, tired, and bummed out, driving on empty from the episode at Mama's. Somewhere inside me was the nagging thought that maybe, just maybe, we could have stopped the two deaths if we'd arrived earlier. Logically, I didn't think so because violence is so difficult to predict or control. Chuck was determined to end it for both of them. Neither Marty nor I could have talked him out of it, but we sure as hell could have tried. That would have left us feeling that we'd done our best; it just wasn't good enough.

Marty spoke as I fired up the engine. "There's an old Aztec belief that if the sun shines the day after a tragedy, then the gods are happy again, things will be good, and the dead will be looked after. Or something to that effect."

"Did you make that up?" I said.

"Partly." She punched my arm and we both laughed. "Pretend it's true. Chuck and Betty will be looked after."

"We need a wake. They'll wait to bury them until Mama's out of the hospital. Maybe Chuck's people will have a say in what happens to his body. Coroner first, though, for autopsies."

"Oh, shit," Marty said. "We forgot Goldbaum." She grinned ear to ear, like a bad child who kept something from a parent. I punched his number into my cell. One ring. "Yes," he said.

"Where's your secretary?" I said. "You're answering your own phone now. Business slipping?"

"I already know," he said.

"Sorry, in all the excitement and confusion, Marty and I forgot to call you. We just gave statements to the police," I said.

The murder of an ex-client hadn't rattled Goldbaum. Grief wasn't an emotion in his usual repertoire. Maybe he reserved it for current clients or his family. I suppose we should be more like him.

"This helps Willie Branner. He didn't do it. Just did surgery," said Goldbaum.

"Our duty is to serve. Betty's not here to tell the truth. We don't have much else."

Goldbaum's voice escalated a notch. "The hell you say. You and Marty could give a deposition or even testify at a trial."

"It might be hearsay. We weren't there. All we know is what Betty told us she did," I said. I felt good, brainy, holding my own with a tough-minded prick of a criminal defense lawyer.

"That's all we need. Maybe Isaacs, too. With the perp dead even hearsay could be enough to create reasonable doubt. Like a deathbed confession. Leave the law to me," said Goldbaum.

Shot down momentarily. Goldbaum knew his stuff, though he'd never win the personality phase of a Miss America contest. "Do you think there'll be a trial for murder?"

"No," he said. He hung up.

"I need a drink more than ever, boss," said Marty.

"Okay to make a quick stop to see Herman and Susie first? It's been too long," I said.

"Sure, let's do that. I love them." Marty reached for the illuminated vanity mirror above the windshield, rearranged it and pulled her make-up kit from her purse. She leaned forward and went to work systematically, transformed herself quickly into the magnificent bright-eyed beauty with smooth, tawny skin, and luscious lips for whom I lusted. "Concentrate on your driving," she said.

I tried to do just that, but as I drove fast toward the nursing home, I was lost in thought about the Webber's health, life in a nursing home, how much I missed seeing them.

We parked in a "staff" parking spot, still bending the rules ever so slightly. At least the yellow lettering on the curb didn't read "administrator" or "director."

We carried the chill inside. Its overheated hallways won out, so off came the parkas as we hurried to Herman and Susie. I'd talked to them several times on my cell phone, but no personal visits since the trips to Flint. "Oh, Christ, I forgot the goodies."

I grabbed Marty and we dashed out before they saw us. The closest convenience outlet had a liquor store next door, so we scooped up a box of Godiva mixed chocolates and a pint of the best Yugoslavian plum brandy. Back to the home. This time I preferred the administrator's parking slot. It had no conscience, absolutely none at all.

Marty displayed the candy for all to see, while I secreted the brandy inside my shirt. Some patients here, with doctor's permission, were allowed one, sometimes two, alcoholic drinks on Friday afternoons before dinner. Otherwise, no alcohol and smoking only in a specified room with a separate ventilation system.

I knocked softly. We entered their room immediately, hit by that distinctive smell of old people. Herman slumped in his chair, a month-old copy of *Sports Illustrated* curled in his lap. Susie deftly knitted without the lamp turned on, sort of like reading Braille, her fingers and needles dancing in the dark. She was awake.

"Well, bless my soul," Susie said. "Long time." Both of us kissed her. I gave her a half-hug, all that was possible in a wheelchair. "Wake up, Herman, company's here." His head shook and he snored at her. She placed her knitting on a night table. I feared she'd use a needle to poke him awake.

"I'm not asleep. I'm up. I didn't fall asleep." He slowly pulled up his head. "It's my Kip. Praise the Lord." He paused for thirty seconds. "And, uh, Marty."

As I hugged Herman, I surreptitiously slipped the brandy inside a pocket in his new Christmas robe. "Glad you're okay."

Marty kissed his forehead. She said, "We've missed you, been busy, back and forth to Flint. Toledo and Flint for us, not exactly San Francisco and New York, but it pays the bills." She handed over the chocolates.

Susie said, "You shouldn't have, but I do love them. I

appreciate it." She slipped the ribbon from the box, opened the lid and sighed admiringly. Plopped a dark crème into her mouth. "TV says that dark chocolate lowers blood pressure. So there." Without offering a piece to Herman, she slid the box on to her bed. "You know, there's something else on TV that bothers me. On that black channel, BET, there's real good movies and songs for us, except for one thing. Every other word is 'you bitch' or 'yo' or 'dog.' Sometimes they call a man a bitch. Disgusting." She reached for the box and ate a second dark chocolate filled with a cherry. "My blood pressure just dropped out of sight."

"Can I get a word in?" said Herman. "You talk a lot, woman. Since I've been back from the hospital, you just go on and on and on." Herman straightened in his chair as best he could, patted his brandy bottle and smoothed his mustache, in that order. First things first.

I said, "Herman, you seem all recovered."

"He's fine," said Susie. "Still in rehab, but he's fine. Can't hurt him."

"Please, woman, can I speak for myself? She's right. I'm doing okay. Use the wheelchair and my walker now and then. Not winning any races. There's something about the golden years. Watch out for them, Kip."

I'd hoped that Herman would be wearing a baseball cap and street clothes. Instead, he still wore pajamas under his red robe.

"We've had quite a time with the case we're on," said Marty.

"I knew you would. Is that the same he-she case where I said the husband did it?" said Herman.

"That's the one," said Marty. "Except for one thing. The husband didn't kill anyone."

"I'll bet the he-she did something bad, too. Lord don't like them people at all. Lord only wants mother and father. No one confesses to all that killing and blood and guts stuff and is completely innocent. Don't make no sense." His cheeks puffed out as the huge grin of pleasure crossed his mouth—he loved being right.

"You hit the nail on the head," said Marty. "Betty did the deed, actually got two women. Tried to blame the husband. I don't think it will work." She rubbed Susie's shoulders slowly while she talked to Herman. "It looks like the husband Willie did some awful things to people but he's not a killer. He was horribly abusive to his family, especially the women, but he's no murderer. So you had them both pegged as bad guys. You helped us a lot."

"Can't you help this guy, Marty?" said Susie. "I mean this guy, my Kip, your Kip, not the other guy Willie. His social life ain't much to brag about."

"Neither is Willie's. He's in jail," I said. We all laughed.

Susie would not be deterred from her mission—my personal salvation. "Kip, I'm old and awful blunt. You seem different. Have you met someone?" she said.

Apparently, both Marty and I were taken by surprise. Our gazes locked momentarily. My heart beat faster. My neck flushed. The scar flared. She wiped an impish grin from her face.

It would have been so easy to declare my feelings for Marty, how beautiful and appealing I found her and how our few brief encounters meant so much to me. To go even farther, to pledge myself to her, to report our liaison to Herman and Susie. Even to brag about it. They always thought the world of Marty. They would have been shocked and terrified by the purpose and goal of our social relationship, by Professor Ruth, and Uncle Kip's ultimate role.

"Not really, not in the usual sense, not exactly met someone, but I do feel more optimistic," I said. "Like I'm ready to get a life again. I've registered for an online dating service. You'll be the first to hear those wedding bells."

Herman turned his head to take a quick nip of the brandy. We all observed him. Why did he turn his head? He wasn't fooling any of us. "Let's have a race," he said.

"What kind of race?" I said.

"Wheelchair race," he said. "You guys push us down the hall. Winner takes all. Kip, you were always competitive. You didn't have much natural ability. You liked to win."

"Susie, you were right. Old people are sure blunt," I said. "A race would be fun but the nurses won't permit it. This damn place, Herman, racing not allowed."

Marty said, "Next time, Herman, next time we come. We'll have a race out in the courtyard." She patted him on the back, then they high-fived each other.

"Thanks, Marty. I'll hold you to that promise. Only way to get the upper hand here. Beat her flat out in a race." He took another swallow directly from the bottle. With all the other meds he received, a little alcohol went a long way. "Need something sweeter."

It was wonderful to see his sense of humor return under any conditions, but I'd bring only a half-pint next time. We kissed and hugged and made our good-byes. Directly to the car.

"Now time for us," I said. "I feel good." I turned the key to the welcome hum of the engine music.

"We can drink and eat and de-brief each other on Betty and Willie," said Marty. Her twinkling eyes confused me.

I wanted to de-brief ourselves about each other over vodka and burgers for lunch at Arnie's place. We'd done what little we could for Herman and Susie.

We arrived amid the wonderful lunch time din. The appealing aroma of greasy fried burgers and hot barbecue, sizzling fries, margaritas, cold English stout or nutty ale, blue smoke, and replayed classic Super Bowl games assaulted me. Quite a relief and a much-needed distraction.

I held up two fingers after we snatched a booth near the quiet side of the place. Our favorite waitress did two things—chewed with empty mouth and then mimicked drinking. I pretended to hold a glass to my lips with my right hand. At ten paces I had ordered two vodkas with olives stuffed with cheese. We'd chew on burgers later. Sign language worked.

Pleasant memories flooded over me even before the vodka arrived. Pavlovian conditioning, the dog salivating before the food arrived, to a bell in Russia but the clink of glasses here, or was it the aroma, or the place, or just being with Marty—maybe all of it, more than any dog could appreciate.

Marty shed her parka and shuddered noisily several times for some reason, maybe to rid herself of the outside chill and adjust to warmth, smoke and noise. Her own brand of conditioning, with the stimulation of Arnie's might lead to a new mental picture. Ridding herself apparently of Betty, Willie, Mama, Herman and Susie. Shake it off. Focus on me, I hoped.

"I'm pregnant, boss. It worked. You're fast, you devil," she said.

I shuddered this time, so wrenching to my torso that it felt like a convulsion. A thousand thoughts raced through my mind. How many cigars would I need? Stupidly, I talked. "Should I order the burgers now or wait until we've finished the first drink?"

"I'm going to have a baby. Timing was perfect, Uncle Kip. I can't drink anymore."

The waitress set the beautiful, ice-cold vodkas on the table in front of us, with spotted and stuffed, dull green, huge Portuguese olives swimming in the translucent ice cubes. "I made a mistake. Two green teas, we can't drink booze today. It's okay to charge us. Two bowls of chicken soup and then two veggie burgers on whole wheat buns. Sorry for the change. Things are different."

I was afraid she'd call the bouncer to shovel us out of the place after changing the order so abruptly. She just gave me a dirty look.

Ecstatic, I reached for Marty's hands. "I won't drink anymore, either. Back to AA, ninety meetings in ninety days. It's the least that a father can do. Are you sure?"

"Yes, so excited I went to the doctor every ten days. Location and timing. Congratulations. Thanks. I could tell you enjoyed it, too, boss."

"I'm overwhelmed. We're biological parents. It's just a lot to take in quickly." Our tea arrived. I gulped too fast. It was hot. My mouth and tongue burned. Could have emptied out my mouth but was too stunned to think of it. Just held in the tea until it cooled enough to swallow. "I love you," I said.

"Professor Ruth and I are struggling right now. She wanted the baby and now she's not sure. She thinks maybe it's a mistake. Our sex life sucks. And don't say anything reassuring, like I've always got you," said Marty. She patted her belly.

"You've always got me, night or day, at home or away."

"Very funny, boss. I know I can count on you." Marty's

demeanor was serious, pleasant but to the point, jaw set with a slight squint to her beautiful dark brown eyes. She sipped tea, then laced her fingers together on the table. "Sex was always great with Ruth before this. Creative, sensitive, and brought us very close to each other. We used to joke that if we could load a strap-on with sperm, we could do it all. Then we'd laugh and work like hell on it."

"It's not unusual for kids or even a pregnancy to change things. Sex produces kids, even when it can't—I mean it still seems like it can. Hell, you know what I mean," I said. I was a father-to-be, and, strangely, I felt fatherly toward Marty. Professor Ruth was a very lucky woman to have her. So was I.

"Professor Ruth's mother gave her a brooch. She cut off the ends which are diamond filigree platinum to make these earrings." She proudly touched both ear lobes.

I said, "Beautiful oval shape. Makes your eyes sparkle even more than usual."

"Please lean over and see if the back of this left one is hooked," said Marty.

"Yes, it is."

"Okay, thanks. Back to your side now."

I said, "Where did you think I'd go?"

Marty ignored my sarcasm. "My professor will adapt. We'll live in the same house. I know that. She's never had a child before. She's probably scared shitless of the responsibility, too. I'm not; my mother did it all. I learned at her feet. Well done, she used to say, is better than well said. Of course, she didn't go to school past the fourth grade." Marty relaxed her hands. She added sugar and lemon to her second cup of tea. She smiled at me, her eyes moist with affection.

"I'm alive again, thanks to you. I'll always love you, in my own way, and you, me. No kiss, no embrace, no sex. Just plain old-fashioned love."

Marty said, "I'm ready for my veggie burger."